Playing with Matches

– A Novel –

Hannah Orenstein

TOUCHSTONE

New York   London   Toronto   Sydney   New Delhi

Touchstone
An Imprint of Simon & Schuster, Inc.
1230 Avenue of the Americas
New York, NY 10020

First Touchstone trade paperback edition June 2018

TOUCHSTONE and colophon are registered trademarks of Simon & Schuster, Inc.

For information about special discounts for bulk purchases, please contact Simon & Schuster Special Sales at 1-866-506-1949 or business@simonandschuster.com.

The Simon & Schuster Speakers Bureau can bring authors to your live event. For more information or to book an event, contact the Simon & Schuster Speakers Bureau at 1-866-248-3049 or visit our website at www.simonspeakers.com.

Interior design by Jill Putorti

Manufactured in the United States of America

10 9 8 7 6 5 4 3 2 1

Library of Congress Cataloging-in-Publication Data

Names: Orenstein, Hannah, author.
Title: Playing with matches / Hannah Orenstein.
Description: First Touchstone trade paperback edition. | New York : Touchstone, 2018.
Identifiers: LCCN 2017037051 (print) | LCCN 2017048167 (ebook) | ISBN 9781501178504 (eBook) | ISBN 9781501178481 (paperback)
Subjects: LCSH: Dating (Social customs)—Fiction. | Mate selection—Fiction. | GSAFD: Love stories.
Classification: LCC PS3615.R4645 (ebook) | LCC PS3615.R4645 P58 2018 (print) | DDC 813/.6—dc23
LC record available at https://lccn.loc.gov/2017037051

ISBN 978-1-5011-7848-1
ISBN 978-1-5011-7850-4 (ebook)

For my family, Audrey, Jack, and Julia Orenstein

- Chapter 1 -

I can count on one hand the number of people I've told about my family's mortifying secret. There's my boyfriend. My best friend. That girl I trusted in high school who leaked it to my whole class. And now, my new boss, Penelope Winslow, founder and CEO of Bliss. I had to tell her to get hired; it was the only way I knew I'd land the job for sure. Anywhere else, the secret makes me a leper; at Bliss, it won me the job. Penelope says it'll make me a star.

I hadn't planned on telling her at all. I just really, *really* needed a job, and I had a hunch that spilling the secret would work in my favor. Up until two months ago, I had expected that People.com, the site I interned for in college, would hire me as an editorial assistant. I had imagined a future blogging about the Kardashians or *The Bachelor*—not exactly my passion, but it would set me up for a life as a writer. But the week before graduation, my boss pulled me aside. She didn't have the budget to hire me. I didn't have a Plan B.

For the next two months, I barely slept—I refreshed Craigslist and NYU's job board every fifteen minutes and sent out dozens of desperate applications. I wasn't looking for just any gig.

You don't get a decent scholarship to study journalism at NYU and still take out a sickening number of loans like I did just to fold T-shirts at the Gap. I spotted Bliss, the matchmaking service, during a Craigslist dive one sweltering night in early July.

"Seeking MATCHMAKERS!" the listing exclaimed. *"Let us arm you with a quiver full of Cupid's arrows."*

ABOUT BLISS: We're an elite matchmaking service that connects New York's most eligible bachelors and bachelorettes. Our clients are tired of meeting the wrong types of people online; they're ready to seek our expert knowledge of the dating world and access to our unparalleled roster of clients, which includes successful entrepreneurs, politicians, lawyers, and artists. Our matchmakers will do whatever it takes to find the right match. If a client is a theater aficionado, a matchmaker might visit the after-party for a Broadway show to get the leading actor's number. If a client needs a brainy intellectual for sophisticated pillow talk, a matchmaker might drop by a MENSA meeting. We're not your grandmother's yenta. Our method is highly individualized, brazen, and bold . . . and it works! Since our launch three years ago, a handful of clients have already sent us wedding invitations.

Matchmakers should be intuitive, creative, and above all, passionate about the quest for love. This isn't your typical desk job. Instead, you'll work around the city, in our downtown office, at home, or out on the town. You'll be dreaming up exciting dates by day, and finding Mr. or Ms. Right by night. (We would never set up a potential couple to meet over dinner and drinks. How dull!)

Skip the traditional, boring cover letter and send us a photo of yourself and a note explaining why our clients should entrust you with the responsibility of finding love.

I stopped cold when I read the description. It reminded me of my family's most shameful secret. Here it goes: My parents didn't meet at a bar, or in college, or through friends (all of which I've claimed). There's no reason a man from the commuter suburbs of New Jersey would ever bump into a farm girl from three hours outside Yekaterinburg, Russia. Not by chance, not through fate, not in some rom-com meet-cute.

My parents met through a certain kind of matchmaker. Dad was lonely, so he chose Mom out of a catalog and paid six thousand dollars to bring her over from Russia back in 1991. The few English words she knew came from Beatles songs. He liked that she was twenty years old, blond, and had boobs too big for her skinny frame. She liked that he owned a car with a cassette player. They weren't exactly soul mates. Mom had me at twenty-two and divorced Dad by thirty after she became a naturalized U.S. citizen and he found an even younger blonde with bigger boobs. So, that's it—don't judge me.

Bliss sounded like the opposite of the way my parents met. Bringing two people together based on a hunch that they would click sounded romantic. I wanted to be a part of it. I sat up in bed in the middle of the night to apply for the job right away. I fantasized about befriending successful, handsome, well-traveled people at Ivy League mixers, gallery openings, and charity galas and making them all fall in love. In those visions, I had a sleek blowout, a less obvious nose, and the toned legs of someone who actually goes to the gym. I laughed at some story from the guy who handed Mark Zuckerberg his first beer at Harvard, then casually slipped him my business card: *Sasha Goldberg, Matchmaker*. The card was thick with sharp corners. Zuckerberg's friend was a Patrick Bateman–type who'd appreciate it.

"I heard you're single," I'd say in that scenario. "Let me know if you're interested in a match."

Then I'd stalk off in a pair of Manolo Blahnik pumps I couldn't afford now, and pick up a fat paycheck.

At my interview four days later, Penelope instantly made me feel at ease. She looked like a modern Marilyn Monroe—platinum curls and a splash of red lipstick and curves poured into a navy dress, with colorful tattoos snaking out from under her sleeves. I thought the interview was going well; she seemed genuinely interested in hearing about my journalism degree and my internship at People.com. But then she threw me a question I didn't know how to answer.

"Why should I hire you?" she asked.

I recited my usual answer.

"Well, I'm a very hard worker. And a quick learner. I'm motivated to succeed here. I'm fascinated by the company."

"Mhm," she said politely. She looked bored.

It was so goddamn hot in the brownstone. A dribble of sweat formed behind my knee and snaked its way down my calf. Up until that moment, I'd been optimistic that I'd get at least a second interview, if not the job. But now I wasn't so sure, and that hurt. I actually *wanted* to work here. So before I had time to panic over the consequences, I dropped the Secret Russian Mail-Order Bride Bomb to convince Penelope that I had to be a Bliss matchmaker. She had to understand.

"The thing is, I'll be a better matchmaker than anyone else you could possibly hire," I announced, maybe a little too loudly. "Because I know exactly how the wrong match can implode. My mom was a mail-order bride from Russia. My dad picked her out of a catalog. They were married for a decade, but they never loved each other. And that's what Bliss wants to do, right? Help people fall in love? I can't think of a more noble thing to do, and I don't see how anyone else could be as motivated as I am."

My words were jumbled and breathless; I didn't have much practice telling people about my family. But it was just bizarre enough to actually work. After Penelope picked up her hanging jaw, she hired me on the spot.

Three days later, I'm at Bliss's office downtown for my first day of training. The office is off the Bowery, around the corner from Whole Foods and Intermix—a stately brownstone with curved wrought-iron railings on either side of the stoop and a heavy brass door knocker. I heave it against the door and hear a flurry of heels clicking against wood inside.

Penelope opens the door. I reach for a handshake, like I did last time, but she clasps my hand in a red-taloned grip and leans in to kiss my cheek.

"Darling, come on in! I'm so glad you could stop by for training today."

She turns and cocks her head for me to follow. The brownstone is the type of place I would sell organs on the black market for. It's on loan from one of Bliss's investors. A marble staircase rises from the foyer and the dark wood floors creak as we walk. Penelope leads me through the dining room—decorated with a massive, glittering chandelier and a deep-red Oriental carpet edged with fringe—and pushes open a door to the study. An emerald green velvet couch rests along one wall and a packed bookcase stretches from floor to ceiling on another.

Penelope slips off her white pumps, folds up her legs to sit bird-like on the couch, and points to a tray of Godiva chocolate truffles on the glass coffee table. "Want one? They're a gift from a happy client—he just got engaged."

I take one. Penelope hands me a pad of paper and a red pen, then sinks back into the couch, touching a long, pointed nail to her lips.

"Matchmaking is the most powerful job a person can have," she muses. "Think about it, what do people really want in life besides love? Success? Maybe. Fame? Not really. Let's say you go to a party and people ask what you do. They'll all work as accountants or in insurance or something dull. The minute you say you're a matchmaker, the room will stop and all eyes will be on you. They'll want you to set them up, give them advice, teach them what they're doing wrong. You'll see. That power is trans-formative."

I've never known that kind of power, but my best friend Caro-line has. When we went to parties together in college, whatever small talk I attempted with the basics and the bros fizzled. But they all instantly fell for Caroline, because she has this bright, fearless thing going for her. People didn't know what to make of her at first, but they always wound up enchanted. She'd tell stories about that time she took nude yoga classes during her meditation retreat in Tulum, that time she slept with her barista and he made her latte art the morning after, that time she took a selfie with Kim Kardashian. People widened their circles to let her in. This wasn't some contrived act; she was really just like that. Once she'd daz-zled them with her absurd story du jour, she'd introduce me with a matter-of-fact, "This is my roommate, Sasha. She's fabulous." And then it wouldn't matter quite so much that I was the quiet, awkward one, because Caroline was in, and we were a two-for-one deal.

In this job, though, I have no one to rely on but myself. That scares me.

"How does all this work? How do you know who to match?"

"Write this down, Sasha. This is all you need to know."

She waits for me to click open the pen and hover it over the pad. I'm hanging on her words and she loves it. She sits ramrod straight with her chin in the air.

"Looks and status," she says slowly, watching me write it down. "Looks and status. That's it. If they're equally as attractive and equally as successful, they don't need to have anything in common. They'll want to hop into bed together and they won't argue about money—the rest doesn't matter."

"That's it?"

She reaches for a truffle, pops it into her mouth, and grins. "That's it. Simple, huh?"

Looks and status . . . are people really that superficial? I want to believe her, but it seems too easy.

"So, you're saying personality doesn't factor in at all?"

"I mean, sure, you could make an argument for that." She grimaces. "Think of looks and status as the minimum requirements— otherwise, your clients will be offended you even consider them to be in the same league."

My parents certainly didn't match up that way. But I guess they didn't last. Sometimes, I wonder if my boyfriend, Jonathan, and I are in the same league. We met when I was a sophomore studying abroad in Paris. I was at a wine bar in the 16th Arrondissement with Caroline when this American guy knocked over my drink. He asked if he could buy me a new one to make up for it. He had sandy hair and deep blue eyes that were lit up by his navy blue sweater, so I wasn't going to say no. I learned that his name was Jonathan Colton, and he was a junior at Columbia studying abroad. He was weirder than his preppy façade let on: he explained he was working on a research paper comparing Hogwarts' architecture to that of real European castles; he also had plans to see a reenactment of a medieval jousting tournament that weekend. I was surprised to learn he was an econ major. Even he looked a little bored telling me about the investment banking internship he had lined up for the summer. I didn't want to break away from our conversation even after our beers were drained. He invited me to join him at the jousting tournament, and that became our first date. That was more than two years ago, and we've been together ever since.

But looks and status? Don't get me wrong, I'm pretty enough. Dad chose Mom specifically for her looks, and I inherited some of them—her clear green eyes, her full lips, her hourglass figure. But I also got Dad's dark, curly-frizzy hair and a nose that's a size and a half too big for my face. And when it comes to status, well, that's a joke. Jonathan's a WASP from Westchester, and an investment banker now. I'm a barely employed girl one paycheck away from moving back home to Passaic County, New Jersey. And not the nice part. I don't know if I believe Penelope's philosophy exactly, but I write her words down anyway and underline them twice.

"So, Sasha, the first thing you'll do when you get assigned a new client is to invite them out for dinner or drinks. The tab is on Bliss, of course. Pick somewhere sexy—hotel bars are great. Not like the Marriott, obviously, but the Bowery Hotel, the Ace Hotel, the NoMad. You know the type."

I do not know the type.

"It shouldn't feel like a stuffy meeting. Your clients should never feel like you're doing *business*, except for the business of finding love. Don't just pick the first place off Yelp. You want to treat them, you know? That's when you do the deep dive into what they're looking for, their relationship history, who they're attracted to, the works."

"How do you get all that?"

"Start off slow, with an icebreaker. Maybe you comment on the weather or compliment something they're wearing. You know, make them feel comfortable."

I flash back to last week, when Penelope gushed over the basic black dress I always wear to interviews. Got it.

"But where do we find the matches?"

She pulls a gold MacBook off the table, opens it, and clicks around.

"Here. The first thing you do is go through our database. We had a developer out in Silicon Valley build this for us last year. It contains thousands of profiles of both clients and potential matches. You can filter by gender, sexuality, age, interests, deal-breakers, income, and height."

Faces flash by, and it's dizzying to think of how many people are in the database. I catch glimpses of their photos—a guy with a shiny bald head, a girl with loose auburn curls, a guy in a shirtless selfie taken on a sailboat, a girl looking serious in a charcoal suit. Penelope stops and scrolls quickly to the top, and their faces blur into one. She stops at the search bar and types in a name.

"I'm thinking Mindy Kaplan will be your first client. She just signed up, and I have a feeling you two will really hit it off. Similar backgrounds, you know?"

Ah. She means Jewish. Or at least Jew-ish. I haven't been inside a temple since my Bat Mitzvah almost a decade ago. Penelope pulls up a headshot of a pretty brunette wearing bright pink lipstick.

"Mindy is thirty-five. She's an executive at a TV network. She just wanted a husband and kids five years ago, you know? Really chic, smart, bubbly."

I lean forward to examine her profile. The numbers jump out first: she's five foot two and makes $150,000 a year. I bet she lives in a doorman building with an elevator. She lists her interests as television, painting, astrology, weekends in Martha's Vineyard, and fund-raising for causes like girls' education and kids with cancer. Her deal-breakers are "not Jewish (sorry), not ready to settle down, poor hygiene, and bad manners." And then, in the section about what she's looking for: "I love my career and I'm great at it, but becoming a mother is the most important thing in my life. Family has always come first for me. I'd hope it would come first for my partner, too." It could have come across as desperate, but she sounds sincere. I like her.

"Our database is extensive, but let's say you don't find Mindy's perfect guy there right away. Then it's up to you to search for single men."

This is what I had imagined—trolling the city's coolest parties for eligible bachelors and flirtatiously adding their numbers to my little black iPhone. One hundred percent terrifying. I've never dated that way. Before Jonathan, I just made out with the know-it-alls in my journalism seminars who seemed to have a lot of opinions about music and drugs and other things they read about in *Vice*. I had somehow survived four years in New York without ever dipping my toe in the New York dating scene for real.

"I go out and meet people, right?" I ask.

"Well, sort of. You definitely can do that. Georgie—one of the matchmakers you'll meet later—specializes in that. She had one client who missed her ex's sense of humor, so she went to stand-up comedy classes until she met the right guy for her. She had another client who wanted to meet a Hindu woman, so she went to a luncheon at a Hindu temple. And last Labor Day weekend, she spent three days hunting around Hyannis Port to track down a Kennedy."

Holy shit. "Did she find one?"

"A Kennedy?"

"Yeah."

She purses her lips. "I mean, technically, he was only a second cousin, but sure. Georgie cares about every client like they're her best friend, you know? She gets so bogged down in finding them the perfect person."

"Isn't that the point of all this?" I'm starting to feel uneasy, like I'm not quite so sure what I signed up for.

"Of course, doll! But there are faster ways." She reaches for her phone. The lock screen is a white background with the Bliss logo in bright Tiffany blue—two stylized capital *B*s facing each other, like two pairs of lips. She unlocks it. "This is the real magic. Look—Tinder, Hinge, Bumble, The League, Raya, Coffee Meets Bagel, OkCupid, Her, BeLinked, JDate, JSwipe, Match.com, eHarmony . . . should I keep going?"

"You have profiles on all of them?" I ask, incredulous.

"All of them. And you will, too. That's one of the reasons we hire matchmakers in their twenties. Young faces are the best bait on dating apps."

"And the other reason?"

She laughs. "We try to hire girls who have actually had sex in the past decade. Our competitors are all women in their sixties."

"Oh." I don't know what to say to that. I have, in fact, had sex in the past decade. As in, like, yesterday. "I almost wonder, though . . . wouldn't it be easier to meet people in person?"

"I mean, I guess you *could* run around the city all day trying to meet men," she concedes, tilting her head to the side like she's unconvinced. "But that's what our clients are doing, and clearly it's not working for them, either. Dating sites and apps expedite the process. I was chatting with a dozen guys at once when you came in this morning."

"A dozen?!"

"There's Joey, the pro-tennis player with a fetish for older women," Penelope begins, ticking him off on her finger. "That's a definite no. We don't want our ladies to feel objectified. Andrew, a lawyer. He seems promising. Maybe a little dull. Raphael might work out for somebody, but it seems like he only goes for real beauties. I'm still sussing out his type, but the size-zero models hanging off his arm in every photo aren't a good sign. Hold on, I need to get to these," she says, gesturing to her phone.

She bites her lip, thinks for a second, then taps out rapid-fire messages on an app I don't recognize. I watch her grin and purse her lips, as if she's actually flirting in real life. Between her pinup look for a casual Thursday at the office and her quick, dry appraisal of these randos, I feel as if I've briefly left planet Earth. Is this my life now? The brownstone is quiet, and suddenly I have visions of lounging for hours a day on this insane velvet couch, typing out messages to older men I don't know. I can't believe this is a real job. I run my hand over the velvet and feel the fibers prickle the wrong way.

She cackles loudly over a message. "Raphael claims to have slept with two Victoria's Secret models. Not with that hairline he didn't."

She tilts the screen toward me, and sure enough, the top of his head is covered with sparse wisps of dark hair. He's twenty-seven.

"Ouch."

"Don't feel guilty, you can laugh," Penelope says. "Most of them are assholes anyway."

"Don't we talk to any women?"

"Sure. Our clients are sixty/forty—more women than men—but straight women are harder to reach on online dating sites because all of our matchmakers are women. So the female matches we find tend to be through our own personal networks."

"Can't you make a profile as a man and look for women that way?"

"Technically, yes. But we don't do fake profiles often. When you're searching for matches, you're searching as yourself. Your own name, your own face, your own bio. The more real it is, the more authentic it feels."

She goes back to typing. I hear the front door open and a voice coo "Hello," then the clacking of heels on the hardwood floor. A few seconds later, two girls appear in the living room. Penelope looks up from her phone and stands up, sauntering over to hug each one. They all exchange greetings. I stand awkwardly, waiting to be introduced.

"Ladies, this is Sasha, our new hire. This is Georgie and Elizabeth."

Georgie is a tiny pixie of a thing in a men's pinstriped white button-down—rumpled, like she had picked it up off a guy's floor that morning—that falls mid-thigh, revealing just the flirty hem of black silk and lace tap shorts underneath, and a messy topknot. She gives me a brief once-over and a half grin—"Nice to meet you"—then turns back to her conversation with Penelope.

Elizabeth is Georgie's polar opposite: she welcomes me with a firm handshake and a genuine smile. Her coral red sheath dress reminds me of something Anna Wintour would wear to terrify some underfed assistant. Unlike Georgie, she actually speaks to me.

"You're going to have so much fun here," she says with the instant ease of a person who knows how to make small talk.

I'm embarrassed to tell her I've never actually done this before, but I do anyway. I babble when I'm nervous. She doesn't seem to care—not about the babbling, not about my lack of experience.

"Look, I dropped out of law school for this. I've never looked back."

"Really?"

"Less money, sure," she concedes. "But way more fun."

She's friendly right away, the way that drunk girls always are at parties, except I get the odd sense she's actually like this all the time. Georgie gossips with Penelope in a low, throaty voice. Out of the corner of my eye, I see Georgie hold her hands eight or nine inches apart and hear a low giggle. Penelope's eyebrows shoot up.

The training continues for the rest of the afternoon—we cover how to use the database, what to write to people on dating apps, how to grill each potential match to determine compatibility with clients. Georgie perches on the arm of the couch behind Penelope, and Elizabeth sits with her ankles crossed on the paisley loveseat across the room. They chime in with tips as Penelope talks. By the time I leave, my notepad is full of scribbles and my mind is racing. Penelope tells me she'll be in touch soon to arrange my first meeting with Mindy.

"She'll love you, darling," Penelope calls to me as she leans out the doorframe over the stoop. "Nothing to worry about!"

Nothing to worry about. I can do this. Right? As I leave the brownstone and walk uptown to my apartment, it occurs to me that this whole matchmaking venture could be a total failure. This job requires schmoozing, and I'm not exactly a people person. But I have to make this work, or else it's back to Mom and my stepdad Steve's house in Jersey.

– Chapter 2 –

"I just want a guy who knows what he wants," Mindy says, wrapping up her breathless rant about the abysmal state of the thirty-something dating scene in Manhattan and stabbing a leaf of kale with her fork.

She chews in silence—the first silence that's fallen over the table since I complimented her blouse as an icebreaker fifteen minutes ago. I'm grateful that she's been doing the heavy lifting in the conversation, since Penelope's training session yesterday feels like a blur. Everything seemed so simple when she explained how to run these introductory client meetings, but actually putting those skills into practice now is terrifying. It's like that required science course I had to take in college. I could follow along when the professor explained how to calculate the distance between two planets using some complicated formula, but when I had to do it myself on the exam, I blanked.

I'm relieved that I like Mindy a lot so far. She's delightful, really. She arrived at Sant Ambroeus twelve minutes after we were scheduled to meet, but texted me an apology in advance: "Running late. My doctor's appt ran long. (Consultation for freezing my eggs.) In a cab now. Sorry . . . see you soon!!! xoxo!!!" She's personable and energetic and doesn't seem to notice that I'm woefully underqualified to find her a husband.

I had suggested this place to Mindy because I know she lives around the corner in the West Village, but also because Jonathan had once brought me here on a date. He hadn't told me that he was a regular, and I got weirded out when the waiters kept clapping him on the arm and calling him Johnny Boy. That day, I had ordered the cheapest thing on the menu, a nine-dollar tiramisu, in case I ended up paying my own half. I didn't want him to think I was using him as a free meal ticket, even though that was occasionally true.

Mindy and I sit in the back at a table crammed between two others. Around us, Ladies Who Lunch types recline on red-leather-tufted banquettes, eat open-faced tartines with foie gras or tuna, and drink tiny espressos. The restaurant hums with chatter in English and Italian and the clatter of silverware against white ceramic plates. Chanel bags hang over the back of almost every chair in the joint. My black Michael Kors tote from Beacon's Closet is stuffed under the table. Mindy's purse is the faintest baby pink and made out of buttery leather. I can't identify the designer, which means it probably costs more than a month's rent.

Mindy finishes chewing her bite of kale and leans forward in her seat, elbows on the table and hands primly tucked under her chin.

"I can't express enough how important it is that he feels very masculine," she says. "He should be strong, decisive, deep voice, broad shoulders. I don't want anyone who's wishy-washy."

"Got it." I nod.

"But the thing is, he's got to be Jewish. That wasn't so important to me when I was younger," she says. She lingers over the word "younger," her eyes widening ever so slightly over the top of her lifted coffee cup. I haven't told her how old I am and don't intend to. "But it is now. I want my kids to grow up the same way that I did."

"Not a problem."

"Some Jewish guys are too soft-spoken for me, too whiny, too close to their moms," she says. "That's not right for me. I mean, of course they should love their moms. But not *love*-love their moms all the time, you know?"

"You're looking for someone who's family-oriented but independent," I rephrase. This was a tip from Elizabeth yesterday—churning out the exact same concept in different words makes the client feel like you're on the same wavelength.

"Yes!"

I never got the same *you must marry a Jewish guy or else* schtick from my family. I'm only half Jewish on Dad's side, and it's not like he ever went for Jewish girls. He likes blondes—Mom, of course, and then his string of girlfriends named Stacey and Tracy and Laci once he moved to Miami. Any Jewish girl claiming to be a natural blonde is just a liar with a good colorist. I've never dated a Jewish guy. I imagine it must be simpler to be born with specific rules about who is available and who is off-limits. It must keep you laser-focused on exactly who you're looking for, the way Mindy is. I didn't exactly have criteria when I met Jonathan—I just wanted someone *normal*, because that was not exactly in great supply when I was growing up.

Mindy's rose-gold iPhone starts to ring.

"Do you need to get that?" I ask.

She barely glances at the screen before sending the call to voice-mail. "No, what would be more important than this?"

But, like, no pressure or anything.

"I just . . ." She stops and sighs heavily. "I just feel like I've tried everything. I've dated everyone, tried online dating, the dating apps, let my friends set me up, went to therapy to get all my baggage sorted out, joined a running club to meet new people, saw psychics, lost weight, did juice cleanses to suck the toxins out of my dating life. . . . I've been banging my head against the wall for fifteen years trying to find my person. I just want to be a mom. I'm almost coming to terms with having a baby on my own—but I'm not ready to stop looking for a husband just yet."

It feels disrespectful to keep eating while she says all this, so I put my fork down. I want to reassure her that I'll find her guy, but I have no idea where to even begin. Instead, I open up the iPhone Note I've been adding to throughout lunch and rattle off what she's looking for. Anything to make myself sound capable.

Her dream guy is in his mid-thirties to mid-forties, I recite, maybe a banker or a lawyer, and hot in a Ryan Reynolds kind of way without being a gym nut. ("Because it's not like *I* have a perfect SoulCycle attendance record, you know?" she points out.) He should be Jewish and smart and want kids. He should work hard but not so hard that she never sees him; he should be funny but not in a snarky, sarcastic way; he should be kind and thoughtful and considerate. Most of all, he should be excited to settle down and start a family.

"You got it," she says, beaming. But the smile doesn't last long. "And that's not too much? You don't think that's too difficult?"

I shake my head and reassure her that I know exactly what I'm doing. I mean, yes, okay, matchmaking sounds crazy hard. But on the other hand, I'm the only one of my friends with a boyfriend, and I think I did a pretty fabulous job finding and keeping him. Girls at NYU couldn't believe that I had found a hot, successful, cool straight guy who willingly wanted to be my boyfriend. (Before I moved here, I had assumed the city would have a Mr. Big living on every block. Imagine my surprise when I discovered every guy at NYU was either a gay theater major or a player who moved through a new girl every week. Straight, single guys in the city know they're a hot commodity, and so they typically turn into assholes.) If I landed myself a boyfriend, I can land anyone a boyfriend. Right?

"I got this. Promise."

I try to push the butterflies out of my stomach. We get the check and I put down my card to expense to Bliss later, praying I haven't hit my credit limit. I don't want to think too hard about failing my way back to Jersey. Outside the restaurant, Mindy initiates a dramatic double-cheek kiss and we part ways. Time to find Mindy's husband. Let's go.

- *Chapter 3* -

I pop in my earbuds and walk east through the West Village. The city is sunlit and stunning. Lush rows of trees give shade to brownstone stoops adorned with black wrought-iron railings. I stroll past the throngs of sunbathers and jazz musicians in Washington Square Park to arrive at Think Coffee near NYU. They have iced coffee that chills my ribs from inside out and enough students with lavender hair and septum rings milling about to make me feel as if I'm still in school. I came here every week in college to work on my pitches and stories for NYU Local, the independent student-run blog. The coffee shop is cozy—the menu boards behind the counter are hand-drawn in colorful chalk, the couches are overstuffed, and the walls are papered in flyers explaining the differences between Ethiopian and Tanzanian coffee beans.

When I get to the front of the line, I place my usual order with the barista for a large iced coffee. Our eyes meet and my cheeks flush. He isn't my type at all—he wears his thick red hair in a man bun and his forearms are covered in intricate geometric tattoos—but there's something appealing in the warmth of his eyes and his even, straight teeth. I suppose that's a prerequisite for matchmaking, falling just a little bit in love with everyone you meet.

The barista hands me the coffee. I toss him a brief smile and circle the crowded shop until I find an open table. I pull my laptop out of my bag. It latches onto the WiFi right away, even though I haven't been here since I graduated. Home is where the WiFi connects automatically. I find the link to Bliss's private database in my email. Penelope had positioned this—working remotely—as a major perk of the job during my training.

"Just think, you can work while getting a pedicure!" she had crowed.

I refrained from telling her that I've never gotten a professional pedicure in my life. When I was a kid, I used to watch Mom at the kitchen table with a paper towel spread under her hands while she did her own nails. She always filed them into long points and painted them cherry red. She never splurged on a salon. I thought home mani-pedis were the height of glamour and beauty. I thought she was prettier than all the other moms who picked up their kids from school in sneakers and ponytails.

By middle school, I realized that different wasn't necessarily better. Tom Braddock, the hulking jock who was the captain of basically every sports team ever, mimicked Mom's walk as she came to pick me up from school one day when we were twelve. He stepped gingerly on his tiptoes, miming her walk in platform sandals, and wiggled his hips from side to side. His hands dripped from limp wrists and he put on a thick accent to say, "Baby, don't hug me, my nails are wet." I ran to the car and bit my lip to keep from crying.

I dive into the Bliss database for Mindy by setting the parameters to straight men ages thirty to forty-five who live in New York; it spits out 2,087 results. The choices are dizzying. I suddenly feel self-conscious—I know that this is New York and weirdos abound, but there's still something ever so slightly embarrassing about on-line shopping for dudes more than a decade my senior. I hunch over my laptop and pull the screen closer to me, then begin combing through the men's profiles one at a time.

No.

No.

No.

No.

No.

No.

No, no, no, no, no.

Oh my god, *no.*

And so on, and so forth, for, like, a half hour.

None of the men are complete garbage trolls. A lot of them come close to what Mindy is looking for. But something is always off. One guy checks almost every box on her list, except for the largest one: he has two kids from a previous marriage and no interest in having any more. Another guy sounds totally sweet and family-oriented just like her, but he works for a non-profit and makes only $40K a year.

I'm on the verge of losing hope when I find Mark's profile. He's number 506 in my results. He looks like a grown-up frat boy with soft brown eyes, ruddy cheeks, and a boyish smile. He works in finance, likes to run along the Hudson River on weekends, and has traveled to three countries in the past year. There's something vaguely Ryan Reynolds–like about his jaw. Mindy might go for him. His profile doesn't give me warm fuzzy butterflies the way I hoped it would when I stumbled across the right match, but reaching out to him is worth a shot.

I dig the notes from the training session out of my bag and copy what Penelope had told me to write in an email from my new Bliss account.

Hey Mark!

I'm Sasha, a matchmaker with Bliss. Your profile stood out to me for one of my clients in particular because you're both well-traveled and have a similar sense of humor. I'd love to learn more about you and see if you're a good match for my client. If you are, I'd be happy to set you up for free. Hope to hear from you soon!

—Sasha

A few minutes later, he writes back.

What is this client of yours like? Can I see a picture?

I immediately hit reply.

Thanks so much for your quick response! Bliss clients remain anonymous—it's just one of the perks of a paid membership. But I'd be happy to tell you more over coffee. Do you have time to meet this week?

I feel like I sound too desperate, but apparently that doesn't faze him. He responds a minute later, making me think I can actually pull off pretending to know what I'm doing.

9 am tomorrow. Starbucks, West between Albany and Liberty. See you there, Sasha—it'll be my pleasure.

The dude's kind of abrupt. But that's fine. I know that Starbucks; it's right by Jonathan's office. I text Mindy that I've already begun the hunt, and she texts back a string of clapping emojis. I schedule Mark's coffee into the calendar on my phone. I don't know if he's necessarily The One, but even if he turns out to be perfect, Mindy purchased the $700/month package that guarantees her two dates a month. I'll need to find her a second guy soon.

I close my laptop and relax at the table while I finish my coffee. I spent four years at Think Coffee, working toward a future as a writer. I figured I'd meet sources for interviews one day, or curl up in the cozy armchair in the back corner to knock out a thousand words, or even hold readings of my work here someday. I'm not ready to rule out that future just yet, but it's time to put it on hold.

When I walk into our apartment on First Avenue and Eighteenth Street, Caroline is flopped horizontally across the couch watching TV and petting our cat, Orlando (named for our shared childhood crush, Orlando Bloom). *Broad City* is on. We've both seen the whole series four times. Our friendship is as solid as Abbi and Ilana's, except we would never have sex with our boyfriends while Skyping each other like they do, because hello, boundaries. Although last weekend, I did spend twenty minutes hunched over her bare butt with a pair of sterilized tweezers to help her remove a splinter she got sitting on a park bench in a short dress. I am a spectacular friend.

"Hi! I thought you were starting work today?" Caroline asks.

"I did! I met my first client and started finding guys for her.

Scoot." I motion for her to move her legs and I curl up on one side of the couch.

"I can't believe you're really going to be a matchmaker," she says, reaching for the Apple TV remote to pause *Broad City*. "That's so fucking cool."

"I'm a real person now, just like you. Thank god."

"Welcome to the ranks of serious adults with serious jobs. Thank you for noticing how dedicated I am to my career," she deadpans.

Caroline works a couple of shifts a week at an East Village shop called Flower Power that sells herbs and is a part-time receptionist at a barre studio, which she mostly hates, but she gets free classes and a lot of time to work on the pilot for her TV show. I mean, theoretically. There has not been much writing going on. Instead, we stay up until one or two in the morning every night, drinking cheap pinot grigio, taking photos of Orlando, and making fun of her Tinder dates. Caroline can eat a whole box of Girl Scout Thin Mints in one sitting, never messes up her winged eyeliner, and has a crippling addiction to *Candy Crush*. She plays it constantly and texts me updates whenever she beats her previous personal record. We met while smoking pot in a dorm bathroom freshman year and are way deep in love.

"You know what? This calls for wine. We should celebrate your first day," Caroline says.

"But we're having dinner to celebrate with Jonathan and Mary-Kate and Toby in two hours."

"So?"

She's already up and rummaging in a drawer for our corkscrew. There's a cheap bottle of wine chilling in our fridge. It was six dollars on the sale rack at the liquor store across the street, but I've made a point of becoming friendly with the owner, so he gave it to me for five. Caroline finds the corkscrew, opens the bottle, and pours the wine into two glass ice cream goblets since neither of us has run the dishwasher lately. She hands me a goblet and I tell her all about my day.

"So, I need your help with Tinder," I announce.

Caroline is single. You know how everyone on *Sex and the City* and *Friends* and *Seinfeld* dated someone new every week? She does that, too, because none of them ever stick. She'll go out with almost anyone who asks because she thinks dating is a numbers game: the more dudes she dates, the more likely she is to find a relationship. But in practice, that doesn't work out. It just means she goes out with a lot of losers with commitment issues. In the four years I've known her, she's never had a boyfriend—just dozens of failed dates and a self-diagnosed case of carpal tunnel syndrome from swiping through apps.

"What do you mean, you need help?"

"Well, I found one guy in the database. But I need another."

"Are you telling me you're getting paid to swipe through dudes?"

"Technically, yes."

Her jaw drops. "I could be a gazillionaire by now! How is that fair?"

"Caroline, you *are* a gazillionaire. Let the little people have a slice of the pie, too."

She starts to stammer out a response, but stops. Her parents are both lawyers who put $2,000 into her checking account every month to cover her "living expenses." (Living expenses, according to Caroline, include things like toilet paper, coffee, and the fur sandals Rihanna once wore on a yacht.) She curls her long blond braid around her fingers and mumbles, "Fine, give me your phone."

Caroline thinks for a moment, types something out, then hands my phone back to me. She shows me the pithy tagline she's written under my photos: "I don't want no scrubs." A TLC reference.

"Seriously?"

"Trust me."

We adjust my settings to find men in Mindy's age range, and then I watch Caroline swipe left on one, two, three, six, twelve guys in a row. She barely registers each guy's face before she makes her decision. She's good at this. Too good, almost, after years on the app.

"Okay, your turn. Swipe right on the guys you like, left on the guys you don't."

I swipe right on the guy in the beanie, left on the guy in the snapback, hard left on the guy whose only photo is a faceless, shirtless selfie in a scummy bathroom mirror. I haven't even finished my first goblet of wine and I'm already drunk on power thanks to Tinder. I keep swiping until I stumble across a gleaming specimen: Adam, thirty-three. That makes him too old for me, but it's fine, since he's not actually *for* me.

Adam has a mess of short, dark curls and a five o'clock shadow. In his photo, he's looking up over the top of an actual printed newspaper, eyebrow cocked, like someone caught him off guard. I tap open the rest of his profile. "I'm an editor at *Esquire* by day and I'm working on a novel by night," he wrote. "Intelligence is sexy, chivalry isn't dead. Hope you like the southern twang. 6'3"." That's it. I scroll through the rest of his pictures—one of him hiking in the woods, a photo with his tiny, elderly grandmother, and another with his arm draped around a girl in a clingy white sundress that makes me jealous in a way I can't explain. I'm smitten. The combination of his hair, his eyes, and the fact that his name is Adam makes me think he's Jewish. I swipe right.

"It's a match!" Tinder announces, our two faces flooding the screen. I get why single people are addicted to this. It's easier to order a boyfriend than it is to Seamless a pizza.

Caroline peers over the screen. "Congrats! He's cute," she says. "Maybe more your type than mine, but cute."

Given her track record, that's a good thing. I refill our goblets with more wine and we swipe on Tinder for a while, making fun of the worst profiles. It's like a sad version of Whac-A-Mole—just when you think you've found the most depressing or poorly written profile, another one pops up.

"You should message Adam," Caroline finally declares. "He's your best bet."

"I don't know. The database is one thing . . . I don't know how to talk to people on these apps."

"That's dumb. You should talk to him."

I struggle to come up with a response. "Girls never send the first message, though, do they?"

Caroline grabs the phone, rereads his line, "Intelligence is sexy, chivalry isn't dead," and types out a response. She hits send with a flourish.

"There!"

"Wait!" I yelp, grabbing the phone. "What did you say to him?"

You say chivalry isn't dead? I don't believe you. I'm Sasha—nice to meet you.

Ughhhhh.

"Caroline, now he thinks I'm hitting on him. That's not how you're supposed to message potential matches."

She blanches. "I'm sorry, did I fuck that up?"

I'm not sure.

I reread her message. It's not bad. If I'm going to be a match-maker, I can't sit around all day waiting for men to talk to me—I should be putting myself (really, my clients) out there, even if the prospect of that makes my skin crawl. If (when?) Adam writes back, I'll let him know the deal with Bliss. But for now, there's nothing I can do.

Two *Broad City* episodes, two goblets of wine, and a handful of obscene Tinder messages from horny guys later, it's time to celebrate my entrance into the world of employed people with a dinner at Hotel Tortuga, my very favorite restaurant in the world. The guest list is small: Caroline, Jonathan, his sister (and my friend) Mary-Kate, and her fiancé, Toby. Tortuga is not a hotel at all, but rather a hole-in-the-wall Mexican place near Union Square that's almost solely to blame for the thirteen pounds I gained freshman year. The restaurant is simultaneously bright and a little dingy, with snug booths, a tropical seascape painted on one wall, the others papered with crayon drawings, and sticky red residue on the tables from spilled frozen sangria. When Caroline and I breeze in, we spot Mary-Kate hunched over her phone in the corner of the back booth. Our usual spot. Toby has one arm slung around her shoulders.

"Hey!" I lean down to give them both hugs. Caroline and I slide into the booth across from them. Mary-Kate doesn't look up from frowning at her screen. "What's wrong? You look upset."

"No, I'm fine. My work wife and I are making fun of our intern. We had to hire her because she's the editor in chief's niece, but her outfits are truly tragic. Think 2008 Kim Kardashian."

I can't fathom anyone wearing that much leopard print these days. "That's terrible."

Mary-Kate is the social media editor for Glamour.com, which means she knows how to make a meme go viral, but has not sustained a full conversation without checking Twitter since she was hired three years ago. She has a trendy long bob tousled just so, crisp red lipstick, and pristine cuticles. Today, she's wearing a royal blue dress that brings out her eyes. Most New Yorkers wear only black, myself included, but Mary-Kate's philosophy is that all black is for lazy people. She has no problem telling me this. We've been close ever since we first met, when she visited Jonathan in Paris during our semester abroad. Mary-Kate and Toby are getting married this summer. I'm a bridesmaid.

Toby flags down the waitress. "Could we have another bowl of crisps, please? Thanks, love."

"Crisps, please?" Caroline mimics his accent. He's British. Some people have all the luck.

"Chips," Mary-Kate tells the waitress.

I've always liked Toby. I've always felt a kind of kinship with him because we both have more or less the same goal: to marry into the Colton family. So far, he's doing a better job than I am; he popped the question last year. Toby's also far cooler than I am. He's the founder of Rolodix, an app that allows serial daters to input biographical information and photos for each of their suitors, lovers, and Tinder matches, Rolodex-style, to share with their friends. (Even I used it when I couldn't remember if Evan was the chef who made Caroline a pork roast or the trust fund baby/aspiring director. Turns out he was neither—he was the scruffy guy who invited her to his improv comedy show, which, spoiler alert, was not funny at all.) Not only is Toby making a pile of money off of it, but *GQ* called him "the hottest brogrammer this side of Silicon Valley" and the *Wall Street Journal* referred to Rolodix as "clever" and "ideally suited to today's swipe-heavy dating culture." I can quote these directly from memory because Mary-Kate does it constantly. Because life is unfair, Toby is also kind of a hunk: six foot one and half black with a razor-sharp jaw. If he weren't so hideously nice, most people would probably hate him out of jealousy.

Our phones all light up at the same time with a text from Jonathan: "Running 15 minutes late, be there soon."

"Duh," Mary-Kate says, rolling her eyes.

She brushes her hair to the side with her left hand, which she does a lot these days—ever since she got engaged. I know people have tics. Fine. But I never saw her fiddle with her hair so often until there was a two-carat, round-cut Anna Sheffield diamond with a pavé band attached to her hand.

"Soooo, tell us about your first day on the job!" Mary-Kate says, ladling us each a glass of frozen margarita from a pitcher. Tortuga's margs are famously lethal.

"Yeah, how'd it go?" Toby echoes.

"Wait for Jonathan," I say. "I want him to get here first."

Jonathan arrives eventually, dropping his Goldman Sachs duffel bag on the floor. I get up to kiss him, breathing in whatever makes him *him*. He smells like sea-salt cologne and office supplies.

"Sorry I'm running late. Mitch needed me to revise the presentation for a deal today. He said it only needed a few tweaks, but you know that means—"

"A lot of tweaks," I finish.

It comes down to this: Jonathan is normal. Better than normal—privileged. He grew up eating pancakes from scratch for breakfast, skiing on the weekends, and wearing Abercrombie & Fitch without caring what was on the price tag. He played lacrosse in high school and went to Columbia because his father did. He was always popular, so he was free to indulge his nerdiest hobbies without fear of judgment: collecting 1970s comic books in high school, joining the trivia team in college. He never had to study sitcoms to understand how regular families communicate or watch the cool girls, hawk-eyed, across the elementary school cafeteria to know what foods were okay to eat for lunch. (Apparently, borscht wasn't cool. My bad.) I crave his easy normalcy the way that addicts crave heroin. And right here is six feet of an exemplary all-American man, ready for me to observe his habits and learn which movies are supposed to induce nostalgia in me and how to use "summer" as a verb.

Jonathan slides into the booth next to me. "How was your first day?" he asks, squeezing my thigh.

I swallow a slurp of margarita. "It's insane. I can't believe I'm getting paid to do this. I just hung out with my first client, Mindy, who's actually really awesome, and then I looked for guys she could date."

Here's the part I can't say in front of Caroline: the job reminds me how lucky I am to be happily settled into a serious relationship.

Mary-Kate squeals and begins to bombard me with questions: How does matchmaking work? Do I have any other clients? Can I find her single bridesmaid a date to her wedding?

"No, set me up first!" Caroline says.

"You don't even need any help," I say.

Caroline contorts her face into a look of mock confusion. "But you're here with your boyfriend, and Mary-Kate's here with Toby, and—" She hoists herself up onto her knees and swivels to peer around the restaurant. "Hold on a sec, I don't see my boyfriend anywhere. Do you see him?"

"Fine, Caroline first!"

I fill Jonathan, Mary-Kate, and Toby in on meeting Mindy and Bliss's database, and how I've already scheduled coffee with Mark for tomorrow.

"And I got her set up on Tinder," Caroline says. Then she leans across me to talk to Jonathan. "Sorry, dude."

"Hey, as long as they know she's taken, I don't have a problem with it." Jonathan shrugs.

"Are you sure?" I ask.

I feel weird putting him in this position. I don't know anyone whose job requires them to download dating apps. Jonathan and I talked about it after my training session, and he said it wasn't a big deal, but I still worry it bothers him.

He stretches his arm around me. "Of course. I know you're my girl."

The words "my girl" still turn my insides warm and mushy. I love him.

"Sasha, I'm really happy for you. I am," Mary-Kate begins, which I know must be followed by a massive "but." "But don't you need experience for something like matchmaking? Why would anyone who wants to get married hire an unmarried twenty-two-year-old matchmaker?"

"They hire young matchmakers on purpose. My boss said she was looking for someone who had actually had sex in the past decade."

Jonathan bites off half the chip he's holding with a loud, smug snap.

Mary-Kate makes a sour face. "Ew."

"But she's right, though, babe," Jonathan says. "I mean, before me, you had hardly dated anyone."

"That's not true. I dated people."

"Sure, just no one tolerable," Caroline points out.

"Look, our food's here," Toby says, pushing the margaritas out of the way so the waitress can set down the platters of burritos and quesadillas.

It's too late to worry about my qualifications for matchmaking. I'll do whatever it takes—I have to.

— Chapter 4 —

We splinter off after dinner. Mary-Kate and Toby head home to binge-watch Netflix, or whatever it is engaged couples do on Friday nights. Caroline and I swing by our apartment to change. There's a birthday party tonight for a girl we knew in college, but that's not why we're going out. We're going because it's a rooftop party on the Lower East Side, which means we're guaranteed breathtaking views of the city, cool-girl fashion eye candy, and the heady feeling of a New York summer night done right. Jonathan darted out after dinner to finish up "just one or two small things" at the office, but promised he'd meet us at the party later if he can.

Three outfit changes, two ice cream goblets of pinot grigio, and one sing-along to the Spice Girls' "Wannabe" later, Caroline and I are ready to head out. I'm in my black slip dress with a long silver pendant and a pair of Caroline's heeled sandals. She's wearing a dangerously low-cut white leather top and half a roll of boob tape.

We indulge in the sweetest of luxuries, a cab. Caroline is texting Wesley, the guy she's been on two Tinder dates with this week, although I don't see why. From the photos I've seen, he's way too Brooklyn for her. His beard swallows up half his face and his arms crawl with colorful tattoos that any self-respecting person would instantly regret (Pikachu, the eggplant emoji, a jumping dolphin).

When the cab pulls up to the curb, Caroline swipes her card without negotiating with me first.

"I'll Venmo you back," I say, watching her tap at the screen to leave a 20 percent tip.

"Or whatever." She shrugs.

Maybe I'll pick up the next cab or the next bottle of wine, but she won't notice or care if I forget. I *do* want to pay her back, just to lessen my guilt: I told her I'd pay her back, so I should. I already mooch off her enough. We don't really talk about how I pay slightly less than my fair share of the rent and she pays slightly more. When she runs to Duane Reade to pick up shampoo, she always offers to pick some up for me, too. I think she feels guilty that she gets money from her parents and I don't, because she's never once brought it up and I've never stopped her.

The party spills out of a walk-up on Rivington Street onto the sidewalk. A hundred years ago, this neighborhood was full of Jewish tenements bursting with immigrants, but now it's all glitzy clubs and vintage boutiques that sell ripped Tupac tees for $300 and brick lofts where independently wealthy models/DJs live. There's a group of girls in tight dresses, clunky platform heels, and chokers. They look like out-of-state girls here for summer internships.

"Should we go up?" one asks nervously.

"I don't know if they'll let us in," says another.

"I thought you said you knew someone who knew the host?" says the third. "What was her name?"

"No, I sort of know someone who knows someone who knows the girl having the party. Do you think that's okay?"

"You here for Victoria's party upstairs?" Caroline asks, cutting in.

They swivel to look at her, wide-eyed.

"Yeah, how'd you know?"

"Come on up. It's fine."

Caroline climbs the three steps up the stoop and finds the buzzer for 4B. Someone buzzes her in and she pushes open the creaky front door with its chipping brown paint. Inside, the hallway is lit in harsh fluorescent lights. Caroline leads the way up the steep, warehouse-style staircase, followed by the three girls. They all have spindly legs and blisters that poke out from the straps of their shoes. A few people walk past us down the stairs, carrying open PBRs and that chain-strap vegan leather Stella McCartney bag that literally everyone in this neighborhood owns. The stairs wind up and up and up and my thighs burn. I can hear the hum of the music upstairs. We pass 4B on the fourth floor and finally reach a heavy, industrial-looking door clearly marked DO NOT OPEN above the sixth floor. Caroline pushes it open and the full force of the party's sound hits me.

There must be a hundred—two hundred?—people crowded onto the rooftop. They're splintered off into groups of three and four and the conversations blur together so all I hear are a few staccato shrieks of "Hiiiii!" as girls approach one another. Drake is on. The rooftop is made of concrete and splattered with red and purple graffiti on one wall. There's a glorious view of One World Trade Center, illuminated in glowing shades of silver and blue against the night sky. Below us, I can see bar patrons crowding around dives and girls in crop tops lining up outside clubs with velvet ropes. Cabs idle in the streets. The air is smoky. This is why people flock to New York every year and never, ever leave.

Caroline removes a pack of American Spirits from her purse and brings a cigarette to her lips. She fumbles through her bag to find a lighter, and a guy in an ironic Hawaiian shirt standing by himself jumps at the opportunity.

"Need a light?"

She smiles and leans in. A little orange flame flickers and the guy cups his hand around the light protectively, waiting for the cigarette to catch. He looks like he's waiting for her to say something to him, but instead, she turns to me, offering the pack of cigarettes.

"Want one?"

I do, but Jonathan hates when I smoke, and I bet he'll be here soon. I've told Jonathan I only smoke when I get really drunk with Caroline, which is true, but what I haven't exactly spelled out for him is that we drink together almost every night. Caroline's cigarette looks so appealing, but I decline. I wish I didn't have to. She switches sides with me so her smoke doesn't blow back into my face and lets Hawaiian Shirt Guy try to impress her for a few minutes before she touches him gently on the arm and tells him she needs to go say hello to a friend. She says she'll be right back. We will, of course, never come back.

We make our way across the party for the requisite rounds of saying hi to people from college. Victoria, the birthday girl, is wearing a red jumpsuit with a plunging neckline that matches the two Solo cups she's double-fisting and a glittery tiara that spells out DIVA. We went to the same parties most weekends in college, but we've never actually had a conversation sober or during the day. She's bugging a skinny guy with a laptop hooked up to the speakers to play Taylor Swift's "22."

"I don't care if you don't think the song matches the party vibes," Victoria insists, stomping one stilettoed foot. "It's my party and I want to hear it!"

I tap her on the shoulder and she spins around, anger dissipating into an exhilarated smile. Her eyes don't focus. She's wasted. She sets her cups down on the table beside her and throws her arms around us in a hug. Her floral perfume is overpowering. Caroline and I wish her a happy birthday.

"Sasha, I saw the craziest thing on Facebook," Victoria says, picking up her cups and guzzling from one. "Something about you being a matchmaker?"

I can't help but smile. "Yeah, I just started working for a dating service."

Victoria's friends descend on our conversation. We weren't ever that close. They had never paid attention to me quite like this before.

The girls pepper me with questions and ask to be set up. I start to explain how Bliss works, but Caroline cuts me off mid-sentence.

"You can't afford her," she announces smugly.

This is what Penelope was talking about when she said that matchmaking was the most powerful job in the world. Suddenly, they're all clamoring to talk to me, just because I do something a little cooler than working as an underpaid blogger or production assistant. I know they just care about the job, not about *me*—they don't really want to be friends—but this is almost better than having friends. It's social currency, and it makes me important tonight. Caroline squeezes my arm and tells me that her Tinder guy Wesley is here. She slips away into the crowd.

"What, did you set her up, too?" Victoria demands.

Before I can answer, my phone lights up with a call from Jonathan.

"I'm here, where are you?" he asks.

I'm relieved. I rise up on my toes to get a better view. I catch his eye, and he nods, wading through the crowd to reach me.

"You have a cool job *and* a boyfriend?" Victoria says, jaw hanging open. "Ugh. I'm getting another drink."

Jonathan is still dressed in his suit and has his Goldman Sachs duffel bag slung over one shoulder. I feel a thrill when I realize that he's probably the most successful guy at this party. Not necessarily the richest (Ruby "Daddy Bought Me a Company" Hoffman is here, and so is at least one rumored Saudi prince), but the person with the most impressive career, for sure. He looks obnoxiously good right now; every other guy at the party is wearing some graphic tee they found at the back of a vintage store, or worse, a pseudo-hipster chambray button-down they paid full price for at Urban Outfitters.

"You're overdressed," I say, giving him a quick kiss.

"You love it," he replies, smirking.

His hand lingers on the small of my back, fingers grazing the top of my ass. Victoria's roommates watch us hungrily.

We head over to the drinks table to scope out what's left of the booze. There are sticky, empty handles of rum, crushed cartons of beer with the bottles gone, and an overturned bottle of cranberry juice leaking sad puddles onto the concrete. I swat a fly away from an open bottle of vodka and pour us drinks. There's only a pinch of lemonade left and no other mixers. Jonathan winces when he takes his first sip.

"Don't make that face," I say. "It's bad for my Russian street cred."

"I think Putin will let you be."

"Tell that to my mom. She'll swoop in and replace you with some guy named Dmitri or Ilya like that." I snap my fingers for emphasis.

"Come on. She wouldn't."

While Jonathan won over my stepdad, Steve, he never quite got on my mom's good side. She doesn't understand why I want a boyfriend at all—she would've killed for the freedom to be single or play the field at my age. ("Look at all the options you have!" she crowed once, forgetting the fact that I am not actually drowning in men who want to be my boyfriend.) I warned Jonathan about this before they met for the first time, and so he amped up his usual charm. It backfired—she found him a little *too* smooth, like he was a player.

He launches into an explanation of the financial concepts behind his latest deal at work, which spins out into a history of the Greek economy over the past century, which reminds him to tell me the story about why his cousin Harrison will be arrested on public indecency charges if he ever returns to Mykonos, which prompts him to recite what he learned about nudity laws in New York City, since he looked those up one time. It's one of the things I love best about him. He's a sponge for detailed, obscure information, and can get lost in tangents like that forever. Sometimes, I have to force him back on track, but I wouldn't want him any other way. He's like my personal library, Wikipedia, and Google all rolled into one.

When I first met Jonathan, I had a constant fear that he'd pull the rug out from under me when I least expected it. I used to wake up furious with him, convinced that he had betrayed me somehow—lied or cheated or humiliated me—only to realize that whatever nightmare I had conjured up was purely a dream. I had to learn to relax, to enjoy him.

Caroline bounds over to us, trailing the bearded, tattooed Wesley behind her. They're a vision in leather: her on the verge of spilling out of her white top, him in a black motorcycle jacket. His dark hair is shaved close at the sides and gelled on top to flop over toward his left ear. He has a slightly chipped front tooth and scrawny collarbones that peek out from his loose V-neck T-shirt.

"It's just that I'm such a nineties kid," Wesley tells Caroline. "Like, it's insane. Those years were the best. I mean, Blink-182 is the shit, man, you know?"

I recall Caroline telling me that he's only going to be a junior in college. He was maybe a toddler when Blink-182 was big. Tops.

"I know, you told me." She sounds bored. "Guys, this is Wesley; Wesley, this is my roommate, Sasha, and her boyfriend, Jonathan."

"Hiya, guys."

He keeps talking loudly about being a '90s kid. When no one responds, he looks around uneasily, then launches into another story.

"I was a little hungover this morning so I didn't want to get up, but my roommate's stupid cat threw up in the hallway, and my roommate was making so much noise trying to clean it up," he says, swaying too close to me. I inch a polite step back. He inches closer, rambling on. "And that made me want to hurl, but I didn't because I was running late to meet with a mom on the Upper West Side. She wants me to photograph her kid's fifth birthday party. She's one of those moms who wears yoga pants and sneakers all day, even when she's not exercising, you know? I don't get it. But I was coming from Brooklyn and the L train had huge delays, so—"

I cock my head slightly and give Caroline a wide-eyed, close-lipped stare intended to communicate one simple concept: *Who the fuck is this guy?*

"Wesley? Why don't you tell Sasha and Jonathan about your art?" Caroline asks gently. Then, to me, "He's a really talented artist. I've seen his work."

"Oh, yeah, right. I do a lot of photographs of handmade sculptures. I just sold a triptych to this independent gallery—I was smoking one day and got the idea to light squares of American cheese on fire. When it melts, you can drape it over shit and it looks really cool. So I melted it over a toy NASCAR car, a Barbie doll, and a dollhouse sofa. It's about how society just indoctrinates children with capitalist values straight out of the womb, you know?"

The silence that follows is just a beat too long. I look down at my feet.

"He's very talented," Caroline says, turning to him and pressing her hand to his chest. I think she tries to beam at him, but the smile doesn't fully reach her eyes.

"Isn't that fascinating," I say.

"So, man, what do you do?" Wesley asks, clapping Jonathan on the arm.

"Nothing quite as creative as what you do," he says. Diplomatic as always.

Wesley takes in Jonathan's suit, frowning. "You're, like, what, a Realtor or something?"

"No." He stifles a laugh.

"Then what?"

"I work in finance."

"Oh, yeah? So, like, what does that mean?"

"I work for one of the bulge bracket investment banks."

"Which one?"

"One of the ones downtown," Jonathan says quietly, sipping his drink.

"Dude, do you work for the CIA or something? What's it called?" Wesley is annoyed.

"Goldman Sachs," he says, like he's embarrassed or something.

He's not, of course. It's a total game. It's like how Harvard grads will tell you they went to school "in Boston" or millionaires will tell you they're "comfortable." Jonathan likes to stretch out the process of telling people where he works. I know he secretly gets a rush from that wide-eyed, impressed look in people's eyes when he finally reveals what he does. If he were actually embarrassed, he wouldn't trot out this little song and dance every time he meets someone new.

Wesley narrows his eyes and nods. "I mean, whatever works for you, man. . . . But don't you have a problem with the way large banks threw millions of hardworking people under the bus with the subprime mortgage crisis?"

Jonathan starts to answer, but Caroline jumps in to smooth things over. "And Sasha just started a new job as a matchmaker! Isn't that cool?" There's a note of panic in her voice.

Wesley ignores her, choosing instead to duke it out with Jonathan. He's losing the argument—hard—when he suddenly checks the time on his phone.

"Do you ever listen to Righteous Mold?" he asks us.

"I'm sorry?" I ask.

"The band."

"Oh. No, I haven't heard of them."

"I got tickets to see them tonight, so I've gotta bounce. There's a one a.m. show around the corner. Sasha, Jonathan, it's been real. Caroline, you're a goddamn daydream." He downs his drink in one long gulp, then suddenly grabs her by the shoulders, kisses her, and disappears into the crowd.

Everyone is silent for several long seconds, absorbing Wesley's absence. The DJ has finally given in and is playing Taylor Swift. Victoria and her friends are screaming the lyrics to "22" in front of the circle congregating by the graffiti wall. Someone's iPhone camera flashes repeatedly. The photos will be on Facebook, Twitter, Instagram, and Snapchat within five minutes.

Caroline breaks the silence first. "You didn't like him."

I try to tread cautiously when it comes to the losers she dates. I know she's embarrassed by how they reflect on her. "I think you can do better," I say.

"Way better," Jonathan says.

"Ugh, don't you think I know that? He's awful. They're all awful. Every single one."

"There has to be someone out there who doesn't suck. You'll meet him, I promise." This would sound fresher—more convincing—if I hadn't already said it a million times before.

"Oh, fuck off, both of you," she snaps. "You don't know what it's like to be single and alone forever." She snatches up a lighter resting on the ledge of the roof, lights another cigarette, and sulks into it. Jonathan waves away the smoke.

"How did I become some soulless Tinder cyborg?" she whines. "I meet so many guys and can't make myself like any of them. I feel like there's something wrong with me."

"No, you're just going for guys who don't deserve you."

"I know it's like that line in *The Perks of Being a Wallflower*—we accept the love we think we deserve. And I know I'm fucking great, so why do I keep going for these idiots?"

I listen and nod and soothe her for a few more minutes until Jonathan gives me The Look that says it's time to go. We're heading downtown together and Caroline's heading uptown, so it doesn't make sense for the three of us to split a cab. I apologize to Caroline again for leaving.

"Yeah, whatever," she says. Her cheekbones file into sharp edges as she takes a drag. She blows her smoke up in a long stream toward the sky.

Jonathan reaches for my hand, but I can't help but teeter toward Caroline.

"Do you want me to stay here with you?" I ask.

I know she does. Back when we were freshmen or sophomores, we would stay out until the parties dwindled down to nothing, then collapse at the nearest diner and scarf down omelets. But that was a long time ago. Tonight, I just want to shut out the noise of the party and crawl into bed with Jonathan. It's an unspoken rule that when you get a boyfriend, the boyfriend becomes your go-to person, and your best friend is . . . well, not less important, but just important in a different way. They fill separate roles in your life. Caroline's never had a real boyfriend, so she doesn't get that.

She sighs. "No, you want to go. Go. Bye."

I feel a little bad leaving her there, but my feet are aching in these heels and I know Jonathan has had a long day. It's time to leave. In the cab on the way to his apartment, I slink down in my seat and nestle my head into his chest. I listen to his heartbeat. My eyelids grow heavy and I can feel myself slipping into a content sleep. Everything—finally—is perfect.

- Chapter 5 -

There's a Tinder message from Adam waiting for me when I wake up in Jonathan's bed on Monday morning. Jonathan rolls over to shut off his iPhone alarm and groans a slurred, "Mmmrrph." He's not a morning person. Usually, he hits snooze once or twice, but he must have an early conference call, because he actually crawls out of bed and slumps off to the shower.

His apartment is a one-bedroom in the West Village with a clear view of One World Trade Center. There's a Métro map of Paris Scotch-taped to the back of his door—a souvenir from our semester abroad—and a high-tech Swedish mattress piled with a rumpled navy duvet. His diploma is propped up on a bookcase jammed with econ textbooks and his old comic book collection. A blue bottle of sea-salt cologne, the gold watch he inherited from his grandfather, and his stack of work and personal phones are splayed out on his nightstand.

I don't hate mornings like Jonathan does, but I'm also not used to working at 6:45 a.m.—which I guess is technically what Tinder-ing with Adam constitutes.

I see you're a TLC fan. What else should I know about you, besides your impeccable taste in music?

You know, the funny thing about swooning is that it can happen even when you're horizontal in bed. Your boyfriend's bed. This is just harmless, work-related flirting. Adam picked up on the "no scrubs" reference, and that's kind of enlightened for a dude. On the "what else should I know about you" front, I should probably tell him that I'm a matchmaker, but I'm not sure how to drop that into the conversation. I really need him for Mindy, and I don't want to scare him off.

I screenshot the message and send it to Caroline for help, but she won't be up for another three or four hours. Later today I have a meeting at Bliss with all the matchmakers, so I can ask for their advice on how to deal with Adam. I have time to kill while Jonathan is in the shower, so I get lost Instagram-stalking a girl I know from NYU who's spending her summer hopping between Ibiza and Geneva as the nanny for a European royal family. She looks tan. I'm jealous.

That's when I hear the click of the bathroom door. Water droplets are sprinkled across Jonathan's shoulders and trickle down toward the white towel wrapped around his narrow waist. I press my phone screen to my chest and sit up in bed.

"Guess what happened while you were in the shower."

"What?"

"I got my first Tinder message from the guy I want for Mindy!"

"Hey, nice!"

He pulls a navy suit and one of eight identical white button-downs—the non-iron kind, since his mom no longer does that for him—out of the closet and drops them on the bed. He removes his towel. He still looks fantastic, of course, but a year of working late nights with no time for the gym and a corporate allowance have filled out his lanky frame.

"You know, it's kind of hot imagining other men drooling over you online." He shakes his head and grins.

I don't know what to say about that, but I don't like the look in his eye. "Don't jinx this for me."

"I want to see who's picking up my girl on Tinder," he says, gesturing for my phone.

I hand it to him and bite my lip. He eyes my meager list of matches and toggles over to Adam's profile, cocking his head to the side.

"Eh. Not sure about this one. I mean, I guess his grandma seems nice."

"What's wrong with him? He's adorable for thirty-three."

"He looks sort of . . . liberal artsy?"

I cross my arms over my chest and roll my eyes. "What do you know about picking up straight dudes?"

"Hey, you could be right." He holds up a charcoal gray striped tie and a solid blue one. "Which do you like better?"

I select the gray one. I'm mildly annoyed that Jonathan doesn't approve of Adam. I'm already anxious enough about meeting with Mark and going to the company-wide meeting at Bliss later today; Jonathan's lack of enthusiasm about Adam just makes me feel worse.

I freshen up with the toothbrush I keep at his place, wriggle into jeans and tank top, and tame my hair into a ponytail. Jonathan shrugs into his suit jacket, dropping his iPhone, company-issued BlackBerry, and wallet into his pockets. He pats himself down to make sure he's remembered everything.

"Alexa, lights off," he instructs his Amazon Echo. He breezes out the front door. "Sasha, let's go," he calls in the same tone of voice.

We take the elevator from his apartment to the lobby. Outside, there's a slow-moving crowd of tourists that clogs both sidewalks. He grabs my hand and pulls me quickly through the mass; his legs aren't even that much longer than mine, but I almost always have to run to keep up with him. He has no patience for anyone who moves slower than several light-years per second.

When we reach the subway, I wish him good luck dodging his managing director's misplaced anger today—apparently, divorce is a bitch. He wishes me good luck with Mark.

Jonathan is at the bottom of Goldman Sachs's totem pole, which means his Very Important Job demands his attention from the minute he wakes up until he crashes after midnight. Technically, he just manipulates Excel spreadsheets and creates detailed PowerPoints, but the *real* work is to look as busy and stressed as possible whenever he's in view of his boss—which, because of the office's open floor plan, is always. That means he gets in early, stays late, and never, ever, ever texts out in the open. I hate not talking to him during the day. Even when I do get to see him, he emails his boss from bed. Sometimes, when I'm trying to talk to him, he gets this detached look in his eyes and it's obvious he's obsessing about work instead of me. Dating a banker isn't for everybody, but I wouldn't date just any banker. The moments in which Jonathan can slide out of work mode and back into his old self—the nerd I fell in love with—make all the sacrifices worth it.

We step off the train at Chambers Street and let the subway doors snap shut behind us. We navigate through the underbelly of the station, paddling through the stream of sweaty commuters, all Connecticut dads wielding briefcases and young people in stiff blazers.

Amid the crowd of New Yorkers and tourists and halal carts, he grabs me around my waist and kisses me, shutting out the rest of the world. I savor being the center of his attention like this. Every kiss is like him affirming *yes, I choose you.*

Jonathan heads to work, and I walk to Starbucks to meet Mark. I'm overwhelmed as soon as I enter. This particular location is surrounded by several investment banks, law offices, and consulting firms, and by a quick visual estimate, a half dozen customers could be Mark. When it comes down to it, what's really the difference between one dark-haired guy in a suit and the next? I get in line and gingerly tap the man in front of me on the shoulder and hope it's him. He turns around, and a look of recognition flickers in his eyes.

"Mark?"

He looks slightly embarrassed to be here, but extends his hand to give mine a firm shake. Mercifully, he looks almost exactly like he does in his photos. Online, he claims to be five-eleven, but I'd eyeball him at an inch or two shorter than that. I make a mental note of his fib. We order coffee and he chooses a table toward the back, away from the mob of men in suits. He hunches over the table, shoulders inching toward his ears, and interlaces his thick fingers.

"So, what's the deal here?"

I launch into my spiel, explaining how Bliss works and why I thought he might be a good fit for my client, keeping Mindy anonymous to protect her privacy.

"Would you mind if I asked you a few questions?" I continue, pulling out my phone to take notes.

"Sure, but if you don't mind, it'd be great if you could keep it down." He cocks his head at the men in line. "My buddies, my co-workers . . . they're here all the time. I don't want them getting the wrong idea or anything. You know, I have no trouble getting girls on my own."

I have no intention of humiliating him. But the thought that I *could* . . . I don't often have that kind of power over these finance bro types. Well, one in particular. I lower my voice and ask him to describe his job. It's a neutral, low-stress opener that softens people up before the tough questions.

He briefly explains his work at Goldman Sachs, declining to go into much detail. "You probably don't care about all the nitty-gritty details, do you? They go right over most people's heads."

I offer him a tight smile. *Hey, asshole, I'm capable of understanding your garbage finance job. I've had sex after hours in a Goldman Sachs conference room, okay?* "You can tell me anything you'd like." I don't tell him about Jonathan.

"It's mostly just assessing risk for mergers and acquisitions in European markets."

"EMEA?" I ask. It's pronounced like one word: eh-MEE-ah.

He looks at me with renewed interest. "Actually, yeah. How do you—"

"European, Middle Eastern, and African markets," I say coolly. Jonathan assesses risk for the overseas subsidiaries of American corporations at Goldman Sachs. You don't date an investment banker for two years and not pick up the lingo.

I turn to his life outside work. He reels off a list of hobbies—running along the Hudson River, playing with his nephews, trying out restaurants and bars around the city—that sounds directly regurgitated from his Bliss profile. Before I can ask him about the types of women he gravitates toward, he pops a morsel of banana bread into his mouth and keeps talking with his mouth full.

"Look, I'm a busy guy. I don't have time to date for the sake of dating. So I'm selective about who I go out with—I only date extremely attractive women. Nines, tens. Eights if I'm slumming it." He gives me a careful once-over, appraising my features. "She should be blond, very thin, very fit, very busty." He mimes holding two heavy breasts with his sweaty hands. "No one over thirty. Oh, and she should make a decent salary on her own, unless she works in fashion or is a model, in which case I wouldn't mind shelling out."

Mark might want Barbie, but he's certainly no Ken. I take in the bags under his eyes, the obnoxiously large Prada logo on one arm of his glasses. He's not exactly bad-looking, but he's delusional if he thinks an entire posse of Kate Upton look-alikes is dying to date him. I get the horrible feeling that he and my dad have the same taste in women.

"Um," I say, taking an intentional slurp of my coffee to buy a few seconds of time. "Right, got it. You have very high standards. Any particular preferences regarding their personalities?"

"As long as they're nothing like my ex," he jokes, cracking a smile. He fills me in on a "crazy," "emotional," "irrational" woman. Then he drops the bomb.

"I've been on about one hundred and fifty Tinder dates since we split up seven months ago. On Saturdays, I stack them back-to-back: a coffee date, a happy hour date, a dinner date. I save the hottest for last—a late-night girl. So, who'd you have in mind for me?"

His words hang in the air for an uncomfortable second. Online, Mark had seemed passably handsome and suitable, and yet now I was sitting across from a Neanderthal. Was my judgment really that bad? When I applied for my job, I had wondered how Bliss stayed in business. Who would actually pay that much money for a stranger to sift through Tinder for them? But if the New York dating scene is full of guys like Mark, it makes sense. Of course successful women like Mindy would drop hundreds or thousands of dollars on the whisper-thin chance a matchmaker could actually find her dream guy. If the options are to fight off guys like Mark solo or to pay someone else to do it for her, Bliss is a no-brainer. How many times had I seen Caroline squirm while retelling the story of a downright disastrous date—the tone-deaf loser who talked about himself for a rambling forty-five minutes before asking what she did for a living, the drunk sad sack who projectile-vomited on her at a bar, the asshole who told a rape joke mid-hookup?

"Mark, it was a pleasure to meet you," I finish, rising to stand and shake his hand. I borrow my next line directly from Penelope's training and it flies out easily. "None of my clients meet your preferences at this time, but I'll be sure to let you know if anyone comes up in the future."

I suck in my stomach and wade through the pool of dad-bod finance guys to exit Starbucks with the most grace I can summon. I'm angry—not just at Mark, but at all the entitled men out there who must think and behave like Mark. If I weren't happy with Jonathan, these are the kinds of duds I'd be dealing with. But I don't have time to dwell, because I have to run downtown for the weekly matchmaker meeting at Bliss's headquarters.

I arrive at the brownstone just in time. From what I gathered from training, the matchmakers meet to fill one another in on their progress, brainstorm potential matches together, and work out issues with clients. The grand dining room is filled with a dozen young women, most of whom I don't know, none of whom are speaking to one another. Instead, they're each attached to one or more devices: some crane over laptops, some tap out messages on iPhones, some pace the floor while talking. Penelope sits at the head of the table, eyes glued to her phone, managing to text while nodding along to something Elizabeth is saying. I don't know where to sit, so I linger awkwardly in the doorway. No one seems to notice me.

I've been dreading this meeting since Penelope first mentioned it to me during training. I don't like to meet new people in a big group like this. It's nerve-racking. It reminds me of my biggest fear in high school, which was to walk into the cafeteria and not have anyone to sit with. Of course, I should be a pro at this by now, because I frequently *didn't* have anyone to sit with, but the bubbling pit of frantic fear in the bottom of my stomach is still there.

One afternoon during sophomore year of high school, I made the mistake of lingering too long near the popular girls' table. The ringleader of the group, a truly beautiful blond girl named Leah who would break her perfect ski-slope nose during an overzealous can-can kick at dance practice a year later, called me over and beamed up at me with her dentist's daughter smile. She asked me to join her for lunch; dumbfounded, I put my tray down in the open space between her dumb hockey player boyfriend, Tom, and her friend Marissa. As I sat down, the girls started to snicker. I could feel my cheeks growing hot and the bottom of my stomach dropping out. *What had I done wrong?*

"Like we'd ever let some tacky trailer-park trash sit with us," Leah sneered. Her lips curled around her teeth and made her look ugly.

She gave a slight nod to Tom, and he bumped my tray with his elbow just hard enough to topple it upside down into my lap. As pasta with tomato sauce seeped into the crotch of my white jeans, I saw Leah swiftly turn her head, withhold a giggle, and bite her lip, refusing to meet my gaze.

But this is a job. It's not a catty high school. I take a deep breath and sit down in the open chair next to Elizabeth. She smiles and moves her laptop to make room for my things. I pull out my phone and text Caroline so it looks like I'm busy.

A minute later, Penelope summons everyone's attention.

"Ladies, exciting news. I'd like to introduce you to the newest member of our team, Sasha Goldberg. She graduated from NYU this year and has a lot to bring to the table. She's currently working with Mindy Kaplan."

I give an awkward wave. The matchmakers quickly introduce themselves, then mostly snap back to their devices. Georgie is huddled in the corner of the room taking a phone call with one finger in her ear to block out the noise of the meeting.

Penelope gestures to the girl on her right, adorned in a gold cursive nameplate necklace that reads ALLISON.

"Want to take it away?"

Allison launches into an animated rant.

"So, Craig went out last night—you all remember Craig, right? The tech guy with three Ivy League degrees who stormed out on his last date because poor Amanda only graduated from Duke?" The other matchmakers nod heavily. Allison swivels her laptop around to show his picture: he's Asian, around thirty, and bundled up in a ski parka on a snowy slope. "Get this: he called Emily 'potentially interesting' and is considering seeing her again!"

Some of the matchmakers cheer. Allison beams.

"Wait, why is he only considering her again? Emily is great," one girl pipes up. I think she said her name was Zoe. She has a cotton candy–colored lob and thick, sculpted brows, like she transplanted her head directly from Pinterest.

"Craig is superlogical." Allison sighs. "He says he needs a few more days to process whether he thinks they're a compatible match.

He's worried that she might live too far away for the relationship to work."

Zoe wrinkles her nose and stops twirling her hair. "Don't they both live downtown?"

"Yes, but he's in Tribeca and she's in the East Village, and there's no direct subway route between the two."

"That's idiotic."

"I know! Especially because she's into him. She dug his intellect."

"Allison, keep trying to persuade him to see Emily again," Penelope says. "Craig is difficult. He's not going to hit it off with many girls, and he shouldn't ruin things with Emily if she likes him back. In the meantime, do you have any ideas for his next match?"

Allison groans and buries her face in her hands. "Ugh. I've been sending out messages on that Ivy League dating site, but no one's biting. I went up to Columbia to see if Craig would think any of the grad students are cute, but he's so particular. I want to swing by the Harvard Club later today, but I don't think I'll have time before six p.m. cocktails with my new client, Richard."

"Ladies, ideas?" Penelope asks.

The matchmakers spring into action, with fingers flying over keyboards. One calls out a five-digit ID code, adding, "She's a surgeon who went to Stanford." Allison enters the code into her own computer, pulling up her photo and information, and shakes her head. "Too old for Craig." One person points at another, snapping her fingers repeatedly, struggling to recall the name of "the therapist who went out with the startup guy to that karaoke bar in Brooklyn Heights the day it was raining." The other person somehow knows exactly who she means and shakes her head no, explaining that the therapist is now seeing someone else. Another matchmaker drums her fingers on the table and suggests her own client, whom Allison kindly dismisses as not smart enough for Craig. There's a silence, and Penelope admonishes the group.

"Most of your clients went to Ivy League schools. Some of *you* went to Ivy League schools. Surely there's someone out there for Craig. Think!"

Another flurry of activity: the matchmakers recommend their sorority sisters, friends of friends, and former clients who might be single again. An idea dawns on me.

"I might know someone." Everyone looks over. "My roommate Caroline's older sister Grace might work. She went to Brown and works at a non-profit. She's twenty-six, if that's not too young for Craig. But she's new to the city and brilliant and looking to meet people."

"Is she pretty?" Allison asks. "Craig is a snob about looks, even though he claims to be a sapiosexual—only attracted to people's intelligence." She looks as if she is trying extremely hard to avoid rolling her eyes.

"Very pretty." I pull up her Instagram on my laptop, scroll past some unflattering, artsy close-ups, and click on a lovely photo of Grace taken at Caroline's graduation party a couple of months ago. I turn the laptop around for Allison to see. Grace looks a lot like her sister except she has rounder features and would never pierce her nose like Caroline did.

"Hmmm. She might work. Does she date outside her race?"

"I'm not sure. I mean, why not?"

"A lot of people don't. The two demographics that receive the fewest messages on dating sites and apps are black women and Asian men. That puts Craig at a disadvantage."

It seems as if people cease to be people here. Instead, they fit into boxes: age, race, neighborhood, height, pretty or not pretty, what school they went to, how much money they earn. I tell Allison that race doesn't matter to Grace.

"And she wouldn't be put off by a guy like Craig?" Allison asks, concerned. "He's an odd duck. Stubborn, ultra-analytical, a little shy."

"She hasn't gone out with anyone in a long time. I think she could be into him."

I haven't exactly answered Allison's question, but it's probably better not to. I'll beg Grace to do it later. If she needs to be bribed with a bottle of wine, so be it. I need Allison and the rest of the matchmakers to like me. Allison asks me to text her Grace's contact info, and I can't help but smile.

The rest of the meeting passes in a rush. I'm impressed by how much the matchmakers know about the people in the database:

Alex can't date Katie because he's allergic to cats and she has two.

Julian won't find Polly attractive because he's exclusively into Latina and Asian women.

Marla shouldn't be set up with Norm because he looks too much like her awful ex-husband.

Harris isn't successful enough for Tom, unless he got that promotion he was hinting at the last time Zoe spoke to him.

Vanessa once might have gone out with Charlie, but she's gotten much pickier since she made *Forbes* 30 Under 30.

Nick is blacklisted after the very rude, sexually explicit voicemail he left for Penelope.

The matchmakers conjure up strings of names in a row, recall a dozen ID numbers off the top of their heads, and remember tiny, precise details about hundreds of strangers' lives. And when the possible database options seem exhausted, they keep going. They shout out names of people they met at dinner parties and music festivals and indie movie screenings. People who once dated their best friend's summer fling's coworker but are now single. People who followed them on Twitter last week who might be attractive in real life. My own social circle suddenly seems so small.

When it's my turn to share, I recap my lunch with Mindy, coffee with Mark, and exploration of the database and Tinder.

"You should check out Sam in the database," Penelope suggests.

Georgie snaps her head up so fast, I'm surprised her thin neck doesn't break. "Sam Nolan?"

"Sam Weinstein."

"Penelopeeeee," Georgie whines. Her lower lip sticks out and her spine sags into a curve. "You know I want him for myself."

I look back and forth from Georgie to Penelope to Georgie again. From the head of the table, Penelope sits up straight and purses her lips.

"He's off-limits. He's in our database," she says firmly.

"Come on," Georgie protests. "You know I'm obsessed with him."

"Georgie, I said no. You know the rules."

Georgie glares furiously at Penelope across the table. "Fine."

Head down, I type Sam's name into the database, trying to tap the keyboard as lightly as possible to avoid disturbing the meeting further. There's a note in his profile that he's been dating someone named Kerry for the past month.

"We're professionals here," Penelope continues, "and we don't mix business with pleasure."

Georgie is still glowering, arms crossed.

"Well, there's one guy who seems pretty perfect for Mindy," I say, desperate to cut through the tension in the room. "Adam.

Thirty-three. He's an editor at *Esquire* and takes photos with his cute, little old lady grandma, and apparently has this sexy southerner thing going for him. But I haven't told him yet that I'm a matchmaker."

"Do it now!" Georgie says. Her fury seems to evaporate. She turns her megawatt smile on me for the first time and leans over the table to reach me. "Here, give me your phone."

I open Tinder on my phone and take a second to read over Adam's last message to me. My stomach tightens into a knot, but I hand my phone to Georgie anyway. She glances at it, types out a message without hesitating, and slides my phone back to me for my approval.

Adam, you're a delight. I'm so glad we connected. But I'm afraid I have a bit of a secret: I'm not single. And I'm not cheating on my boyfriend, either. I'm a matchmaker for a dating service, and I've been hoping that you would be a perfect match for one of my clients. She's beautiful and vivacious and witty and I know she's dying to meet a gentleman such as yourself. Could we meet for drinks sometime? I'd love to tell you more . . . xoxo Sasha.

It sounds nothing like anything I would ever say—ever—but Georgie probably knows what she's doing. I hesitate over the intimate "xoxo Sasha," but hit send anyway. My heart is racing. What if the message is so crazy, he doesn't respond? I guess there are more fish in the sea, but there's something about this particular catch. I don't know what it is—just a gut feeling that tells me he's the right guy for Mindy. Maybe it's my newfound matchmaker intuition coming in strong.

When the meeting ends ten minutes later, the matchmakers disperse: some spread out into the study to chill, others dash out the door for meetings. I scoot my chair back and gather my laptop and purse. I know I shouldn't be nervous about joining them in the other room, but butterflies form anyway. They're all just so polished and opinionated—I wouldn't even know where to begin to connect with them. Even though Elizabeth has been friendly to me, it doesn't mean they'll all be like that.

That's when my phone lights up with a Tinder message from Adam.

Sorry, but I was interested in you, not your "client." I don't think this is going to work out.

– Chapter 6 –

Here's what I wish I had known before Jonathan took his job: when
you date a finance guy, you have to be okay with getting neglected.
I am now, most of the time. They don't mean to eff you over like
that—it's just that the job comes first and everything else comes,
well, dead last. But I've been waiting outside Ruchi, the Indian restaurant near his office, for nearly a half hour, and my neck is starting to ache from craning down at my phone to pass the time. I'm
bored and annoyed. Jonathan was supposed to pop by for a bite to
eat with me, then run back to finish up his work. My phone rings.
Jonathan only calls when it's bad news.

"Hey," he whispers, "I'm so sorry I'm running late. I know I told
you I'd try to be better about this."

I exhale just loudly enough to let him know I'm not thrilled.
"No, it's fine."

"I feel really bad for having you trek down here, but Mitch sprung
this fire drill on me at the last minute and I can't get out right now."

I got used to this a long time ago. A fire drill is when a boss
throws an urgent task at a junior banker and sees how quickly he
can get it done. It's not Jonathan's fault, but this is the second time

he's canceled last minute this month. He wasn't like this when we first met. His job changed everything.

"I mean, I'm already at the restaurant. You can't leave the office just for a half hour? You'll need to eat *something*."

I'm pleading. I hate pleading. It makes me sound needy. There's a long pause on the other end of the line.

"I'm so sorry, babe. Tonight's not gonna work." At least his voice sounds tender as he shuts me down. "I have to go."

The phone clicks off. It's been a shitty day: Mark disappointed me, Adam disappointed me, and now, completing the trifecta, Jonathan is disappointing me, too. Men are the worst.

Ruchi is overpriced, and so even though I could kill for some chicken tikka masala right now, I cross the street and pick up a slice of dollar pizza instead. The pizza guy hands it to me on a paper plate and I sit at one of the low gray tables under harsh fluorescent lights. A late-2000s pop song blares from the speakers. I open Tinder, go through twenty-five profiles, swipe right on five, and match with three. I copy and paste identical messages to each of them, taking care to personalize them with names so each man feels special—a tip gleaned from our staff meeting this afternoon.

Hi Jason! I know this might sound unusual, but I'm actually not on Tinder for myself. I work as a matchmaker for a dating service called Bliss, and I think you could be an amazing match for one of my clients. Would you be interested in learning more? I'd love to hear from you.

Although I'm sending a ton of messages, my inbox is frustratingly empty. I double-check just to be sure; no new messages from Adam.

I'm curious if I can find him outside Tinder, which turns out to be surprisingly easy. Researching potential matches for Bliss uses the same skill set I honed as a freshman reporter at *NYU Local.* I Google "Adam + Esquire + editor" and up pops his page on the website—Adam Rubin. (Rubin! So, he *is* Jewish.) He writes about music: album reviews, industry news, interviews with rock bands and rappers I've actually listened to. I get sucked into reading his work. Then I type his name into Instagram and scroll till I find his profile. The most recent photo is of a dimly lit drink on the rocks, posted twenty minutes ago. Guys never know how to properly edit photos. Hello, saturation and brightness filters.

"The usual watering hole never fails," the caption reads. I tap open the location tag: Tanner Smith's, a bar on West Fifty-Fifth Street.

I flip back through Adam's photos. I'll admit it: he's a hunk. I have a crush—a work-sanctioned, totally productive crush that I want to spin into a match for my client. So sue me. Georgie goes out to pursue matches in person all the time. Maybe I can, too.

Before I lose my nerve, I scarf down the rest of the pizza, dump the plate into the trash, and speed-walk to the subway, darting between workers filing out of office buildings. *You can do this, you can do this, you can do this*, I tell myself with every step. *This is your job now, this is your job now, this is your job.* I hop on the train uptown. I realize that Adam might have already left the bar, or maybe that was an old photo he just posted now. It's not like real life is a *Law & Order: SVU* episode, where the bad guy is always at the same neighborhood pub that the cops just so happen to visit. New York is sprawling, and Adam could be anywhere by now. I don't want to sit alone in that pizza shop all night. I want to be bold, like a real matchmaker would be. I don't have a plan for what happens when I find Adam; I just know that I have to win him over for Mindy. When I get off the subway and reach the bar, I take a deep breath and push open the door.

It's darker inside than I expected, and it takes my eyes a second to adjust. The bar is all gleaming wood and old-fashioned black-and-white tile and swirling wallpaper. It looks like the kind of place where cocktails are 80 percent elderflower liqueur and cost a minimum of fifteen dollars. Pretension aside, it looks comfortable, like everyone here just happened to drop by their hippest friend's place for a drink after work.

I take a few hesitant steps forward, scanning the row of people at the bar. There's a guy with a dumb handlebar mustache reading from a Kindle, two women in off-the-shoulder tops clinking wineglasses, and a pack of four dudes who probably work in marketing who are all wearing identical blue button-downs with light sweat stains under their arms. Every stool is taken, and from what I can tell, Adam isn't anywhere. He could be at the back of the bar, I guess, but I'm too self-conscious to poke around. That's when I lose my nerve. I shouldn't be here. Adam doesn't want to be bothered. He doesn't want to be tracked—fine, stalked—via social media. What am I doing?

I leave the bar. I slump against a wall and feel embarrassed. I really thought I could do this job—be bold and flirty and fabulous. Instead, I'm chasing down a dude I've exchanged three messages with on Tinder on the slim chance he's actually down to date Mindy. But I'm not brave enough to pursue Adam. I want to go home. I'm only a half block from the N train. I trudge toward it, but stop at the top of the stairs leading down to the station.

I didn't come all the way to the bar just to turn around and go home. I'm already here, and even if I feel silly and self-conscious, I'd feel even worse going home on the subway without making a real effort to find Adam. I turn around and walk the half block back to the bar. I pull myself up to my fullest height, take a deep breath, and head back inside. I have to do this.

I walk along the bar. Same Kindle guy, wine women, marketing bros. No Adam. The bartender, a guy with a slight build in a tight vest, catches my eye.

"Can I get you something?" he asks, picking up a cocktail menu and offering it to me.

I smile and shake my head. "Maybe later."

I move toward the back of the room, where tables line a rosy brick wall. And there he is: Adam, alone at a two-top, nursing what looks like whiskey and hunched over a black Moleskine notebook. At least, I think it's Adam. He has dark curls, an olive tan, and two days' worth of stubble. I pull my phone out of my purse, open up his profile on Tinder, and swipe quickly through his photos to confirm his identity. It's definitely him.

I have never approached a guy in my entire life. Like, not even once. I rack my brain for an opening line, but I'm coming up with nothing. I know if Caroline were here, she'd tell me I don't need an opening line—because I'm hot (according to her), guys will talk to me no matter what. I don't really believe her, but right now I need some advice. I take five quick steps in Adam's direction.

"Adam, hi!" I wave.

He looks up from his notebook, startled. His dark hair sticks up in the front, like he recently ran his hands through his hair. "Hi!" Then a short pause. "Er, do I know you?"

"Sort of. Well, no. I guess you don't. I'm Sasha. From Tinder." I can feel my face turning bright red.

He tilts his head and gives me a blank look.

"The matchmaker."

His expression changes as it sinks in. He runs a hand over his stubble. "Jesus Christ."

"I swear I'm not stalking you."

"I don't know if I believe you." A hint of southern drawl laces through his vowels. "How'd you know I was here?"

Time to think fast. I can't let him slip away. "How about I tell you over a drink?"

"Don't you have a boyfriend?" he says, a hint of a challenge in his voice. His eyes gleam. He's cuter in person, should that even be possible.

"I mean, yes. But that's not the point. I just want to get to know you. I really think you'd hit it off with my client."

"You know, the more you use the word 'client,' the more this sounds like an escort service gone wrong."

"I promise it's not. Let me buy you a drink?" I will him to not reject me in public.

Adam scratches his chin and looks around, then gives an ex-asperated sigh. He closes his notebook and stands up from his chair. He's massive—six foot three, a wingspan like a basketball player's, shoulders that slope endlessly under his worn-in charcoal gray T-shirt, and an aura that extends a good two or three inches beyond that. He moves to the open chair and pulls it out from the table.

"All right, take a seat."

I'm shocked, half by my bravery and half by his chivalry. I sit; he waves over a waiter.

"Could we get a cocktail menu?" he asks.

"Oh, I don't need anything special," I say. I don't want to waste his time. "Just a vodka tonic, please. Thank you."

"I'll do another bourbon, neat," he tells the waiter. He's close to finishing his drink.

Adam takes a sip from his glass. "So, Sasha—Sasha, is it?—you should probably start by explaining how you found me here."

"It wasn't rocket science. You're easy to find on Google, and from there, your Instagram told me where you were."

"That's creepy." He cocks an eyebrow.

"Yeah, maybe, but I wouldn't have tracked you down if I didn't think you'd be the perfect match for my client."

He shakes his head. "There you go again with that word— 'client.' You're gonna have to explain that to me. This whole 'matchmaking' deal." He actually makes air quotes. "I don't want to buy anything, if that's what you're after."

"No, that's not what I want to do at all," I counter quickly. "I work with a company called Bliss. Our clients tend to be too busy or too high profile to go out and find dates themselves, so they turn to us to help find suitable matches. Clients pay for personalized matches, but recruits like yourself don't pay a dime."

The more often I churn out Penelope's words from training, the more they feel like my own. Every conversation I have on Bliss's behalf makes me feel a sliver more like a bona fide matchmaker and less like a kid faking her way through a grown-up, glamorous person's life. The waiter returns with our drinks.

Adam leans back in his chair, stretching his arms up and inter-locking his fingers behind his head. I can see a hint of his stomach and the trail of hair leading into his jeans. I snap my eyes back up to his before he can notice.

"You know, what the hell?" He laughs and leans his elbows for-ward onto the table. "It's not like I'm meeting my dream woman on Tinder."

"God, it's the worst."

"Oh, yeah? How long have you been on it?"

I bite my lip and consider lying. "Three days?"

"Come on." He groans. "That's nothing."

I can feel my cheeks flush again, and I know it's not just the first sip of my drink. There's a tiny spark between us that needs to be extinguished.

"So, um, can I ask you a few questions about yourself? To see if you're compatible with my . . ." What's another word for client? "With the woman I'm working with?"

He laughs, spreading his elbows wide and resting his chin on his knuckles. "Shoot."

"Are you looking for a serious relationship, or something more casual?"

It sounds so clinical when I ask it like that. But I have to say it—I mean, I met him on Tinder, so for all I know, he could just be looking for a casual hookup.

He rolls the edge of his glass on the table, avoiding eye contact. "It's probably time for something serious. That's one of the reasons I left the South. I grew up and went to school in Georgia, but everybody down there paired off years ago, and then it was just me. Third wheel extraordinaire." He laughs, but in the way Caroline laughs about being single; it's not funny anymore.

"You want marriage and kids?"

"I mean, I'm not opposed to having a little fun along the way." He grins. "But yeah, a family would be nice eventually."

I'm relieved to be on the right track.

"Cool. Can you tell me about the type of women you typically date?"

"Type?" His accent draws the word into two syllables. *Ty-ype?*

"Like, in terms of looks, personality, interests, age." I feel like a creep probing him for this information—like it's too personal for me to ask. But I have to stick it out. It's my job now.

"Oh, I mean, I don't know . . . smart, funny, pretty?"

I nod encouragingly, but that doesn't actually give me anything to work with. It's too vague.

"When you say 'pretty,' what specifically do you mean?" I try.

"Well, I swiped right on you, didn't I? I've mostly dated brunettes with, uh, a few curves on them. I've dated petite girls in the past, but it's not on purpose. It just worked out that way." He gives me a sheepish smile. "Sorry, I know you're tall."

"No, no, I'm not offended at all." Actually, I'm irritated on principle. It works out best for everyone to pair off by height. But whatever, Mindy's Olsen-sized—five foot two.

I draw out the rest of the information slowly: he likes women who aren't afraid to call him on his bullshit and put him in his place. He wants someone with a little fire in her personality, someone with a delicious laugh. The most romantic thing he's ever done was back in college, when he crammed into a bus seat for ten hours overnight with a bouquet of sunflowers and a tub of chicken soup to surprise his long-distance girlfriend when she had the flu. (Mindy will die—that is too freaking cute.)

The conversation dances in lazy circles away from the subject at hand—the novel he's working on, how he always felt out of place in the South, the creepy Pigeon Man with graying skin in Washington Square Park we're both scared of—but every once in a while, he stumbles onto another note for me.

"I don't always date Jewish girls, but I guess it could be nice. It would make my mom happy. But not a JAP. I'm done with those princessy types, you know?"

I nod and jot it down. No Jewish-American Princesses—he means girls who carry Rebecca Minkoff bags to brunch and spend Christmas eating Chinese food with their grandparents in Boca Raton. Mindy isn't a princess.

"Oh, and you know what drives me crazy? I once went out with a girl who made the most disgusting noises when she chewed. This woman you have in mind for me, she doesn't do that, does she?"

"She's a perfect lady."

He mimics the chewing noises, and they're awful, like a trucker slurping down food in the front seat of his eighteen-wheeler.

"Ew, stop it!" I reach out and swat his arm.

His eyes flash to mine, and I suddenly pull back, embarrassed. I shouldn't have touched him like that. Besides, he's for Mindy. They're perfect for each other—how could they not be? I adore her, he's charming, and they both seem to like me. That's how the transitive property works, right?

"I should probably get going," I tell him.

"Of course." He signals for the check. "Will I hear from you again? I mean, for Bliss."

I'm surprised he remembered the company's name. "I have to run the match by my boss, but I have a good feeling about this. From what you've told me, I think you two will really hit it off."

The waiter comes by with the check and we both spring to give him our credit cards.

"Hey! I told you this one's on me," I say.

He shoos away my hand. "Come on. I can't let a beautiful woman buy my drinks."

I redden. "Seriously. It's on my company." I love that I can say that now.

"A southern gentleman would never let a woman pay her own way."

It's silly, because I know he can probably afford the tab with no problem. It's just important that I keep this professional—and let Bliss cover the bill.

"Split it down the middle," I tell the waiter after a tense beat.

Adam goes quiet. I think we both feel flustered. The steady lull of other people's conversations fills the space between us.

He recovers from the awkwardness first, saying, "If your client is half as lovely as you are, I can't wait to meet her."

I break into a grin, but force myself to cut that shit out. "Oh, well . . . she's really fantastic, I promise."

We each sign the check and I follow him out of the bar. He holds the door open for me; he's exceedingly well-mannered. I don't know how to part appropriately. A hug seems too intimate, but a handshake would be too businesslike. He pauses, too, like he can't figure it out, either. He steps forward, like he's going for a hug, at the exact moment I give an awkward wave.

"Er, right, bye," he says.

I turn and hurry down the street to the subway station. I take the stairs to the train two at a time. I happily swipe my yellow MetroCard through the machine—after all, I'm about to hit payday for Mindy and Adam's date. The subway is humid and grimy, but there's a four-piece jazz quartet on the platform playing "What a Wonderful World." The trumpet player, an older man in a fedora, winks at me when he catches me listening. I let myself sway to the beat until the train pulls into the station.

– Chapter 7 –

Jonathan caved. He always does—eventually. Two and a half hours after Caroline and I popped open a bottle of victory pinot grigio to celebrate my successful stalking mission, Jonathan called. He was getting a cab home from work, he said, and did I want him to pick me up? It's out of the way, but he wouldn't mind. Caroline and I were in the middle of a deep dive through Adam's Facebook photos dating back to 2007—it's all we can see thanks to his privacy settings. But the minute Jonathan's name popped up on my phone screen, I knew what he'd ask and that I'd say yes. I always do.

"I'm so sorry I couldn't do dinner earlier," he apologizes when I climb into the cab. I slide across the seat to give him a sloppy kiss. He pulls back a little too fast and I curl into the nook of his arm. "Oof, how's the wine tonight?"

"*Delicious*, thank you very much."

There's a white plastic takeout bag in his lap that smells spicy and familiar.

"I brought you chicken tikka masala from Ruchi," he says sheepishly. "I wound up ordering in."

"For me?" I squeal. I cringe a little when I hear how drunk I sound.

"Just for you."

The cab, the meal; it might sound special, but it's not. Goldman Sachs lets even junior employees expense up to twenty-five dollars for dinner after 8 p.m. and any amount for a cab after 9 p.m. I'm not above enjoying his job's perks. I almost feel entitled to them after all I put up with.

As the cab turns and zooms downtown, I tell Jonathan all about tracking down Adam and winning him over for Mindy. I amp up the parts where I really sold Adam on Bliss; I gloss over the stomach-churning chemistry between us and the way he called me "beautiful" in that languid, stretched-out accent.

"I wasn't actually sure I was cut out for this matchmaking stuff, but I'm actually not . . . bad?"

"Of course you're not bad." He squeezes my thigh. "No guy in his right mind would say no to you."

"But it's not actually *me*, though. I'm just the . . ."

"Bait?" He turns to look at me, grinning, and his hand moves farther up my thigh.

I swat his hand away. "The middleman. The wingwoman."

He smirks. "Call it whatever you want."

My tongue still feels thick with cheap wine when Jonathan's alarm blares the next morning.

"You can sleep in," he says quietly as he shrugs into his suit jacket. "Just lock up on your way out."

"Mmmrph."

Eventually, the sunlight glinting off the glass office tower across the street makes it impossible to sleep. I get up, shower, savoring the ocean-scented bath products that leave me smelling like him, and tackle some work for Bliss. Penelope made it clear in training that I don't have full autonomy—none of the matchmakers do. Before I can set up a date, I have to email Penelope a match proposal detailing why Mindy and Adam are compatible, including photos of each of them. ("Looks and status," she had repeated. "Looks. And. Status.")

Mindy Kaplan, 35, is a TV exec who hopes to settle down and start a family. She is bright, fun-loving, and hard-working. She seeks someone masculine and assertive, yet kind and considerate. Ideally, he'd be Jewish.

Adam Rubin, 33, is a writer who moved to New York from the South specifically because his friends had all settled down and he felt left out. He's ready for a more serious relationship. He has impeccable manners, the broad shoulders and height that Mindy likes, and he's Jewish.

They're equally attractive and equally successful, and appear to be each other's preferred physical types. (Her celebrity crush is Ryan Reynolds; he likes petite, curvy brunettes.)

I have a hunch they'll click. He's charming and suave; she wants someone assertive and masculine. She's outgoing and he's a little quieter. I think they'll balance each other out nicely. I like the idea of them together!

I attach photos of Mindy and Adam and send the email off to Penelope. A jumble of energy and good nerves snakes through the pit of my stomach.

I pull on a pair of light-wash boyfriend jeans and a white eyelet top from the pile of things I keep at Jonathan's place, and I'm in the middle of doing my makeup when Penelope emails back.

"Excellent work! You have wonderful instincts. Please schedule this date."

I have wonderful instincts. I shoot off a text to Mindy.

"Good morning! Just wanted to let you know I had drinks last night with a handsome, charming gentleman for you. A. is an editor at a magazine and criminally attractive. When can you meet him?"

Penelope had taught me to never use people's first names—initials only—before a first date. Bliss instituted that rule after a client Googled her match before a date, then stood him up because she didn't find him attractive on Facebook. Plus, initials create mystery, and that only adds to the client experience, or so I'm told. Mindy writes back instantly.

"Sasha!!! I was just thinking about you. I was just reading my horoscope and apparently Venus's return bodes well for my love life this month. CANNOT WAIT to meet A. Is Sunday night too soon? Any time after 6?"

"Let me check with him and get back to you."

"Thanks, doll. BTW, do you know what sign he is? I'm a Cancer. Not that we have to be astrologically compatible. But it's fun to think about."

I look up Adam on Facebook. His birthday is in March. I Google his sign, then text Mindy that he's a Pisces. This is so stupid.

"Phew!! I just really cannot date another Aquarius after what happened with my ex. Sorry, forgot to mention that earlier. K, can't wait to see if he's free Sunday."

I start to text Adam, but another text pops up from Mindy.

"Sunday doesn't sound like I'm too available, does it?"

I reassure her that it does not and finish my text to Adam. He takes longer to respond—enough time for me to finish my makeup and make coffee—but texts back to confirm Sunday evening. I wonder if he's lounging around his apartment, or if he's waking up in someone else's, or if he's already writing a story for Esquire.com.

I stretch out on Jonathan's beautiful brown leather couch intending to plan the date. But I wind up reading Adam's stories on the site. There's an interview with a producer on a highly anticipated upcoming indie album, a story mourning the loss of the famed New York City concert venue Webster Hall, and an essay defending country music from barbs thrown by what he calls "northern snobs" (guilty). I catch myself reading them each in his deep drawl before I close the site and force myself to get back to work.

Penelope had emailed me a Google Doc with creative date ideas, but they all seem too eclectic for Mindy's tastes. One date involved pretending to be engaged and shopping for a diamond ring at Harry Winston together; another involved a scavenger hunt through Washington Square Park; a third sent the couple to an improv class on their first date. Those all sound absolutely mortifying to me. Instead, I call The Garret, a speakeasy in the West Village on top of a burger joint, to make a reservation for drinks. Simple.

I'm afraid of disappointing Penelope with my boring date. The job description for Bliss I had spotted on Craigslist had called drinks dates "dull." I know she's banned them because they turn dates into interviews, but I don't think Mindy wants to play Truth or Dare while minigolfing, or whatever Penelope thinks would be exciting. She's a pretty conventional girl. So to appease Penelope, when I enter the date into Bliss's system online, I instruct both Mindy and Adam to bring a special object with which to identify each other. I decide that Adam should carry a single red rose and Mindy should bring a box of chocolates. Their icebreaker is to prepare a story about their first date ever, even if that was a sixth-grade outing to an ice cream shop. I hit send and the system emails both of them with the date information. Thirty seconds later, Mindy texts me a string of salsa-dancing lady emojis and "Thank you! Xoxoxoxo!!!"

It feels really, really good to have finally set up my first date. I set a calendar event in my phone for 7 p.m. on Sunday, when Mindy and Adam are supposed to meet. But I don't feel self-congratulatory for long, because a few minutes later, my phone lights up with another text from Mindy.

"Obviously very excited to meet A., but just curious—any leads on date #2?"

"I'm on the hunt," I type back.

So I fibbed. But I'll find the second date soon enough.

At 11 a.m., I head uptown to meet Mary-Kate at La Petite Coquette, the lingerie boutique in Greenwich Village, to shop for her wedding-night lingerie. She took a day off from work to iron out last-minute wedding details. I'm on the L train, squished between a college-aged guy loudly blasting Britney Spears from his headphones and an elderly woman shooting him disapproving frowns, when I spot a potential match for Mindy.

He's in his late thirties with wire-rimmed glasses and a thick head of dark brown hair. He holds the subway pole in one hand and a copy of this week's *New Yorker* in the other. He appears to be reading the articles rather than skipping to the cartoons.

Would Mindy like this guy? Probably. He looks like he's cut from the same future-quasi-DILF-y cloth as the photos she sent me of her past two exes: tallish, dark hair, nice teeth. He wears that same J.Crew blue gingham shirt that every man in America owns. I would never say something to him for myself if I were single. But I said something to Adam first, didn't I? And that (miraculously) turned out to be a success.

I decide it's least awkward for me to say something to Subway

Man right before I get off, in case he turns me down. I have one more stop, just one more minute, to make my move.

I maneuver past Britney Guy, who's starting to groove and mouth along to the lyrics. No wimping out now. I stand firmly in front of Subway Man and try to use my steadiest voice.

"Hi."

He looks up blankly from his magazine. New Yorkers do not speak to one another on the subway. Ever.

"Hi?"

"I know this is ridiculous, but I work as a matchmaker for a dating service, and I, well, I can't help but wonder if you and my client would get along. I have a hunch that you would."

I sound insane. Even Britney Guy stops dancing.

"Oh, jeez. Um, wow," Subway Man says, grinning and running a hand through his hair.

That's when I see it. His left ring finger encircled by a gold wedding band. How could I forget to check for a ring?

"I'm flattered, really, I am," Subway Man tells me. He shakes his head and laughs. "But I'm married. My wife will get such a kick out of this. She's a huge Patti Stanger fan."

I emit a squeaky "Okay!" and slink over to the door. It's only the first week of my matchmaking career and I'm already hitting on married men. Great! The subway hums along for another fifteen humiliating seconds. I swear the doors open even more slowly than they usually do. I scurry onto the platform at Union Square and up the stairs away from Subway Man as fast as I can without breaking into a run.

Aboveground, Union Square is bustling like always. I lived in three of the NYU dorms in this neighborhood, and a wave of nostalgia hits me as I wind through the crowded plaza. The square is ringed by huge chain stores—Whole Foods, Forever 21, Best Buy—but the park in the center has lush green grass dotted with people stretched out on picnic blankets. A dozen Hare Krishnas in long orange robes beat drums and tap bells as they chant. Two teenaged guys whiz by on skateboards. Caroline and I used to sit on the concrete steps here and talk about how much it would suck when we had to get real jobs.

Mary-Kate is already flitting around the boutique when I walk in. Signed black-and-white photos of celebrities ("Your bras—wow! Thank you!" wrote Jennifer Aniston) line the store and a rainbow of underthings made of silk, lace, and chiffon greet customers at the entrance. The bride-to-be stands in front of a wall of flimsy white items, head tilted, tapping her foot to the beat of the Mariah Carey ballad playing softly in the background.

She holds up two white bras. One is a millimeter-thin lace dream, complete with delicate daisy-chain straps. The other is a padded, frilly creation, trimmed with dainty ruffles.

"Which looks more me?" she asks, pursing her pink-lacquered lips at each one.

I examine both. I can feel the saleswoman's hawk eyes from behind. Mary-Kate's a lace girl.

"How about this one?" I ask, picking up a G-string of iridescent pearls. Mary-Kate grimaces and swats it away.

When she disappears into the dressing room, I wander slowly around the store, letting the luxe fabrics slip through my fingers. They feel like something a character in a romance novel would wear. I pause at a glossy black kimono with wide bell sleeves. The neckline is cut in a sultry V and cinches at the waist with a belt tie. I want to wear it to pad around the Bliss brownstone under the sparkling chandeliers and sink into the green velvet couch with a vodka martini while Tindering away the hours. I flip over the price tag: $278. It's all I want to wear for the rest of my life, and it will never, ever happen—at least, not on my own dime. Mary-Kate calls my name and peeks her head around the plush pink curtain of the dressing room, motioning for me to come inside.

It's a tight squeeze with two of us in the dressing room, but even up close, I can tell that she looks fantastic. Her boobs are hoisted high by the daisy chains and look soft and round. Her stomach is the flattest I've ever seen it, thanks to her wedding diet of grilled salmon, grapefruit, and Adderall. And she swapped my joke pearl G-string for a matching pair of lace briefs. She is religious about her barre classes, and it shows. I tell her how gorgeous she is, and she beams.

"I'm so glad you're here with me," she says, hugging me close. "You're like family. And I wouldn't be surprised if that's official in a few years anyway."

Wait, what? I step back from the hug and search for clues in her eyes.

"Did Jonathan say something to you?"

"Maybe I shouldn't say anything."

She turns back to face the mirror, coyly trailing a finger along the seams of her zillion-dollar lingerie and studying her reflection. She flips her hair to the side, and the overhead light catches on her diamond ring, making it glint a half dozen colors in the mirror. She seems pleased with the effect.

"Mary-Kate! C'mon. Tell me."

She hesitates, bites her lip. "I shouldn't saaaay anything."

I can tell she wants to give in, and I glare at her in the mirror until she does. She's such a pushover.

"Jonathan mentioned that he wants you to move in with him. Has he said anything about that to you yet?"

I lean back against the cool pink wall and shake my head. "No," I say, stunned.

Jonathan and I have only talked about the future in vague, abstract terms before. The most specific he ever got was his panicked promise to "do the right thing" the one time my period was mysteriously late. If we move in together, the next logical step is to get engaged, and then to get married. I want to marry him. Who wouldn't? He's Jonathan Colton—and in a series of bizarre, incomprehensible events, he's decided that *I* am the girl he wants to be with. Not the girl from his country club. Not his Kate Middleton–look-alike ex-girlfriend from Columbia who legitimately works for NASA. Me.

The morning after the first time he said "I love you," I signed my Starbucks receipt as Sasha Colton. With a swooping capital *C*, the sharp cross of the *t*, and the curled flourish at the end of the *n*, the name looked regal and sharp against the thin white paper. I signed my name like that every morning for a week before I forced myself to stop, afraid it would become a habit and I'd accidentally slip up in front of Jonathan one day.

It would be a long engagement, probably. We're still so young. Even if Mom was married at twenty-one—causing me to down vodka shots the night of my twenty-second birthday and announce to the party that I was officially an old maid—that didn't mean I wanted to get married at that age. It would be nice to be married at twenty-seven like Mary-Kate.

But then, thinking of marrying Jonathan, I get a gnawing feeling in the pit of my stomach, which reminds me how tense and closed off he can be, usually when he's stressed about work. Which is all the time. I don't know how to open him up or take his mind off the office. We would have plenty of time to work all that out if we were engaged. He'd be all mine. Forever.

Mary-Kate snaps her fingers in front of my face.

"Sasha, pay attention."

I jerk my head up to see her wrapped in a sheer, floaty white robe over her bra and underwear. The sleeves are embroidered with daisies to complete the matching set and the hem grazes the floor. She looks like a goddess. I force myself to remember that Jonathan is just thinking about asking me to move in with him. Nothing more.

"You like the robe?" I don't respond right away. "Please don't tell Jonathan I told you. I shouldn't have said anything."

After another ten minutes of fretting over her reflection, Mary-Kate plunks the credit card her mother still pays down at the register. She watches with pride as the saleswoman wraps up her purchases and congratulates her on having such good taste.

− Chapter 8 −

On Sunday, I wake up in Jonathan's bed to the sound of my alarm. I roll over to turn it off, and he pulls me back toward him with one arm.

"Don't go," he mumbles into my hair.

His body curves around mine, heat radiating from his chest and his hips snug around my ass. Moments like these make the whole day brighter.

"Why are you awake?" he asks, rubbing his eyes. Sleep slurs his words.

"It's Steve's fiftieth birthday party today, remember? We talked about this."

Jonathan rolls over, slides a pillow over his head, and doesn't say a word. I get up and pull on a pair of denim cutoffs and an old NYU T-shirt I sometimes keep at his apartment for occasions like these.

"You said you'd come with me," I remind him. "We haven't spent the whole weekend together in a while."

Jonathan grumbles into his pillow and sits up, squinting and mussing his hair.

"Um . . . let me check in at work. I told you I'd *see* if I could come."

He reaches for his iPhone, then his BlackBerry, and scrolls

through them both. I sit on the edge of the bed and watch him read work emails. I wonder how many hours I've spent watching him do this. Dozens? Hundreds? Over the course of our lives together, it will eventually turn into thousands. Millions.

"Yeah . . . I'm sorry. It's going to be a heavy workload today."

"But it's Sunday morning," I protest.

I can't stop thinking about what Mary-Kate told me. A Sunday afternoon away together, even if it was just to Jersey to see Mom and Steve, sounds so relaxing. It would be a break from our regular routine—and maybe even the perfect opportunity to talk about what the future might hold for us.

"Sasha, you know if it were my choice, I'd be right there with you."

He's always saying that, although he really does look apologetic this time. He crawls across the bed to sit behind me, kissing my cheek and massaging the knots in my shoulders. I'm caught between the impulse to stand my ground and openly sulk, or be the chill girlfriend who can roll with anything. One gets to move in together, the other doesn't.

"Hey, if you're ever missing out on male company, you can always talk to one of your Tinder guys, right?" he says, snickering at his own joke.

I whip around.

"That's not funny. You know Tinder is for work only."

"I know, I know. Sorry. I was kidding." He stares at me with wide, gentle eyes until I turn back around, letting him finish the massage.

As he finishes working out a particularly gnarly knot in my shoulder, I vow to act less bitchy toward him. It's not really his fault that he has to work so much. He's a little more than a year into his three-year analyst program. If he gets promoted at the end of the three years, he becomes an associate, enjoys a cushy salary bump, and regains control of his life. He'll finally have time to go to the bar trivia nights he's always telling me about; he'll have time to relax; maybe we could travel together. I fantasize about his promotion more than I'd ever admit out loud.

On my way home, I text Caroline a quick plea to be my date to Steve's party, then check in with both Mindy and Adam. Mindy sends a flurry of outfit photos for me to choose from—we wind up agreeing that her red fit-and-flare dress strikes the right note between bombshell and wife material—while Adam just asks if he needs to bother with a tie (I tell him no). And Caroline agrees to come. Back when I was single, she was always my plus-one for family holidays and birthdays and special occasions like these. Sometimes, I miss when it was just the two of us. I know she does, too.

Mom picks us up from the train station in her silver Kia. "My princesses!" she trills. "Get in. We have so much to do this afternoon before the party."

I move three white ceramic coffee cups with dried brown coffee rings in the bottoms from the front seat into the console before sitting down. Mom leans over to kiss me on the cheek, then licks her finger and rubs the lipstick off my face. She does the same to Caroline, who—to her credit—does not flinch when Mom rubs her wet finger onto her cheek.

"Irina, so good to see you," Caroline says.

Mom launches into the list of preparations as we drive home: make the salad, frost the cake, set the table. I never noticed she had an accent when I was a kid, but now I hear it loud and clear when she speaks in front of my friends. It's thick and guttural—not ugly, exactly, but clearly not American. When we pull up to the house, the sting of shame kicks in, as it does every time Caroline visits. Caroline's summer house in the Berkshires is nicer than Mom and Steve's regular (only) one. It's the smallest on our street and could probably use a fresh coat of paint. The lawn is stubby and uneven. Caroline has never said anything about it to me, but that doesn't mean she hasn't noticed.

Inside, Mom sets us to work chopping tomatoes and onions for the salad. She busies herself in front of the oven, putting in the chicken. Steve comes downstairs and peeks his head into the kitchen. He's bald, shorter than Mom, and wears dumpy sweaters, but he makes her happy. They've been together since I was fourteen. He's always felt more like an awkward uncle than a dad to me, but I know he tries hard.

"The yenta is here!" he says, voice creaking. "Looking lovely as always, girls."

"Hi, Steve," Caroline and I chime together.

"You'll have to tell all my friends about what you do when they arrive. They're completely fascinated."

"Now, how exactly does this work? You use a catalog of girls?" Mom squints, pursing her lips.

"No, Mom, it's not a catalog. It's a database of people who have already expressed an interest in Bliss. And I use Tinder and other online dating sites and apps." I'm only a little exasperated; I've explained this to her at least once already.

"I don't know how I like that," Mom says. "These girls, how do they feel about you sending them out on dates with strange men?"

"No, they ask to be set up. They pay for dates, too. It's nothing like . . ." I start, trailing off when Mom flares her nostrils angrily and cocks her head in Caroline's direction. Caroline pretends not to notice and chops her tomato with gusto. Mom doesn't know that Caroline knows about her past. "It's a really nice company, I swear."

"Tell them the story about how you tracked down Adam," Caroline prompts.

"Oh! It was kind of cool, actually." I launch into an explanation of how I stalked him to that bar, and they seem genuinely impressed by my diligence. But there's something else I need to say. It won't go smoothly or easily, but at least I can rip off two Band-Aids at once—Mom and Caroline.

"So, I heard from Mary-Kate that Jonathan might ask me to move in with him."

Caroline's knife stills. "Wait, what?" she asks, annoyed, at the exact moment Mom exclaims, "Oh! *Honey.*"

"It's nothing concrete yet," I admit. "He hasn't even asked me. But sharing a one-bedroom with him would be so much more affordable than what I'm doing now."

"But . . ." Caroline slides her knife sharply through a tomato slice and juice spurts up onto the cutting board. "I love living with you."

"I know. And I do, too. But I'd save so much money this way."

She stares down at the cutting board and starts on another tomato, knife flying. Her mouth squishes to the side. I can tell she's working up the courage to say what's really on her mind.

"It's not really about the money, though, is it? You just want to move in with Jonathan." Her tone is sharp. Accusatory.

"That's part of it, yeah." I shrug, but instantly regret how flippant it makes me look.

"What about me? Who would I live with?"

"You could find a new roommate. Or your parents could spot you money for a one-bedroom, right?"

She grimaces. "I'd feel bad asking them for more money."

"But you *could*," I point out. I know she hates whenever I bring that up, but I'm annoyed that she isn't being supportive. It's so like her to act all pouty whenever things are going well with Jonathan. "They already pay most of your rent anyway."

"Better my parents than my boyfriend," she shoots back coolly.

"That's your moral high ground?"

Mom darts her gaze from me to Caroline like she's about to jump into two opposing lanes of traffic. She tentatively interjects herself. "Sweetie, do you really want to live with Jonathan? It's a big commitment, living with somebody."

"Yeah, I think so?" I don't mean for it to come out sounding like a question.

When we spend time together at his apartment—and it's almost always his apartment, because his place is bigger and brighter and has a fancy doorman who greets every resident by name—the hours just slip by. I feel like I'm at home already. Why not make it official?

"That boy works too much," Mom says, shaking her head. "That's the problem. If you want to see him more often, make him see you more often . . . but don't move in with him to make the relationship work."

"He can't help his work schedule." It's one thing for me to complain about how busy he is, but it's another for Mom to do it.

"If he made more time for you, you wouldn't feel the need to move in with him so young."

"You had been living with Dad for two years when you were my age," I point out.

"Which is exactly why I'm telling you not to make the same mistake."

Mom can give me her opinion, but ultimately, the decision isn't hers to make. Unlike Caroline's parents, mine don't actually have any financial strings to steer my decisions. I'm not naïve enough to think that living with Jonathan would be like playing house; we don't cook, or make DIY furniture, or garden. Life together would be less about achieving domestic bliss and more about avoiding the half-hour slog between each other's apartments.

"I love him." My voice sounds small. I hate that they're ganging up on me.

"I know you do," she says, sighing. "I'd just rather see you live with Caroline. Have fun. Be young. There's no need to rush."

We've had variations on this conversation before: whenever I explain how important Jonathan is to me, Mom pushes back. *You're so young*, she says, or *There's no need to jump to conclusions that he's the one for you.* I think it comes from a place of fear: she doesn't believe a rich guy like him would really choose a Jersey girl saddled with loans like me. I want to prove her wrong. I keep chopping at my onion. It burns my eyes. The kitchen feels too cramped right now.

"I don't know. He hasn't asked me yet. It was just an idea. I'm just not making very much at Bliss. And Caroline, you know this has nothing to do with our friendship. Really. I promise."

"We can talk about this later," she says curtly.

"Caroline, I love you. You know that."

"Mhm."

I hate fighting with her. We almost never do, and this is precisely why—neither of us is very good at it.

Steve, who's stayed silent, claps me on the shoulder.

"I see Uncle Jim and Aunt Joan pulling into the driveway now. Why don't you go open the door for them?"

As I put down the knife to go to the front door, I see Steve and Mom exchange strained glances.

The party keeps me and Caroline busy and flitting around separately for the rest of the night. Guests trickle in around six, an array of Steve's relatives and friends who all sport matching pleated khakis, beer bellies, and receding hairlines. They ask over and over for me to explain my new job, and I can't help but relish the attention. Caroline looks less thrilled; Steve's elderly aunt Joan has her cornered on the loveseat in the living room and is grilling her about all the cute boys she must be meeting in the big city. I feel guilty about what happened earlier in the kitchen, and I swoop in to divert the conversation.

"Aunt Joan, did Caroline tell you about the TV pilot she's writing? It's really impressive. You'd love it."

Caroline mouths *Thank you* while Aunt Joan skewers a pig in a blanket with a toothpick.

"Well, it's only in the early stages right now, but it's a supernatural romance series, kind of like if *The Vampire Diaries* met *The Bachelor*. Magical creatures competing to find love, that sort of thing."

Aunt Joan chews slowly and nods. One of her penciled-in eyebrows is smudged down toward her left eyelid. She feigns interest for a minute until she totters off to the bathroom. I sink into Aunt Joan's vacant spot on the loveseat and rest my head on Caroline's shoulder.

"I'm really sorry about the apartment. I didn't mean to upset you," I tell her softly.

"No, it's my fault. I overreacted. If you want to move in together, that's fine. It's just . . ."

"Just what?"

Caroline looks down and fidgets with the hem of her skirt, unable to look me in the eye. "I'm going to miss you. It's just not fair that you have Jonathan, and now you have Bliss, and soon you're going to have this cozy apartment. It's like you're living this real, adult life, and I'm all alone with a stupid retail job." She uses the corner of one fingernail to very carefully wipe away a tear, so as not to smudge her winged eyeliner. "I didn't think life after college would be like this."

I feel awful. I had never pictured the situation from Caroline's point of view. After all, she's always been the one with the fancy summer house and a mom who wears real pearls and hair that dries straight right out of the shower. And now, Caroline's jealous of . . . me? Me! It's both very flattering and very sad. Our friendship has always relied on ignoring certain unshakable facts that shape our lives: money, family, looks. She has advantages in all three in ways that I just . . . don't. It's easier for both of us when we gloss over those points.

I hug her and kiss her temple and tell her that good things are going to come: a screenwriting job, an agent who likes her pilot, a great guy. But the moment she softens into the hug, an alarm on my phone goes off.

"Oh, shit. Mindy's date is in ten minutes. I promised I'd call her. I'm so sorry, one sec."

Caroline slumps back onto the couch. Guiltily, I imagine that's exactly what I look like whenever Jonathan takes a work call in the middle of a date. I vow to be a little more understanding of the demands of his job. I take the stairs two at a time and head toward my old bedroom.

Bliss calls this date-sitting. I'm technically on call before and during each date, in case the two people can't find each other, need a pep talk, directions, last-minute wardrobe advice, or anything else. The day I met Georgie, she'd suggested I avoid scheduling dates late on Friday and Saturday nights in case I might be wasted and forget to pick up a call. The phone doesn't always ring, she said, but if it does, you need to be coherent enough to answer it.

I push open my bedroom door and dial Mindy's number for a pre-date pep talk. The room is small and decorated in childish pastels, with waist-high piles of books lining one wall and a row of Russian nesting dolls on top of the dresser—a birthday gift from my grandparents, whom I've met just twice. Mindy picks up on the first ring.

"How's it going?" I ask.

"Everything's great. I have the box of chocolates for him. I got here a minute ago and sat at the bar stool closest to the door, but then it occurred to me that he might meet me outside the bar? So I went outside again. But now I'm wondering if it's better to wait inside. But what if he doesn't see me? Oh god."

I can hear the click of her heels against concrete. She must be pacing. Penelope says to never give out a client's or a match's phone number before a date, in case they don't want to see each other again. It would be a breach of privacy. But it also leads to problems like these. Imagine finding anyone in public without a phone—it's like the '90s all over again. Or what I assume the '90s must have been like, anyway.

"Mindy, take a breath." I'm gearing up for a pep talk, but I don't know where I'm headed with this. I wonder if I'll ever stop feeling like a fraud at this job. "First of all, I'm really proud of you for going on this date. Thank you for putting your trust in me to find a great guy for you. I think you're going to love him. And he's going to die when he sees you—you're beautiful in that dress."

"Aw, babe. Thank you."

I pace, gesturing wildly with my free hand, trying to conjure the right words out of thin air. I speak slowly, giving my brain enough time to catch up with my mouth. "Just remember, you're smart and charming and outgoing and have nothing to worry about tonight. Just be yourself."

"Right. Be myself. Be myself. Be myself. Ha! God, I don't know why I'm nervous. It's only the most expensive date of my life." She gives a short, harsh laugh.

A $300 match puts a lot of pressure on her, sure, but it puts even more pressure on me. And on Adam, even if he doesn't know it yet. Please, whatever higher power might be listening, please let them be obsessed with each other.

"Why don't you go get comfortable at the bar? I'll text him and let him know you're inside."

"All right. Oh, I'm really excited. Thank you, Sasha."

"Bye, Mindy. Knock him dead."

I hang up and flop onto my bed in relief. The date is in five minutes.

"Hey! M. is sitting at the bar inside," I text. "She's the brunette in the red dress with the box of chocolates. Have a great time!"

"Running five minutes late," he writes back.

Ugh. I relay the info to Mindy. I'm nervous; I want the date to feel promising. Mindy deserves that much. And considering that Adam gives even me—very committed, very taken *me*—the fluttery feeling of a crush whenever I see his name light up on my phone screen, I can only imagine how she'll fall for him. It'll be perfect. It has to be.

"Headed into the bar now," Adam texts eventually. "I guess it's never too late for a first blind date."

I head downstairs and pour myself a strong vodka soda. Caroline is chatting with Mom. She shoots me a small smile when she sees me coming. The conversation about our living situation isn't over, but it's tabled for now. I join their circle. I don't intend to talk about my work call, because it suddenly feels gauche to flaunt my job in front of her, but Steve's best friend, Ron, appears by my side and grabs my arm.

"Now, what's this I hear about you setting people up? You gotta get me a hot date." His thick mustache bristles against his upper lip as he talks.

I don't have the heart to tell Ron that he probably couldn't afford Bliss, nor do I know too many women who are dying to be set up with a twice-divorced middle-aged plumber who could use a nose hair trimmer. So I give him a one-sentence summary and make a vague promise to "email him more information." I can feel Caroline slouch and start looking around the room for a better conversation—one she hasn't already heard a dozen times tonight—but I'm her best bet.

After the party, on the train back to the city, we're mostly quiet. It's not a comfortable silence. The list of topics we can't talk about has grown too long: Bliss, Jonathan, Caroline's string of terrible dates, the apartment, money.

"Mary-Kate's wedding is coming up," I say finally.

"Yeah, I know," she says, hardly turning her head from its resting spot against the window.

"I think one of Toby's friends works in TV. I'll try to talk you up to him." It's the least I can do.

She sighs heavily. "Thanks, you're the best."

I can't tell if she means it anymore.

- Chapter 9 -

"Hi, I'd like an everything bagel, toasted, light on the scallion cream cheese, please, and a large iced coffee, skim, no sugar," I spit out to the cashier at David's Bagels.

After reciting this every morning for the past year of living across the street on First Avenue, I have this line down pat. The cashier, a tiny Asian girl with a ponytail threaded through the back of her navy blue David's Bagels baseball cap, already has my coffee waiting.

The bagel shop is an unpretentious mom-and-pop shop with cool, dim lighting and smudged windows. The customers are mostly neighborhood people who have been coming here for years to read the paper in faded T-shirts and sweats and chew silently by themselves. Sometimes, doctors and nurses clad in light blue scrubs ferry trays of coffee cups back to the hospital next door. When I was in college, I'd come here on the weekends to work when I was too lazy to walk twenty minutes back to the library on campus, and it's been my home away from home ever since. It feels like an extension of my apartment, which is why I feel perfectly all right strolling in here with messy hair that could use a wash and no bra whatsoever underneath a Columbia sweatshirt I stole from Jonathan.

My usual table by the window is open. I sit down, unroll my bagel from its paper wrapper, and lick up the extra ooze of cream cheese just in time. At 10 a.m., the time we agreed upon yesterday, Mindy calls in.

"Hiiiii, hon," she singsongs.

"How did it go? I'm dying to hear."

"Girl, you are a genius."

I tilt the bottom of my iPhone away from my face and squish my palm to my mouth to muffle a squeal.

I want to say *"Really?"* Instead, I manage the marginally more professional "Tell me everything."

"Well, don't get your hopes up just yet. Long-term, I don't think we're right for each other."

"Oh. Huh." I take a bite of my bagel, disappointed, and listen.

"But wait, let me fill you in. So, he walked into the bar—great place, by the way. I've been meaning to go but never have. And he was a little, like . . . schlubby? Like, his shirt was untucked and he was a little sweaty. He said he almost forgot the rose, which is why he was running late, and why he was sweating, from all the running. I mean, annoying, but whatever. You're right, he's really cute."

"He's definitely cute," I agree.

"There wasn't initially a spark, but we ended up having a good time! I mean, maybe it was all the cocktails. We got three at the bar, then went around the corner to this sushi place I knew for some sashimi, and then he suggested a nightcap. So I guess we drank too much. But he's totally sweet. A little immature for me—like, I told him that I had hired a decorator to help me choose upholstery for my new couch, and he said he's had the same couch since *college*."

I can tell she means this as a bad thing. "Oy," I commiserate, even though I have no plans to get rid of my own college couch anytime soon. I don't tell her this.

"I mean, how old is he?"

I hesitate. If I lied, she would never know the difference. But I can't do that in good conscience. "Thirty-three."

"Oh. I mean, two years younger is fine in some cases. But here, it showed. *Anyway*, I hate to kiss and tell, but . . ."

I can tell she wants me to drag it out of her. This feels exactly like the post-hookup recaps I have with Caroline, except Mindy is more than a decade older and has this manic bubbly quality to her voice.

"But?"

"We made out. I mean, actually, we hooked up a little bit. But no sex! Definitely no sex." She giggles. "He was such a gentleman, though. After he helped me wave down a cab, and before I got in, he kissed me. The cabbie was honking at me to get in, but he didn't care and just held me and kissed me."

"Mindy, that's adorable. I'm melting."

Actually, I'm cringing. Why does this feel like hearing about my parents hooking up? It's gross.

"I know. Thanks so much for introducing us."

"So, what's the problem? He has bad taste in furniture?" I feel like there's a lot about adulthood that I don't quite get yet.

"No, it's not that. I just get the sense that he has a lot of growing up to do, and I don't have the time or the energy to wait around while he does it. Been there, done that. He says he wants to get married and have kids, but I think he just feels like he's missing out because all of his friends are doing it."

"So no second date?"

She sighs. "No. I just want to focus on the people who will be in my life long-term right now."

I'm bummed it won't work. I suddenly realize what a fluke matchmaking is. I can do all this research to set up the perfect couple—and Mindy and Adam really were perfect, Penelope said so herself—but the only way to know if they'll really work out is to have them meet in person. This job isn't easy. Chemistry can't be controlled.

"All right, then. On to the next one. I'm working to find your second match. I met the *worst* guy for you the other day, some i-banker douchebag named Mark, so I'm back to square one."

"Ugh. Well, I trust you. But this is all confidential, right? I don't want to hurt Adam's feelings."

"I won't tell him what you said." What I *would* say, exactly, was totally lost on me, but I could worry about that later.

"Good. Thank you. Hon, I have to run, but I had so much fun last night. You're brilliant. I know you'll find me the right guy soon. Kisses, dollface."

She makes a kissing noise into the phone and clicks off the call. I try to imagine what I could possibly tell Adam without betraying Mindy's confidence or hurting his feelings. She's going out of town for the next month? She's seeing someone else? She's fresh off a bad breakup and not ready to get seriously involved with anyone yet? None of these sound very believable.

While I finish the rest of my bagel, I swipe through a few different apps and send more messages on Mindy's behalf, then demolish my overflowing Bliss inbox. There's no nine-to-five in the matchmaking industry, I'm discovering. Working from home apparently means working all the time—whenever clients need a match or a pep talk or a post-date phone call. My emails right now are mostly automated messages from the database, which are sent whenever any matchmaker adds a note to a client's profile. I try to read them all to stay up to speed. Among this morning's crop: Georgie has dibs on Tyler B. for her client Amara after his next date with Katrina; Elizabeth needs a match ASAP for her client Connie, the one who only dates evangelical Christian Republicans (in Manhattan, of all places!); Allison wants to know if anyone has heard if Frank is still dating Eve, that cute yoga instructor in Bushwick? I'm still trying to untangle who's who. The names and faces all swim together. I had an inexplicable hunch that Frank *was* still dating Eve. Hadn't someone mentioned it during a meeting? But, ah, no. Five minutes later, Penelope emails to explain that Frank had never dated Eve, but he'd dated Eva, the nutritionist who worked on the Upper West Side. I'm still learning.

After breakfast, I walk ten minutes to the Strand, the famed bookstore near Union Square. It's a stately cream building on the corner, the kind that could be mistaken for City Hall. The red-and-white awning that runs the perimeter of the second floor advertises 18 MILES OF BOOKS. I asked one of the employees about that once, and he told me that if you counted every foot of bookshelf in the entire place, it would equal eighteen miles. I still can't fathom that.

I flock first to the table of new fiction. The covers are all smooth and bright, and I run my hand over them. I read the jacket copy on the prettiest ones. I can't really afford to drop twenty-five dollars on a book—they're a third of the price on the Kindle app, even though choosing to support a giant website over my own local, charming bookstore makes me feel guilty. But I get lost in browsing that table, then the next one, then the back alleys with older fiction and the upstairs table of coffee table books. I wonder, like I always wonder, what it would be like to write a book and see my name on shelves here. I've made false starts at a novel before, but the prospect of committing to write a real book has always scared me off writing more than a few amateurish pages.

It's midday and there aren't too many tourists. For an hour, I don't worry about checking JDate or OkCupid notifications or fret about someone else's date—I just wander through the stacks. When I finally do check my phone, I have an unread text from Jonathan.

"What are you up to tonight?"

"Nothing in particular, why?" I reply.

I don't expect him to respond right away, but he does. "Let me take you out to dinner. Someplace special. I should be able to get out of work early. Wear something nice. I'll pick you up at your place."

I can't help but grin as I lean against the stacks and type out a yes. When he first got his job at the bank, I was hurt by how little I saw him. I went so far as to Google "how to date an investment banker," which led me to a hilarious online forum from 2007 where the wives of the men who were busy tanking the economy commiserated over how little they saw their husbands now that they were locked up. As strange as it seemed, I sympathized with these women—the ones who just wanted their husbands home from work before midnight on a Tuesday, the ones who wanted to know without a doubt that they could make weekend plans and not have them canceled at the last minute, the ones who felt invisible whenever their husbands immersed themselves in their BlackBerries, which was always.

I know Jonathan's hard work is paying off; he earned the highest possible bonus after his first year on the job (it was $35K—slightly more than I can expect to make for the whole year at Bliss). And I want to be supportive of his career, especially if we're in this together for the long haul. But I wish he could be more like himself, or at least more like he was when we met. He used to spend weekends immersed in giant history books about the Reformation of the Church of England or military strategy in Vietnam, popping his head up from behind the huge covers to read his favorite tidbits aloud. Now he only reads me lines of infuriating work emails. And I'll admit it: sometimes, his long hours leave me lonely. Days like these, days when he sweeps me off my feet with a surprise, make the disappointment of playing second fiddle to his career worth it.

At 6 p.m., I blow-dry my hair into submission. I rarely style it like this, but Jonathan prefers it sleek. Over the hum of the hair dryer, I hear our front door groan shut.

"Hi!" I call, voice echoing off the white tile walls of the tiny bathroom. I'm bent over with my head between my knees, the nozzle of the blow dryer aimed toward the nape of my neck.

I hear the familiar drop of Caroline's purse on the couch and the skittering of Orlando's paws down the hall, followed by footsteps.

"Hey," she says, leaning against the hallway wall, just outside the bathroom door. She crosses her arms and slumps her head against the doorframe.

We haven't really spoken since we left the party in Jersey. The silence wasn't exactly on purpose, even though I waited to get out of bed until after Caroline had headed to her shift at Flower Power this morning. It was unnecessary; I'm not mad at her. And I don't think she's *mad*-mad at me. Our friendship is just strained right now.

I straighten up, click off the hair dyer, and put down the toilet lid. "Take a seat."

She sits and watches me finish my hair. I blow the final pieces straight and brush the resulting silky mane into place. The blowout makes me look rich, like the women in the Bliss database.

"Want me to do your makeup?" she asks.

A truce? "I was hoping you'd ask."

She switches places with me, pulling her makeup bag out from underneath the sink. I hug my knees to my chest as she starts to blend tinted moisturizer up and out over my cheekbones.

"Where are you going tonight?"

"Jonathan's taking me out for dinner."

"Where's he taking you?"

"I don't know. Somewhere nice, he says."

I don't want to tell her my hunch that he's going to ask me to move in with him tonight.

"Mm."

There's a short silence as she caps the moisturizer and rummages through her bag to find Orgasm, the cheekily named NARS blush, and swirls it over my cheeks. I look right at her, but she avoids my gaze. It's not my fault that my life is sort of, almost coming together and Caroline's has stalled. In college, she was always the one with the life worth talking about—the glitzy internship at *SNL*, her lavish spring break trip to Belize, that time an *America's Next Top Model* contestant offered her coke while in line for the bathroom at Fat Baby. And now she's lost. We don't know how to navigate this new dynamic.

Caroline applies liquid liner to my lash line and flicks it out into a perfect cat eye. She repeats the technique on the other side. "Open."

Before I can even readjust to the light, she holds the eyelash curler frighteningly close to my eyeball and squeezes it over my lashes. I'm tempted to blink but can't.

"Didn't you say you have a date tonight?" I ask.

"No, not a date." She releases the eyelash curler. "Grace is coming over later with a bottle of wine. We're gonna order in Chinese and watch *The Graduate* again."

"Oh, again? Nice. I'm jealous."

Her voice goes flat. "No, you're not. You actually have real plans tonight."

Her surly mood makes me nervous, especially when she's holding a pointed mascara wand so close to my face. I make a last-ditch attempt to steer the conversation back onto happy turf.

"Hey, did Grace go out with that guy from Bliss yet?"

"Oh, yes!" She grabs my chin. "Hold still, I'm trying to do your mascara. Yeah, she said he was a pompous asshole."

"What?" It sounds like a whine.

Even if I'm not yet confident in my own matchmaking skills, I had assumed that Allison would know a good match when she saw one. She had seemed so confident during the meeting. They all had.

"He kept bragging about how he's a CEO. But he's, like, the CEO of his own company. He doesn't have any other employees—just an intern." Caroline rolls her eyes.

Grace doesn't put up with bullshit. She's the kind of girl who posts all those really serious, heavy articles from *The Atlantic* on Facebook about the Syrian refugee crisis and how we need to put an end to female genital mutilation in the Third World. Fluffed-up startup titles wouldn't impress her.

"Argh. She was a champ for going through with that, though. It really put me in a good light at work."

"I know." She sounds tense, like our fight in Jersey is still playing in her head.

I hate it when she sulks. I try to coax her out of her bad mood.

"So, how was work today? How are things with Barbara?" Her boss.

She rolls her eyes dramatically. "The worst." There's a hint of relish in her voice. I know she wants to give me the scoop on whatever ridiculous demand Barbara shoved on her today, and she does. It's a long, complicated story about filling an order of herbs for a reiki healer who runs a practice out of her living room in Montauk and involves Barbara, Barbara's ex-husband, Barbara's ex-husband's dog walker, and a confusing chain of events I can barely follow. She tells the story slowly, indulging in every detail. If she's aware I still need to get dressed, she doesn't show it.

I owe her this—sitting here to listen, even if this small allowance of friendship makes me late for Jonathan. Caroline and I need each other, even when what's between us feels insurmountable. That's why she's here, painting me up with half of Sephora's finery. She wants to be here with me, here for me, even when it hurts. That's real love.

Caroline steps back to admire her handiwork. She sighs heavily. "You clean up good, kid."

I get up and check out my reflection in the mirror. "No, you're just talented," I correct her. I really do look polished. "Thanks. I love you."

"I know." She opens her mouth to say something, but then closes it. "Go get dressed."

I pull an olive green halter dress from my closet. It looks like nothing else I own. The color makes my eyes glow green and reveals just enough of my chest to be considered alluring. The fabric of the dress clings to my waist and swishes around my thighs. I bought it on impulse when Jonathan and I first started dating. I was high on him and Paris and the prospect of transforming into a chic, cosmopolitan, jet-setting swan. I'm not that girl yet. But maybe, if I keep wearing the dress around real chic, cosmopolitan jet-setters, I might become her one day.

Jonathan texts. He's in a cab one minute away. I spritz on the perfume Mom bought me for graduation, step into nude pumps, and head outside.

Sure enough, a yellow car is pulling up right outside my building. Jonathan rolls down the window and lets out a low whistle.

"Hey there, beautiful," he says, letting his eyes roam over my body. "Come on in." Then he instructs the driver, "Twentieth between Park and Broadway, please."

It's only been two days since I saw him, but it feels so good to slide across the pleather seat and kiss him. I missed him. Even though I want to sniff out any clues about moving in together, he first asks about my day. Last year, Jonathan had graduated and was already working at the bank, and I was still stuck in school. I felt like a child sometimes, embarrassed to tell him about my professors and my midterms when he had an impressive job and a ludicrous salary. Now that I'm employed, too—and not just working, but working in the most scintillating industry—I can't get enough of showing off my gorgeous grown-up life in front of him. He listens and laughs and cringes at all the right parts.

The drive is short, and I don't bother pretending to offer to pay for the cab. Jonathan made more this week than I'll make this month. I stand on the curb as a trio of women a few years older than I am enters Gramercy Tavern. One gives me the once-over. I flick my hair over my shoulder and give Jonathan another kiss when he joins me. He smells like sea salt.

If you've ever flipped through *Vogue* and wondered exactly who was purchasing $1,200 monogrammed spoons or artisanal leather sandals designed specifically to wear in St. Barts, well, the Gramercy Tavern crowd would answer your question. The food is award-winning, but above all else, the restaurant is a place to be seen. The dining room is furnished with colorful abstract murals and intricate white crown molding. The host who leads us to our table looks like a baby-faced Ryan Gosling. When he hands us the menus, I wonder if the prices are in another currency—like maybe Canadian dollars. Jonathan puts down his menu, leans his elbows on the table, and takes one of my hands in his.

"I'm so sorry I wasn't able to come to Steve's party this weekend. I know I should've been there. I feel really bad about it."

"You don't have to apologize. Work comes first." I have that line down pat by now.

"Sometimes, yeah," he says, shrugging. "But I don't ever want you to feel like I take you for granted."

"I don't feel taken for granted," I say defensively.

"Good. I'm glad." He rubs my hand, his thumb massaging the spot where a diamond might be one day. "That's why we're here. I'm so sorry, I wanted to do something special to make up for it."

He knows how to make me feel important when it counts. It's enough for me. And in turn, I like to think that I make him feel important, too, especially when he's at the bottom of the totem pole at work and the youngest child of parents who weren't always attentive.

The waiter comes to take our order. Jonathan scans the menu on the spot, trailing his finger down the long list of expensive bottles. We both know that he has no idea how to choose a wine, but he would never admit that to the waiter. He orders a bottle of Malbec, then the rabbit appetizer and the flank steak. I ask for the fig-infused foie gras and the lobster ravioli. When the wine comes, the waiter pours a drop of it into a glass for Jonathan to taste. He swirls it around in his glass and makes a show of sniffing it before tasting it.

"Excellent," he pronounces.

The waiter pours us each a glass. I sit back in my seat, satisfied, and watch my glass fill with the inky liquid. Jonathan and I look like we belong here, and that makes my skin buzz. I didn't know that restaurants this luxurious even existed before I met him. If only the girls I went to high school with could see me now.

Jonathan is explaining the complex details of a deal he's working on at the office when my phone rings. Normally, I would ignore it, but since Bliss is a 24/7 job, I feel obligated to at least glance at the caller ID. I pull my phone out of my bag. It's Adam.

"Oh, shit. I'm so sorry. It's for work. Would you mind if I take this?"

Jonathan holds up his hands and laughs. "The tables have turned, workaholic. Go ahead."

"Hello?" I totter my way through the restaurant and push open the heavy glass door. Another woman lingers nearby on the sidewalk, smoking a cigarette. I'm dying for a drag.

"Hey," Adam says. "Sorry for not texting you back earlier. Is this a good time?"

"Um . . . I guess I have a minute?" I steer away from the restaurant and drift a few paces up the sidewalk.

"Good."

"I'd love to hear about the date." I only hope he talks fast.

"Have you spoken to Mindy yet?"

"Not yet," I lie. I haven't figured out how to gently tell him Mindy's not interested.

He pauses. "This is confidential, right? You won't tell her what I say?"

"One hundred percent confidential." That's not true at all. Giving Mindy feedback is part of what she pays $700 a month for.

"All right. Well, she was cute and sweet. Not exactly my type, but we had a great time anyway."

Damn it. Maybe my instincts aren't right after all.

"What do you mean, not your type?"

"Eh . . . ?" His voice jumps an octave. I recognize that tone. He's trying to phrase this in the least insulting way possible. "I thought she was a little ditzy."

I narrow my eyes. "Adam, she's ridiculously successful."

"Sure, doing what, reality TV? Takes real intellect, I'm sure."

"Wow. Okay. *Well*, then." I don't do a very good job of masking the irritation in my voice.

"Listen, we had a lot of fun anyway. Thanks for setting us up." His southern drawl makes this sound sincere.

"Yeah, of course. No problem."

"And if you ever have another girl for me, I'm happy to go out again. I trust you."

Our appetizers have arrived by the time I return. Jonathan hasn't touched his. Instead, he's tapping away on his BlackBerry. He doesn't acknowledge me as I take a seat. I wait for him to finish the email, nudging my fork into the foie gras without actually lifting it to my mouth. I'm starving. Finally, he sets his phone down. We finish our appetizers, then our entrées, then the bottle of wine. We're too stuffed for dessert. It's been two decadent, heady hours since I first got into his cab, but he still hasn't asked me to move in with him. Didn't he just discuss this last week with Mary-Kate? Isn't that what this fancy dinner is all about? It's tough to focus on whatever Jonathan is saying; half of me wants to blurt out some-thing about moving in together, but the other half knows it's better to wait for him to bring up the subject first. I don't want to sound pushy. The waiter brings over the check, which is close to $200. Jonathan doesn't flinch. He signs the receipt with a flourish and flips the bill book shut.

Back at his place, he leads me into the bedroom and doesn't bother to turn on the lights. He wraps his arms around my waist and places a trail of kisses down my neck. I can't help but swoon. My disappointment fades away and I feel like putty in his arms.

"God, this dress is incredible on you," he says, untying the knot at the nape of my neck. The dress slides over my body like water down to the floor. "You know I love you, right?"

I tilt my head back to kiss him. "Right."

If only I had known then that it would be my last blissful night, I would have savored it.

- Chapter 10 -

"Oh, hi. It's you," Georgie says when she opens the door at Bliss's brownstone the next day. She parts her lips into what might be considered a smile, but it doesn't extend all the way to her eyes. She hasn't exactly been quick to embrace me.

I need to make serious headway on finding a second match for Mindy before her month's membership is up, so it's time to get over my social anxiety and make nice with the other matchmakers. They can teach me which idiots to ignore and which fine specimens to follow up with—because I learned the hard way yesterday that my judgment isn't as finely honed as I had hoped.

Today, Georgie wears white denim shorts and a flimsy white camisole under a fire-engine-red kimono. She cocks her head and motions for me to cross the threshold into the building and lets the door swing shut. When she turns to climb the marble stairs, a fire-breathing dragon embroidered between her shoulder blades stares back at me. Does she ever wear real clothes, or just repurposed lingerie?

I follow her up the stairs, past a half dozen ornate gold wall sconces and a Grecian-style sculpture of a nude woman on the landing, and down the hall. She pushes open a door to a sitting room. Allison, Zoe, and one of the other matchmakers from the meeting last week lounge on an enormous brown tufted leather couch in the middle of the room, flanked by end tables with identical vases of orchids spilling over the top. The walls are paneled in a sexy, dark crocodile print, broken up only by what looks like a Warhol over the fireplace. It's a lot to take in at once, and I can't help but blurt out something stupid.

"That can't be real, is it?" I ask, pointing at the painting.

"Why wouldn't it be real?" Georgie asks. There's a mocking edge to her voice.

"Because it must cost, what, millions?"

"Knockoffs are tacky. Andy was a friend of Bliss's investor's dad."

I wish I had kept my mouth shut. Manhattan makes middle-class life mortifying.

Georgie settles into one of the armchairs across from the couch, and I sit down in its pair.

Allison, the sweet one, asks about Mindy's date. I tell her all about it—how I tracked down Adam on Instagram and followed him to the bar, how sure I was that they'd be a hit, and how both of them claimed to have had fun together, despite no interest in a second date.

"I know how frustrating that can be," she says, nodding sympathetically. "Especially after you put all that effort into setting up the date."

"Right!"

"Clients don't always know what's best for them. See if you can push them toward agreeing to go out again. Worst-case scenario, they have a drink and leave; best-case scenario, they realize they actually like each other a lot. And it'll look better if you can show Penelope that your clients go out on second and third dates."

"You can do that? Make your clients go out again?"

"Hey, they're paying us big bucks for our 'expertise,'" Zoe, the one with pastel pink hair, says, putting snarky scare quotes around the word "expertise." "When we say jump, they ask how high."

"But that's the thing. I don't really *have* any expertise. It's not like I know what to tell women who want to get married. I'm only twenty-two." Georgie, Allison, and Zoe are all in their mid- or late twenties, and I feel self-conscious and immature when I admit this.

Zoe laughs. "None of us have any expertise!"

"You don't?" It's a relief to hear.

"No way." Zoe shakes her head emphatically. "Sure, we might talk to dudes all day about what they're looking for in a relationship, but it would be a mistake to think that any of us have unlocked this magical secret about how to find love. Impostor syndrome's real."

That explains the panic, the feeling like I'm fumbling along in the darkness, making things up as I go along. So I'm not the only one.

"I totally get that," I tell Zoe.

Georgie looks up from swiping through Tinder and rolls her eyes.

"Don't undermine your own authority. We work hard at what we do. We know a thing or two. At least *I* do."

Allison and Zoe exchange strained glances.

"Don't worry about it. You'll find your groove eventually," Allison says, leaning forward and putting a reassuring hand on my knee.

She's in the middle of telling me about the client she's working on when Georgie punches the air triumphantly and leaps up from her seat.

"Yes! Finally, a real catch." She trots over to the couch to thrust her phone in the girls' faces.

Zoe glances at the screen. "He's another finance bro. So what?"

Georgie juts out her hip. "No, he's not just another finance bro. I have five clients that would eat him right up—he's tall and cute and just sent me a flirty message."

I know that in order to be accepted into their circle, I need to put myself out there.

"Can I see?"

Georgie turns back to me and hands over her phone.

The shock doesn't sink in immediately. It's not like jumping into a pool of water and feeling the rush of cold hit my skin all at once—it's more like easing into a deep, frigid ice bath, where the pain creeps up steadily and doesn't stop. There on Georgie's phone is a Tinder profile filled out with Jonathan's name and photos. I see a photo of him lounging on a pool chair at his parents' house in the Hamptons (didn't I take that photo last August?). Below is his name, age, and a short bio that reads: "Columbia, Manhattan, Goldman Sachs. I'm 6'2", if that matters."

"Not impressed?" Georgie asks.

"I, um . . ."

A hard lump forms in the back of my throat. My chest tightens, like I'm about to hyperventilate or explode. If I open my mouth, I'm going to cry. I can't break down here at work in front of these girls I hardly know.

"He's a liar," I eke out, handing her back her phone. "He's only six feet, not six foot two."

"What? How do you know that?"

The other matchmakers are very still. I wipe away a tear that slipped out, roughly shove my laptop back into my purse, and rise from the chair.

"That's my . . . He's my . . ."

"Boyfriend?" Georgie asks, gaping.

"I have to go."

I fly down the marble staircase and out the door. My sandals make loud slapping noises against the sidewalk as I run halfway down the block. When I turn the corner and am safely out of sight from Bliss, the bubble in my chest pops and I finally burst into tears. I slump against the glass wall of Whole Foods and slide down to the ground. In my head, I see Georgie's childlike delight, followed by Jonathan's face on her phone, churning in an endless loop. It just doesn't make sense. Why would he cheat? Or has he even cheated? He was just on Tinder, right? That doesn't necessarily mean anything bad has happened yet. Right?

I work through each possibility, but it all seems so hopeless. If anyone could get away with cheating, it would be him—between the late nights at the office and his constant attachment to his phones, I'd never even notice if he was having an affair. It would just look like par for the course.

Fuck.

Dinner at Gramercy Tavern was so easy and lovely. Or maybe it was *too* lovely, like he felt guilty and had to do something extravagant to make up for it? I think about his hand on my waist. The flash of his white smile. The confident swagger of his walk. I want to throw up. A group of teenaged boys skateboards down the sidewalk. The nearest one gives me a long, pitying look as he skates by.

"Sasha?" Georgie stands five feet away. She looks uncertain. "I thought I should check on you."

"Oh, you didn't have to." I hastily stand up, brush the dirt off my palms on my thighs, and wipe the tears from my cheeks. "I'm fine."

"I'm so sorry you had to find out like that. I had no idea when I showed you, I promise."

I can't help it, but I start to cry again. My face screws up and I cover my mouth to muffle my sobs. It is humiliating to do this in front of her. She closes the distance between us and squeezes me into a hug, then strokes my hair.

"Shh, shh."

I let her hold me for far longer than is probably dignified. Even though I'm a head taller, she coaxes my head onto her shoulder and rubs my back in small circles.

"I'll be fine. Really."

"You don't have to pretend to be strong, you know," she says after a long time. Her voice is low. "I wasn't when my ex cheated on me."

"This happened to you, too?" I sniff.

"Mhm." She nudges away a crumpled Diet Coke can on the sidewalk with the toe of her pristine white sneaker. "My first real boyfriend after I moved to New York. He cheated on me for months."

"That's awful."

"I was a mess. The Duane Reade cashier started giving me free packs of tissues because he'd seen me buy so many of them. But then I picked myself up and resolved to be better than ever. Smarter than ever. And I haven't been hurt since. You'll get there, too."

A terrible thought dawns on me. "You don't think this was happening for months, do you?"

She shrugs and shoves her hands into the pockets of her kimono. "Who knows?"

The sun is hot overhead and I feel slightly faint. I haven't eaten anything today. A manic energy begins to unfurl.

"I have to go. I have to talk to him. I have to know what I'm dealing with."

Georgie high-fives me. "Fuck yeah. Go get him."

I stride quickly down the Bowery toward the R train at Prince Street. The sidewalk narrows due to construction, and I'm trapped behind a group of slow-moving morons for half a block before I run around them and into the street. A car stops short and the driver honks, then flips me off. I sprint past him and the remaining three blocks to the subway. I'm out of breath and the skin between my toes feels on fire where my sandals rub the flesh raw, but I can't slow down. I skip down the stairs two at a time and swipe my MetroCard.

The train pulls up just as I reach the platform, and I hop on. It's almost entirely empty at this time of day, so I take a seat. I'm too jittery to sit properly, so I jiggle my feet against the floor at a frenzied pace. The guy across the aisle eyes my flying knees. In my head, I rehearse what to say to Jonathan. I want to sound confident and calm and collected, but I feel scary high on adrenaline. I need to know what he's done—if anything. Maybe there's nothing to worry about at all. Why is this train taking so long? I feel like I could vomit. Fuck. Fuck, fuck, fuck. It's taking forever.

Four thousand years later, when I reach the Goldman Sachs building in the shadow of One World Trade Center, I dig in my heels to push the heavy revolving door through to the other side. Jonathan once explained that a man goes through the doors first if he's with a woman to get it started, but he'll allow her to take the lead if the door is already spinning. I told him that was bullshit. The lobby boasts sky-high ceilings and what seems like half the world's granite supply, and like always, is crowded with deliverymen holding plastic bags of Chinese, Indian, and Mexican takeout.

Whenever I visited in the past, I texted Jonathan and waited in a corner of the lobby for ten minutes for him to come down. Not this time. I saunter into the middle of the grand room and dial his work number, which he always picks up. He answers on the first ring.

"This is Jonathan Colton."

My heart is racing.

"I'm in your lobby," I announce evenly. "Come downstairs now. We need to talk."

"Wha— Sasha? This really isn't a good time. You know I can't leave in the middle of the afternoon and—"

"Jonathan."

"Yes?"

"We need to talk."

"Later, babe? I have a lot of work to do."

I pour as much venom into my voice as possible. "Come. Down. Now."

"Okay," he says, lowering his voice. "Give me one minute."

– Chapter 11 –

Jonathan pushes through the security turnstile a minute later, eyes flickering up to mine. His shoulders are hunched, and despite the tailored suit, he looks like a scared child. He kisses me. I forget to refuse; it's muscle memory.

"Is everything all right?" he asks with concern, his eyes wide. What a sociopath.

"I'm fine." I straighten up to embody every inch of my full five-foot-eight frame and place one hand on my hip. "But we may not be."

His brow furrows. He does a very good impression of a worried boyfriend.

"What do you mean?"

"Jonathan, what do I do for a living?" I say, taking a step back. I wish I'd worn heels so I could look directly at him, eye to eye.

"You're a matchmaker . . ." His eyes dart nervously over my shoulder to the line of deliverymen and guys in dark suits pushing through the revolving door on their way back from lunch. I want to scream at him to look at me.

"Correct. It's my job," I say slowly, exaggerating my hand gestures like I'm talking to a five-year-old, "to use dating sites and apps to find matches for my clients."

He nods. "I know."

"So why the *fuck* did you think you could flirt with other girls on Tinder and it wouldn't get back to me?"

The words are hardly out of my mouth before his hand connects with the small of my back and he steers me out of the lobby.

"We are not having this conversation here." His breath is hot on my ear. He shoves us along quickly.

"Jonathan!"

"We are leaving," he hisses.

I break free of his hand, toss him a nasty look over my shoulder, and stride out of the lobby, throwing my weight at the revolving door. Jonathan follows in the next compartment, then takes my hand and leads me thirty feet down West Street. I yank my hand out of his and stop, dumbfounded. He keeps walking, and I have to hustle to catch up.

"What? You're not going to defend yourself?" I ask, incredulous.

I fold my arms across my chest so he can't see my hands shaking. This angry, bold version of me feels powerful. I like her. It's exhilarating to tell Jonathan exactly what's on my mind without worrying if it's something a "good" girlfriend would say. Jonathan presses his fingers into his temples and rubs them in small circles.

"Look, I . . ." He glances around, searching for the right words. I've never seen him speechless like this. "I'm so sorry you had to find out this way. I was going to tell you about her eventually."

Hold on. "Her? I didn't know there was a her. I just knew you had a Tinder profile."

He drops his head. He stops in his tracks to pound his fist against a wall, then crumples his hand by his side and keeps going.

"All I know—all I knew—was that you were flirting with one of the Bliss matchmakers on Tinder. Georgie? That's my Georgie.

I've told you about her." There's no flicker of recognition in his expression. Apparently it's too much to ask him to listen to a single thing I say. "I had come here to talk to you about it, but you, oh, you just dug your own hole even further."

I thought I'd cry or scream when he confirmed his infidelity, but I don't have the energy to do that again. I'd already assumed the worst—I don't have to wonder anymore. Jonathan turns to me. His eyes are hungry like he's firing up to turn around a flagging presentation to his boss. He fires off excuses to see which, if any, will stick.

"It meant nothing. It was just sex. I love you, you know that, don't you?"

"Tell me what happened."

I'm not sure I'm brave enough to know, but I can't walk away from here with any lingering questions. That would keep me up at night, I'm sure of that. Jonathan looks like he's about to speak, but his gaze goes above my head. He turns pale.

"Get in here," he says suddenly, pulling me into a Dean & De-Luca and leading me toward a display of gourmet nuts. "There's a guy who works on my floor. Down the street. He can't see this."

"Can I help you?" a young, chubby-cheeked guy in an apron chirps.

"No," I say, unable to shake the anger out of my voice.

"Let me know if you need anything. My name is Tim," he says sweetly.

Jonathan gives him an exasperated nod. We both watch in silence as Tim retreats to his station by the cash register.

"Tell me who she is."

He picks up a container of candied cashews and stares at the lid intently, running his finger over the plastic lip. He doesn't look at me when he speaks.

"Her name is Cassidy. I met her three months ago."

Cassidy. She has a name. I make a mental note of it so I can look her up later.

"You met her on Tinder?"

"No, at a bar. I was out with people from work. Really." He looks at me intently, almost as if to say *believe me just this once.*

"Go on."

He swallows. "Nothing happened at first. We were just texting. But then you were out with Caroline one night and I was frustrated about work and lonely, and something happened between us."

"You slept with her."

He hesitates, then nods once, swiftly. I bite down hard on the inside of my cheek to keep myself from giving him the satisfaction of a reaction. When I stare back at him, stony-faced, arms crossed, he lowers his voice meekly. He looks like a bad dog about to be punished for shitting on the carpet.

"And then I got curious about who else was out there. I downloaded Tinder. I meant it as just a game. I talked to girls, but I never did anything with them."

"What happened with Cassidy?"

He clutches the container of cashews tighter. I grip his forearm and repeat the question.

"I saw her again on Sunday while you were in New Jersey," he admits quietly. "I'm so sorry."

"What about us moving in together?"

"Huh?"

"Mary-Kate told me."

He looks annoyed. "Sasha, I love you. I want us to be together. I messed up, okay? I really messed everything up."

"Clearly."

"It meant nothing, all right? Sasha, you have to believe me." His voice is desperate.

"I don't have to do anything."

His knuckles turn white and the container of cashews he's holding bursts open, nuts flying everywhere. He chucks the box into the aisle as I step past him, toward the door.

"You have to pay for those!" Tim calls angrily across the store.

Jonathan flails, then grabs my arm.

"Don't go. You have to give me a second chance."

"Hey! You can't leave without paying for those!" Tim interjects, his voice shooting up an octave.

Jonathan exhales angrily, releases his grip on my arm, and pulls his wallet out of his suit jacket. He marches over to the counter and slams his credit card down. Tim tells him his purchase will be seven dollars and eighty-nine cents. Jonathan and I will be over the minute I exit Dean & DeLuca, and I'm not quite ready for that yet. I stand by the door and wait for the transaction to finish. I notice I have two bleeding hangnails I don't remember picking at.

Jonathan snatches his credit card back from Tim and pushes the door open to the street. I follow. He tries kissing me, but I'm fast enough to pull away this time. His face falls.

"I'm so sorry," he insists, his voice wavering. I've never seen him cry before. "I'll stop talking to Cassidy. This won't ever happen again. Look, I'm deleting Tinder off my phone right now."

I see Jonathan in front of me, but it's not really him. It's Dad, pleading with Mom, telling her that he'll never stray again. Jonathan taps hastily at his phone, but I interrupt him with a soft touch to his elbow.

"Stop. I don't care if you delete it. I'm done."

His eyes fall and his mouth sets in a defeated line.

"We're over," I say, refusing to let my voice shake. My stomach feels like it's about to lurch into a dry heave. "Goodbye."

I walk toward the curb, suddenly very aware of my frantic heartbeat and the squareness of my shoulders. I spot a taxi and raise my arm. The driver slows to a stop in front of me.

"First and Eighteenth, please," I tell him. "Fast." I can't look at Jonathan as the cab pulls away.

- *Chapter 12* -

The magnitude of what I've just done hits me all at once. I lean against the window and let the tears come as I think about the first time Jonathan kissed me, the girl in my eighth-grade science class named Cassidy who always smelled like soup, the pair of jeans I left at Jonathan's last week that I will probably never get back. The countless hours we'd spent lounging in bed together, limbs tangled, his fingers woven through my hair. His skin like a furnace next to mine. The taxi's TV blares an irritating commercial. I hit the button to turn off the TV, but it doesn't work right away, and I end up pounding my fist into the screen until it finally flickers to black.

"Rough day?" the driver asks.

"I don't want to talk about it."

He either doesn't hear me or doesn't care. "If it's boy troubles, let me tell you, miss, love is a beautiful thing. Something worth fighting for, eh?"

I dig my nails into the bare skin of my knees to avoid snapping at him. The backseat of a cab is the one place a New Yorker can feel truly alone, and I hate him for infiltrating my bubble. This is supposed to be my space to wallow and break down and wipe the dripping snot from my tantrum into the underside of the worn-out black pleather. I grimace when I swipe my credit card to pay the cab fare. I wish I hadn't gotten into the cab at all, even if it did make for a sleek exit.

Back at my apartment, the lights are off, which means Caroline must be at work. I'm glad to be alone. I don't have the energy to tell her what happened. I scoop up Orlando and collapse onto the couch. I nuzzle my face into the cat's furry body, but he wriggles away. I'm exhausted by the betrayal and the anger and the storming up and down the city. Jonathan is gone. Jonathan is really gone. Jonathan is no longer my boyfriend. And I'm the one who cut the cord.

The only person who knows about the breakup is fucking Tim at Dean & DeLuca, which means I have to tell people, one by one, that the relationship I was so proud of is over. Mary-Kate's wedding is in four days. That is, if I'm still going—I'm not sure if I'm still invited. My skull aches. My eyelids are glued shut with goopy mascara schmutz and the dry, crusty remains of tears. My eyeballs are swollen like grapefruits.

I want to feel better, not worse, but I don't know how to do that. So, instead, I pour myself a double or triple or quadruple vodka tonic from the kitchen. Jonathan's Columbia sweatshirt is still draped over the back of a chair; I hurl it toward the living room wall. Then I sit down, open my laptop, and click over to Facebook. I search Jonathan's list of friends for the name Cassidy, and exactly one result pops up: Cassidy Greer. Her profile is locked away under privacy settings, so all I can see is a small square photo of a laughing blonde. Of course he went for a blonde.

I Google Cassidy and instantly wish I hadn't. Her name appears in a gushy feature titled "The It Girls of Instagram," published last year on The Cut. I'm simultaneously engrossed and repulsed. I skim past the sections featuring the Instagram-famous DJ and the leggy redhead who scored a modeling contract, and land on Cassidy, a food blogger with more than 250,000 followers. She's a bottle blonde, obviously. Her eyebrows are two shades too dark for her buttery Blake Lively hair. And her pale pink, carefully lipsticked mouth is too big for her face. But I can't delude myself into thinking she's not attractive—she's beautiful. The reporter reveals she maintains her slender frame at Pure Barre, and that her father happens to be a retired vice president at Bain Capital and a close personal friend of Mitt Romney's. She went to Yale. Of course she did.

It gets even worse once I pull up her Instagram. Every photo features a mouthwatering meal bathed in bright white light. There's the açai bowl topped with juicy red strawberries, the avocado toast sprinkled with black pepper, the kale salad drizzled in olive oil. Her delicate, long-fingered hands sit at the edge of each photo, holding a fork or cupping a latte. Her face is always just tantalizingly out of view. If I didn't hate her on principle, I would've followed her, too. I scroll back through six months of photos before I slam my laptop shut.

Orlando is meowing on the floor, wrestling with Jonathan's limp sweatshirt. He has the sleeve caught in his daggerlike claws, and he's batting it into the corner of the living room. The sweatshirt will be ripe with dust bunnies, and I don't feel like rescuing it.

My phone buzzes with an incoming text. It must be Jonathan; my fingers fly to my phone so fast, I'd be mortified if anyone were around to see. My stomach drops at the sight of a different name on the screen.

"Just sent out a bunch of new messages on Tinder. Very nerve-racking. Don't know how you do this all day for work, but I'm impressed," Adam writes.

His text is the first thing in hours that's made me not want to kill myself or somebody else. I start to type back a response, but I realize I have no idea what I want to say. I delete the whole thing, then impulsively hit the call button.

"Hello?"

"Skip the Tinder dates," I hear myself say. "Would you want to go out with me sometime?"

I feel like I'm at the top of a roller coaster, right before I plummet a thousand feet toward the pavement. This is the worst idea I've ever had.

"I thought you had a boyfriend."

"So did I."

"Oh, jeez. I'm so sorry."

"Don't be," I reply.

I should hang up and go live in a post-apocalyptic Siberian cave where I can't embarrass myself like this in front of other human beings, but it's too late for that.

"Well, in that case, yeah. We should get drinks sometime."

"Drinks! Yeah. Tonight?"

"Tonight, uh, let me think. Um . . . I actually have plans."

"Oh." Could I have sounded like more of a desperate loser? I'm tempted to Sylvia Plath myself, but I don't really know how to turn on the oven.

He rushes to fill the stretched-out lull in the conversation. "Next week, then?"

"Yeah. Next week."

"I'll text you," he promises.

We do that awkward thing where he starts to talk, then I start to talk, and then we say goodbye. My cheeks are burning and I feel like I've had a triple espresso shot. If Jonathan can sleep with other people, so can I.

- *Chapter 13* -

None of the traditional post-breakup options appealed to me. I didn't want to chop off my hair (too unflattering), or wallow forever (too depressing), or get a sick revenge body (too much effort). So, instead, I threw myself into work.

Bliss matchmakers work on commission: clients pay $700 a month for two dates, and I get to keep 35 percent of that, or just over $120 per date. That had sounded like a lot when Penelope had first explained it, but now that I'm seeing how much work goes into every pairing, I'm realizing exactly how much work I need to do to stay afloat. Patti Stanger made this look easy and lucrative on *The Millionaire Matchmaker*, but she had me fooled on both counts.

That's why, on my first morning as a single person, I actually iron my most professional-looking white button-down, pat concealer onto the bags beneath my eyes, and walk to the Bliss brownstone to talk to Penelope. I find her in the dining room, tethered to her usual array: laptop, iPhone, and extra-large iced coffee. Her nails clack rapid-fire over the keyboard and I see a Bumble conversation in progress on her phone.

"Hi," she says, eventually making eye contact after pausing midword to check her phone. If she notices that not even Maybelline's finest could disguise the puffiness around my eyes, she doesn't say anything.

"Hi. I've been thinking—I'd love to take on more clients. If possible. I just feel like I'm finally getting the hang of this."

"It's going well with Mindy?"

"Well, she says she had a great time on her first date. I don't think they're going to go out again, but I'm searching for other matches for her."

"She went out with Adam, the *Esquire* editor, right? Tall, Jewish, thirty-three?"

There are more than five thousand people in Bliss's database. Penelope is truly frightening. Almost as frightening as the tiny jolt of electricity in my stomach when she says his name.

"Yeah, that's Adam."

"Not a bad start. I can give you more clients. But are you up for a challenge?"

I need the money. "Sure." I sit down.

Penelope opens our database on her laptop and pulls up a client's profile.

"So, he's not quite as 'cool' as Mindy," Penelope begins slowly, making sharp air quotes around the world "cool." "But don't let that scare you."

Then I take in what's on the screen. His name is Eddie Hyman. He's five foot four and lives an hour away in the Bronx. His database photo is a selfie taken against the backdrop of a ratty couch. His shiny bald spot, uneven smile, and massive gut are not promising. He says he's an accountant and "has minimal relationship experience."

"I'm not scared," I lie.

"Let this scare you, then." Her voice goes flat. "He's forty years old, just moved out of his mother's house last year, and has never had sex."

Oh, dear god. And his last name is *Hyman*?

"He's the sweetest guy you'll ever meet, I swear. He was working with Bella, one of the other matchmakers, but they just didn't have the right chemistry. He asked to be transferred to someone a little more sympathetic." She pauses. "And Bella doesn't work here anymore, of course."

I'm not ballsy enough to ask why.

Penelope sends me his contact info, then flits out of the dining room, citing a meeting with an investor. I slump over the cool surface of the table and press my forehead to the lacquered wood. I can find Eddie a girlfriend. Sure, no problem. Tons of women want sweet, smart, sensitive men. Sexual experience isn't necessarily a deal-breaker. Height isn't necessarily a deal-breaker. Right? Ugh. I'm not even able to convince myself.

I borrow Georgie's fake-flirty tone and type out an email to Eddie, explaining that I'm so excited to work with him and that I'd "love to arrange a cocktail or coffee meeting" at his earliest convenience to introduce myself.

Eddie's earliest convenience, it turns out, is that afternoon. It's his idea to meet for coffee rather than drinks; it's my idea to travel to his neighborhood, Riverdale in the Bronx, which is so far from my apartment I might as well be somewhere in the Atlantic Ocean. I just want to be polite. My subway ride to meet the forty-year-old virgin extraordinaire takes an hour.

I arrive at his chosen coffee shop and spot him instantly—he's hard to miss. I chose to wear my flattest flats so I don't tower over him, but there isn't a pair of shoes in the world that would make our four-inch height difference less awkward. The coffee shop is cute, with windows draped in cheery gingham curtains and glass pastry cases holding mouthwatering cheesecakes.

Fifteen minutes have passed since we introduced ourselves, and despite amping my practiced charm up to eleven, I was having trouble breaking the ice. Eddie is flustered. He pushes up his glasses, fixes the collar of his shirt, clears his throat. A thin bead of sweat rolls down from underneath his sparse brown hairline toward his temple, and he mops it up with a wrinkled handkerchief. I pretend to fiddle with the clasp on my bracelet to avoid staring and making him feel even more uncomfortable.

"Let's talk about your previous dates with Bliss," I suggest. "Any feedback on what wasn't working with Bella would be so helpful, so we don't run into the same problems again."

"I did not find Bella very professional." His voice is stiff and a little nasal.

I prod him for more information. Jesus, I've had more forthcoming conversations with my cat.

"She sent me on a date to walk around Chelsea, which is extremely far from me," he began slowly. "Which I didn't mind. But when I got there and found my date, we ended up in the middle of the Pride Parade. Now, I don't have a problem with that, but it was . . . a bit loud. Bella said she didn't realize the parade was that weekend."

I love the Pride Parade, but it's the last place I'd ever send a date. Picture literally two million people flooding the city, half of them in rainbow-striped jockstraps dancing on floats. Add in sweltering summer heat, booming Mariah Carey and Britney Spears songs, and street vendors selling flags and glitter, and it's a lot. It's hilarious to imagine Eddie trying to carry on a real date there, but it's also kind of sad.

"And then Bella disappeared. Never set up another date, even though I had paid for a second one already. I mean, I get it, I'm not the easiest person to match. But there has to be someone out there for me. I'm not asking for much. I'm just a little socially awkward. Meeting people makes me anxious."

He looks at me with weary eyes, then looks away.

"I get it, Eddie, I do. I get anxious when I meet new people, too." I make a fluttering motion by my stomach. "Butterflies, nerves, you know."

"How could you possibly know what this feels like?"

He gives me a withering glare, and suddenly, I hate myself for what I said. He leans back in his seat and crosses his arms over his chest. I feel acutely aware of the sugar in my voice and the bright smiles I've been sending him across the table. He must think I'm the biggest simpering fake in the world.

Time for a new tactic. I ask him to tell me more about himself. When he falters, I lead him through the conversation one question at a time. Eventually, he describes a quiet life to me. He works as an accountant. He goes bowling once a week with the same league he's been playing in for a decade, roots for the Mets, and has been considering getting a dog. Maybe a beagle. He doesn't have many friends.

"But a few months ago, well, I . . . I was sort of dating a girl. She taught high school marching band," he says, dropping his voice to a whisper and blushing furiously, "and made ends meet by writing erotica on the side. We were together for three weeks."

Well, well! I can't bring myself to ask if he's actually a forty-year-old virgin after all, so I smile maniacally and tell him that sounds very, um, exciting. He doesn't look like he wants to offer any more information. Instead, I push for details on his ideal match. Eddie tells me he's looking for a girl—"er, sorry, a woman"—who's smart, extroverted ("to balance me out"), wants a family, and likes sports. He's shy about describing his physical preferences.

"Pretty, I guess," he says, looking down at the table. "Blondes or brunettes, doesn't matter to me. And, um, petite would be nice. You've probably noticed I'm not the tallest guy."

After we drain our coffees and scrape the last of our pies from our plates, Eddie walks me four blocks to the subway. On the way, I catch our reflection in the window of a Barnes & Noble. We make a jarring pair, but my hour with Eddie has softened me. He's awkwardly lovable. At the entrance to the subway, he goes for a handshake and I give him a quick hug.

"I'm going to find someone for you," I tell him. "I promise."

Back at home, I get into Serious Work Mode (translation: hair up, bra off, sweats on) to find Eddie a date.

I open Bliss's database and set the search parameters for straight women ages 30 to 40 in New York City. Two thousand results pop up, and I groan. I start by reading through every profile, but after three that are way off-base, I realize there's a faster way to do this, even if it feels mean. I scroll through the results in search of the least attractive photos. Within fifteen minutes, I have three potential options to review. Finally, I have hope!

But that hope is short-lived. As I delve further into their profiles, I have to cross each one off my list. Nell, a thirty-one-year-old accountant, says that she's new to dating and wants a more experienced partner—that's definitely not Eddie. Marie, the thirty-seven-year-old special education teacher, is 5'11". Liz, a thirty-three-year-old nurse, specifically requests "no bald men, please," although personally, I think she could stand to be less picky. So I'm back where I started. I email Penelope to see if she has any ideas. She responds quickly.

Eddie is a tough one. I don't have any women in mind off the top of my head, but you might want to try creating a dummy profile on OkCupid as a man. You can fill in a little of his information if you'd like. Reach out to women and explain that you'd like to set them up with a friend of yours. Whatever you do, don't use the word "matchmaker" in your message, because that tips off OkCupid that you're a professional and they can shut down your account. I've been kicked off the site seven or eight times already—they don't like us poaching their users. Good luck!

I spend the next hour glued to OkCupid. It's something to do other than wait for Jonathan to text (he won't) or refresh Cassidy's Instagram (I shouldn't). First, I create a fake email address, which I then use to create a fake OkCupid account. The site's interface doesn't feel half as current as swipe-based apps like Tinder do. Now that you can search for a husband using just a few photos and an optional one-liner bio, anything more than that feels like you're trying too hard. I fill out the bare minimum of biographical information about Eddie—just enough for it to feel like a real profile and not a front for a serial killer. Then I dive into the pool of available women.

One profile jumps out at me immediately. Hilary86's photo shows a woman with enormous brown eyes. She describes her life as a travel reporter, which has taken her hang gliding in Brazil, on a kayaking tour of Indonesia, and to a safari in Kenya . . . and that's only this year. "If you have a passport and a sense of adventure, you might be able to keep up with me," she writes. "Keyword: might." I'm jealous of her confidence. She's approximately eleven thousand light-years out of Eddie's league. I click back to the list of potential matches and start to browse. I keep getting lost down rabbit holes like Hilary's, but after an hour, I've sent identical messages to three women.

Hi! I know this sounds weird, but I'm actually a woman. My friend Eddie here asked me to help him out. He loved your profile and I think you'd really get along. He's a gentleman with a heart of gold, smart but not show-offy, and would sincerely enjoy meeting a kind, down-to-earth woman such as yourself. I know this is far-fetched, but is there any chance you might be interested?—Sasha

Of course, the problem with this method is that women typically receive more messages than men do. The numbers point to a grim reality: none of these women will even open my message, much less write back to me. It hurts to imagine that someday soon, I might have to sift through OkCupid—or some other site or app—for myself, not just for Eddie. I'm not ready for that yet. I'm barely ready to get a drink with Adam.

My phone pings with a new email. It's an OkCupid message from one of the women I was interested in for Eddie—thank god! In my haste to read it, I knock an old coffee cup onto my laptop. Luckily, it's empty and there's no harm . . . but even if I did spill coffee, it would be a small price to pay if it means Eddie the forty-year-old virgin will not die alone.

Hi. I'm not sure if you messaged the right person. Are you sure he would want to meet me?—Diane

Diane's profile reveals a drawn face, prematurely lined, with small, beady eyes behind outdated square glasses. Caroline has a similar pair she bought at a vintage store, but she wears them ironically. "I'm a little shy. I don't have much relationship experience. Just waiting to meet the right person," Diane's profile says. If Eddie had a female replica, Diane would be it.

Diane, of course he would. Could I call you to tell you more?

She writes back quickly.

I don't think so. I don't know who you are.

Diane, don't make this difficult for me. I'm doing you the favor of a lifetime.

I'm a friend of Eddie's. Look, I know this is ridiculous, but I'm trying to help him meet people. He's a great guy—just a little shy. I'm sorry for bothering you, and if you want me to stop sending messages, I will. I just have a hunch that you two would enjoy each other's company.

I leave my phone number. A couple of minutes later, she calls. Her voice is higher-pitched than I had expected, with a strong Staten Island accent. After I thank her for calling me, I struggle with how to phrase my next line as delicately as possible.

"I know I told you that Eddie is a friend of mine, but actually . . . well, I work for a dating service. I'm a matchmaker. Eddie is my, um, well, he's my client."

She goes silent—not that she was particularly talkative to begin with.

"Diane? Are you there?"

Finally, she speaks. "Yes."

"I'd love to learn a little more about you. If it turns out that you and Eddie are compatible, then I'd be happy to send you on a date."

"I don't want to buy anything."

"It would be at no charge to you."

"So all I have to do is answer your questions?"

I try to project a sense of confidence. "Exactly."

Another long pause. "All right."

It takes forever to draw out information because she only speaks in one or two syllables at a time. She lives on Staten Island and works in the financial department of the local school district. She doesn't go out often. She doesn't like loud restaurants or concerts. She doesn't drink, she doesn't drive, and she doesn't like cats. She has allergies to shellfish, most nuts, and some fruits. When I ask what she *does* like, she takes another long pause before answering.

"Sometimes, I watch baseball on TV." Even her voice sounds mopey.

"Do you root for the Mets?"

"I like them. Yeah."

That's Eddie's team. It's a done deal. I don't even bother asking her what kind of guy she's attracted to, because that opens a conversation I don't want to get into. No one's dream man is short, fat, and bald. But then again, Diane is miniature—only four foot eleven, which makes Eddie a strapping stud by comparison. Or something like that. They'd be into each other, right? She has nice—well, she has fine teeth.

"You know, Diane, I have a really good feeling about this. I think you and Eddie will hit it off. I'm going to check in with my boss before I schedule the date, but expect to hear from me soon."

"Okay."

I hang up and feel like a rock star. I'm getting Eddie a date! I dash off a match proposal to Penelope and she approves it a few minutes later. "I'm impressed by how quickly you handled this. Good luck to them," she had written. I spend the next hour futilely researching a spot that's somehow convenient to both Eddie in the Bronx and Diane on Staten Island. The trek between their two boroughs involves transferring from a subway to a ferry to a bus. I check their availabilities over text (wide open, both of them) and decide to send them for a walk along the waterfront at Brooklyn Bridge Park soon. Penelope had taught me during training that people are always more attractive when in motion.

Good luck to them, indeed.

– Chapter 14 –

Four days after my relationship imploded, and my faith in love, fidelity, and honesty shattered, I'm racing across the lobby of the Bowery Hotel with a paper grocery bag brimming with a cocktail dress, heels, and enough industrial-strength undergarments to out-fit the entire cast of *Real Housewives*. Mary-Kate called me earlier this week and asked if I would still come, despite the breakup. I wanted to say no until she called me "basically a sister."

The hotel lobby boasts red Oriental rugs, intentionally worn in spots as if to show decades of wear, and dimly lit with small wrought-iron sconces holding golden-orange orbs of light. A familiar-looking girl with angular cheekbones and black leather leggings jabbers under her breath in French by a leafy green potted plant; I think I've seen her on a billboard somewhere. I jam the elevator button several times in a row. I was supposed to be in the bridesmaids' suite on the eleventh floor ten minutes ago.

Finally, the doors open, and I gasp. A sandy-haired guy hunches over his BlackBerry, typing at lightning speed. My stomach lurches. I haven't seen or spoken to Jonathan since our breakup. Now that I've had time to reflect (and cry, and drink countless bottles of wine with

Caroline), I'm starting to wonder if I made the right decision. I broke things off in the middle of Dean & DeLuca due to a dizzying cocktail of rage, adrenaline, and confidence. I had been brash and impulsive. Of course I'm hurt by his cheating, but that doesn't mean I don't miss him. The elevator dings again, a clear, high bell, and the figure looks up from his BlackBerry. The features are all wrong—the nose is too sharp, the eyes dirt brown. It's not Jonathan. The man slides past me and holds his arm across the threshold while I step inside.

"Thank you," I stammer.

My heart slows from a staccato sixty miles an hour to a mere forty-five as I relax against the cool metal interior of the elevator. I'm not prepared to face Jonathan. But whether I like it or not, I'll have to see him today. And not just him—Mary-Kate, their parents, and every last aunt, uncle, and nosy cousin who wants to know when Jonathan will put a ring on it.

Today was supposed to be my grand entrance as a contender for a coveted spot in the Colton family. Instead, well, I press my palm into my torso and resist the urge to vomit. The elevator doors open and I race down the hall to the bridesmaids' suite. I rap on the door and Jessie, the pug-faced one who got so wasted at Mary-Kate's bachelorette weekend in Austin that she *peed herself*, lets me in.

Inside, a cacophony of loud female voices, an old Beyoncé song, and the steady hum of a hair dryer sounds. The suite is enormous. Mary-Kate, her mother, Nancy, five bridesmaids, Toby's mother, and an army of hairstylists, makeup artists, nail technicians, photographers, and wedding planners are sprawled out amid a sea of nude strapless bras, cans of hairspray, and extra camera lenses.

"Watch out for the cords," Jessie warns, leading me through the maze. "We have, like, seven curling irons plugged in."

I step carefully over an iron and lean down to kiss Mary-Kate on the cheek. She sits in the hotel's chintzy armchair with three ladies in waiting: one crouching on the floor to paint her toes shell pink, another painting her fingernails a matching shade, and a third weaving an intricate braid into her updo.

"There's my single girl!" Her expression shifts into a sad puppy's. "My brother's such an ass. I'm so sorry."

The rest of the bridesmaids go quiet until only Beyoncé's voice cascades up and down octaves. They're listening for dirt, so I put on a brave face.

"Yeah, I know. It . . . sucked." My throat constricts and I can feel tears welling up, so I cast around for another topic. "But I wouldn't dream of missing your big day. You look stunning. Toby's a lucky guy."

Her little rosebud mouth spreads into a self-satisfied smile. "Thanks. Now, where's your robe? My gift to you. All the girls have them."

Mary-Kate is wearing a white silk kimono with a deep V-neck and wide bell sleeves, the same one I'd been admiring at La Petite Coquette, save for the color. She snatches her hand back from the manicurist and twists around in her seat to show me her back. "Mrs. Warren," her married name, is spelled out in delicate silver beads. I look around and realize the rest of the bridesmaids are wearing matching kimonos in sapphire blue with—thank god—no kitschy beading in sight.

"Mom, get one for Sasha," Mary-Kate calls. She turns back to me. "It's my little treat to you for being my bridesmaid. I saw you looking at them in the lingerie shop."

Nancy springs out of her armchair like a gazelle, unfolding the long, lean limbs she's honed on tennis courts. Jonathan gets his straight nose and piercing blue eyes from her, and my heart does a back flip when she makes eye contact. I want to shrivel up and disappear.

"Come, Sasha. They're in the other room."

I follow her into an adjoining sitting room, which is empty except for the photographer's assistant.

"Can we have a moment, please?" Nancy shoots the assistant a pointed look, and she scurries away.

Nancy sets down her mimosa on the windowsill, rummages in a bag from La Petite Coquette, and selects a robe, then looks me up and down. Her eyes linger on my chest.

"We weren't sure what size to get you," she says carefully. "I hope the medium fits."

Like her daughter, Nancy is fine-boned, small-chested, and slim-hipped. I am precisely none of these things. They have lanky, slender bodies made for golf and sailing and brightly patterned Lilly Pulitzer sheaths. Mary-Kate convinced me to try on one of her Lillys once, and blanched before noting that pastel paisley isn't flattering on everyone.

"Thank you," I say, taking the robe from Nancy. "That should be fine."

Nancy stares, her eyes unflinching and unkind. Her voice drops to a harsh whisper.

"I want to ensure that whatever disagreement you're having with Jonathan has no bearing on the wedding. Today will be seamless." She raises one eyebrow sharply at me. "Understood?"

My throat feels tight. I've never been totally comfortable around Nancy—her cool, reserved elegance has always intimidated me—but this is something else.

"Y-you know what happened, don't you?"

"I'm aware."

"He cheated on me," I clarify.

Nancy leans one bony hip against the cherrywood desk and

takes a sip of a sunny mimosa from a champagne flute. She examines me with her ice-blue eyes for a second too long, a second that grates on my nerves.

"I thought you loved my son."

"I do. Er, I did." I exhale heavily. "I thought he loved me. I didn't think he'd hurt me like this."

"But you were in this for good, weren't you?"

"Of course. I want to be with him forever," I say. "Wanted."

The words burn on my cheeks. It feels like such an intimate thing to admit to her; I had never managed to say as much to Jonathan himself.

"Then don't be foolish, Sasha," she snaps. "Husbands will stray. But a smart wife—a wife who knows what's best—will follow."

"I don't understand."

"You must." She tilts her head toward me.

"I don't."

"I normally wouldn't confide in you like this, but for whatever reason—and I can't even begin to imagine why—my son is quite taken with you. He's crushed."

I ignore the brazen backhanded compliment and cross my arms over my chest, waiting.

"Men will have their . . . let's see, how can I put this? Dalliances," she says. "Don't make the mistake of letting them ruin your relationship. Men stray when they're bored—so a smart woman will make things interesting again."

"I see."

Her thin lips curl into a small smile. "When I found Frank in other women's beds, I joined him."

Imagining Frank and Nancy's affair or threesome—no, that word is too vulgar, they'd probably call it a *ménage à trois*, pronounced in a crystal Parisian accent—makes me feel queasy again. I suddenly realize how warm and stale the air is in here.

"And that . . . worked for you?"

"It did. Some women choose to turn a blind eye. Jacqueline Kennedy, for example. And look how that turned out."

I narrow my eyes. "Her husband was assassinated."

"Regardless," she says, waving a hand. She straightens up and brushes an invisible piece of lint from the sleeve of her jacquard jacket. "I don't want whatever tiff you're having with my son to ruin the wedding."

"I'm not sure that's possible," I say, raising my chin.

"Darling, it's not my choice to have you here." Her tone makes it clear she doesn't consider me "darling" at all. "I've never thought you were right for Jonathan. But he says he loves you, and Mary-Kate insisted on including you. You're here as our guest, but you'll do as I say. Now go, change into your robe. Your makeup artist is waiting."

She returns swiftly to the main part of the suite, and I hear her fawning over Mary-Kate's hair. What the hell was that? I don't know whether to laugh or cry. I can hear Jessie admonishing Faye (Toby's sister, the bridesmaid tasked with putting together this afternoon's playlist) for letting Beyoncé's "Single Ladies" slip into the mix. The song cuts out short and a new jam fills the room. I peel off my tank top and shorts and wrap myself in my new blue silk kimono. I cinch the belt tight, take a deep breath, and head into the other room to be painted up like a good Colton girl.

An hour later, I've been contoured, tweezed, and perfumed into a Madame Tussauds wax replica of a rich Ivy League girl. I'm standing on the roof of the Bowery Hotel with the rest of the bridesmaids to take photos before the ceremony. We're a dizzying seventeen stories up, and an extravagant array of gleaming glass towers, rows of brick town houses, rushing avenues, and quaint side streets of the East Village and Lower East Side sprawls out beneath us. Bliss's headquarters is down there somewhere.

I'm barely encased in a navy chiffon dress on loan from Caroline's closet. I can't inhale too deeply because I'm afraid it might split at the seams. Mary-Kate had deemed matching bridesmaid's dresses tacky, so we were instead instructed to wear dresses in shades of blue. (Of course, they had to pass muster with Victoria, Mary-Kate's work wife.) Victoria had outright rejected my sale rack pick, but Caroline had just the right dress: high neckline, cinched waist, hem hitting right above the knee. It's both the most expensive thing I've ever worn and the most conservative dress Caroline owns. She wore it on election night when her father ran for Congress two years ago. (He lost.)

"Don't you dare stretch out the top," she had said when she lent it to me. "Dad says the next election cycle may be better, so I might need to wear it again."

So I hold my breath and freeze my eyes wide for the camera. I smile so hard my cheeks ache. The photographer snaps a dozen portraits of the five bridesmaids lined up around the beaming bride, dressed in a simple, strapless Vera Wang ball gown. Her grandmother's string of sapphires, as blue as the Mayflower blood running through her veins, glitters around her neck.

"Gorgeous, gorgeous," he says, clicking the shutter repeatedly. "Remember, think skinny arm thoughts. Think light, natural hands on hips."

He peeks around the edge of the camera, frowns, then nudges one of his assistants and points at me. "Fix that."

The assistant rushes over to arrange my right hand on my hip. She presses her thumb into the back of my hand and gently splays out my fingers one by one. I've been relegated to the farthest position on the right, as far away from Mary-Kate as possible. Nancy's orders.

"Let's loosen up your grip," she says softly, like she's coaxing a scared kitten. "There you go."

The flashbulb pops three more times, white and harsh, then the photographer releases us. I stare up at the cloudless blue sky for a moment and blink to restore my vision. When I look back down again, I notice Jonathan emerging from the elevator onto the rooftop. He's devastating in a tuxedo, so heartbreakingly beautiful that he shouldn't even be allowed to wear one. The black and white suit is in high contrast with his golden complexion, and sits smoothly across his broad shoulders. His eyes—the ones that match his mother's—cast toward mine and freeze.

The chiffon tugs across my chest as I gulp for air. I feel like I'm falling down the hotel's seventeen stories with nothing to grab on to. I've thought about what this moment would be like for four days straight now, and it's not any easier than I thought it would be. Jonathan pauses by the elevator bank, then strides over to me. I steel myself for whatever he's about to say, but the photographer swoops in front of him and pulls him toward Toby for a photo. Right before the flash pops off, his eyes shift toward mine.

I'm not ready for this. I'm not ready to face him. What kind of moron dumps her boyfriend mere days before she's a bridesmaid in his sister's wedding? My presence in the bridal party isn't fooling anyone. I'm not here as one of Mary-Kate's best friends; I'm here because I'm Jonathan's girlfriend.

Was Jonathan's girlfriend.

My first week as a single girl had started off strong—I found Eddie a match, and even sort-of, kind-of, possibly secured a date for myself. But then I spent the next few days in the fetal position in my bedroom with the blinds drawn, alternating between sobbing and reading through every tweet @CassidyGreer had ever written, dating all the way back to 2009. I had no appetite for food, but I did manage to keep down several vodka tonics and a whole lot of wine. The apartment reeks of cat shit because I don't have the energy to scoop Orlando's litter box. The thin skin around my eyes is so raw and puffy that earlier today the makeup artist tried to console me before I even mentioned my breakup. And now, Jonathan is standing less than fifteen feet from me, so handsome in his tux, just an hour away from standing across the aisle from me as his sister promises to stay faithful to her one true love for as long as they both shall live.

It's not so terrible for a bridesmaid to strand a bride at the altar, is it? She has four others to count on. If I kicked off my heels, I could run the twenty blocks home and be safely locked in my apartment in no time at all. But I've already been caught on camera by the photographer. Damn it. I regret passing up Caroline's offer of Xanax this afternoon.

The rest of the groomsmen—Toby's Rolodix cofounder, Charlie, a cousin, and two other friends—join Jonathan and Toby near the edge of the roof for more photos. Each one of them is a catch on his own, but together, they're a terrifyingly ambitious, successful, and well-groomed bunch. Jessie and Victoria are whispering and giggling a few feet away, and I can only imagine which ones they're picking out for themselves. I bet Jessie goes for Toby's cofounder, Charlie; she seems shallow enough that his net worth would outweigh the fact that he reeks of frat-president vibes the way some guys reek of cologne. I wonder if Charlie has ever cheated on a girl. Probably. Has Toby? If he hasn't yet, would he ever? Fifty-five minutes to go till he exchanges his vows with Mary-Kate.

The photographer leans down to switch out his lens, and the groomsmen relax out of their ramrod-straight poses. Jonathan shoves his hands into his pockets and stares down at his black leather dress shoes. He fidgets, as if he knows that I'm watching. He looks up suddenly, but just as our eyes connect again, the photographer raises the camera and calls him to attention.

Once Toby and the groomsmen finish taking their set of photos, it's time for the group portrait. The photographer barks directions: Mary-Kate and Toby in the center, surrounded by the bridal party. I cross over to the bridesmaids' side, trying to give the groomsmen a wide berth. Charlie swerves. I dodge him and stumble directly into Jonathan's back. He whips around to face me.

"Hi," he breathes, reaching out an arm to catch me from toppling over in my heels.

His fingers are warm on my skin, and his touch is still electric. Something churns low in my stomach—nausea? Or desire? All I have to do is say it doesn't matter. Take him back. If I can do that, my life will fit neatly back together like a puzzle. The cracks between the pieces will always be there, sure, but the pieces will fit.

But the burning sense of betrayal still bubbles under my skin. Maybe I don't want the pieces to fit together anymore. Mom and I were better off once Dad left. That kind of lesson is hard to forget.

"Hi," I say quietly, my voice catching in my throat.

"You look beautiful," he says.

Jessie darts over to us. "You two can make up later. You're holding up the photographer," she hisses, grabbing my arm, and deposits me at the end of the line of bridesmaids, as far from Mary-Kate as possible.

A dozen fake cheery smiles later, the photographer decides he's gotten his fill of this pose.

"Pairs, please, pairs, please," he calls, snapping his fingers.

His assistant guides us to a shabby chic taupe loveseat in the corner, where she instructs Toby and Mary-Kate to sit, and fans out Mary-Kate's massive cloud of tulle over his lap. Bridesmaid-groomsman pairs surround them: Jessie sidles up to Charlie. Faye makes a beeline for her cousin. Jonathan is the only one left, and the thought of being cradled in his arms for however many minutes it takes to get the right shot frays my nerves. I glance over help-lessly at Mary-Kate, who shoots a look at Jonathan.

"Faye, trade places with Sasha," Nancy orders, cutting in. "That way, the bride and groom's siblings will be together. It's a nice shot, isn't it?"

The ceremony is formal, and if I were in a better mood, I'd think it's beautiful. Instead, I want to bolt. Jonathan stands stoically next to Charlie, Toby's best man, his attention focused on the happy couple. I gaze down the aisle toward the back of the room where Mary-Kate's other single friends undoubtedly are hating every minute of this sappy nightmare, too. When the ceremony ends, I slip through the crowd and head to the ladies' room. I just need a second alone to decompress.

The restroom is decked out in white marble. I file into the first stall, flip the toilet lid down, sit down hard, and slump forward with my palms pressed to my cheeks. *Breathe*, I tell myself. *Just breathe.* My mind spins in circles: the night we first kissed in Paris, the first time he brought me home to his parents, the easy confidence in his smile. And then, the image shifts: Jonathan's face on Georgie's phone, Cassidy's glossy pink lips, Cassidy's 250,000 fans, cheering her on daily with likes and praise. It's too much.

I hear the door open and two more sets of heels clack into the ladies' room and stop in front of the sinks and mirrors.

"You'll never guess what Carol told me," one says, voice dripping with gossip. Carol is Jonathan's aunt.

"About Mary-Kate's nose?"

"No, she's very coy. She never confirmed that."

"Oh. Well, then, what?"

"Did you see that tall bridesmaid?"

I snap to attention. What?

"Which one?"

"Dark hair, busty?"

I'm torn between opening the door and revealing myself, and staying put. I know it's about to get dishy. I lean my elbows on my knees and listen as intently as possible for whatever's about to come next.

"That's Jonathan's girlfriend. Her mother is apparently some kind of Russian mail-order bride. Picked out of a catalog and everything."

"No . . ."

"Mhm. Can you believe it?"

Part of me can't believe that my secret leaked through the Colton family like that. But part of me feels naïve for ever expecting I could keep a lid on it forever. Of course Jonathan told, or Mary-Kate told, or Toby told. Of course *that* was the thing that would precede me—not that I'm a matchmaker or that I just graduated magna cum laude from NYU. Of course the dirt would travel fastest.

"How trashy," one of them continues. "I didn't even know that Jonathan was seeing anybody."

"Well, obviously they're not trying to show her off."

They fall into silence, probably reapplying lipstick or fluffing their hair. It's all clear now. I don't belong here. I can try as hard as I want—borrow a dress from the daughter of a would-be congressman, have my face contoured beyond all recognition, sit idly by as Jonathan cheats on me—but I won't ever be one of them. I'm not thin, I'm not blond, I'm not old money. What's the point in trying anymore? I stand up, unlock the stall door, and step up to the middle sink between the two women.

"Excuse me," I say, turning on the faucet and running my hands under the stream.

I look into the mirror and make eye contact with each woman's reflection, my lips curling into a smug smile. They're both middle-aged, lightly tanned, with sun spots on their chests and thumbnail-sized pearls dangling from their ears.

"I couldn't help but overhear what you were saying about Jonathan's girlfriend." They both go wide-eyed, thin lips parted as if about to apologize. I'm relishing this. No fucks left to give. I twist off the faucet, grab a rolled-up fluffy white hand towel from the stack on the vanity, and unroll it with a sharp flick of my wrist. "But before you call me trashy, just know that I don't sleep around like some of your relatives do."

The smaller one sucks in her breath, eager for gossip. "Who do you mean?"

I wipe my hands with the towel and toss it into the bin. "Oh, Frank. Nancy. Jonathan. The whole family is quite charming. You can imagine my relief when I caught Jonathan cheating, dumped him, and no longer have to be a part of it."

I sweep a glossy sheet of hair over my shoulders and stride out the door as their jaws drop. If this family has taught me anything, it's that you don't get anywhere by being nice. I'm shocked at my own boldness. Normally, I'm the last person to spill a secret, but I don't feel any remorse. Instead, I just feel a beautiful, limitless freedom.

Back in the hall for cocktail hour, I ignore the black bow-tied waiters passing silver trays of Mary-Kate and Toby's signature cocktail—some prissy champagne lemon thing—and head to the open bar for an extra-cold dirty vodka martini. I ask for it very, very, very dry, with three olives. The sound of ice clanking inside the shaker calms my nerves. The bartender pours the drink and hands it over, glass filled to the brim and trembling with surface tension. I take a sip and discover it's biting enough to cut through the jazz quartet and the mumble of voices that reverberate throughout the hall. I thank him and head over to an empty cocktail table in the corner of the room.

"Mind if I join you?" a man with a British accent asks minutes later, appearing at my elbow.

I look up from my phone. He has a dark shock of hair gelled up in the front and a pleasant face. It takes a second to place him, but we met last year at Mary-Kate and Toby's engagement party. He and Toby grew up together; he's the friend who works in entertainment whom I promised Caroline I'd talk to.

"Oh, hi! Gordon, right?"

"Yes, Gordon. Sasha, right? Jonathan's girlfriend?"

"Oh, um. Yeah. I mean, no. We just broke up this week," I say, trying to fake a lighthearted laugh.

"I'm so sorry to hear that." He puts down his glass of Scotch, looking concerned.

"It's fine, it's fine . . ." I insist, taking a gulp of my drink to stall. "You work in TV, don't you?"

"I do."

"My best friend is working on a pilot and I know she'd love to run some questions by a person who actually works in the industry. It's like *The Vampire Diaries* meets *The Bachelor*, if that makes any sense."

Gordon laughs. "I mean, I work at PBS. But I could take a look at it."

"Really? Oh, thank you! That would be amazing."

"Of course. So, how's it going? What's new with you? Aside from, you know."

"Ha. Well. I graduated from school and started working . . . it's kind of an insane job. I work as a matchmaker for a dating service."

It takes Gordon a second to wrap his head around that. "You do . . . what?"

I launch into my usual explanation of what I do at Bliss. After weeks of reciting it multiple times a day to potential matches, I have my lines down pat, down to the exact inflections of my tone. I love watching the intrigue build behind Gordon's eyes. It's so simple to dangle Bliss into the conversation and captivate people. Even this room, filled with Colton blue bloods from Westchester, Toby's tech mogul buddies, and Mary-Kate's glitterati or Twitterati or whatever, I'm the most interesting one.

It occurs to me that Jonathan could very well be watching us, so I make a show of touching his arm and laughing. Talking about Bliss reminds me: I need another date for Mindy. And here's Gordon: a cute, successful man with a gloriously posh accent who's hanging on my every word. What's not for Mindy to like?

"Hold on. You don't happen to be Jewish, do you?"

"There's some Jewish ancestry on my mother's side, actually."

Close enough. "You know, I just realized that you might really hit it off with one of my clients. What do you think about letting me set you up?"

He swills his Scotch, considering the idea. "What would that involve?"

"Tell me . . . what do you look for in the women you date?"

"You mean in terms of personality?" he asks.

Men who want to appear sensitive always rush to ask that. They don't want to give me the impression they care chiefly for looks. I nod.

"Well, passion is huge," he says. "She has to really love something, whether it's her job, or her friends, or her travels. Spontaneity is important, too. Quiet, loud, doesn't matter to me . . . but I want someone with a good heart. A caring, considerate person."

I have no idea if Mindy would consider herself spontaneous or what exactly constitutes a "good heart." I nudge Gordon on, trying to land on anything that would make him and Mindy a compatible match. He says he could see himself settling down in a few years and would love to have kids one day. He's mostly dated brunettes in the past. Boom, boom, boom. I slide an olive from my drink between my teeth, bite, and swallow.

Matchmaking is not as straightforward as I'd imagined. But at least I know thus far that Gordon's breath smells fine, he's not wearing a wedding band, and he doesn't have any jarring speech impediments or facial tics. Not bad. That's essentially what I'm here for as a matchmaker—to weed out any total disasters and introduce my clients to people they wouldn't necessarily encounter on their own. It's impossible to predict with 100 percent certainty if two people will hit it off, but it's pretty simple to tell if someone is a disgusting scumbag. I ask for Gordon's number and tell him I'll follow up soon. He reaches into his suit jacket and pulls out a thick card. I don't have a purse with me, so I tuck it into the neckline of my dress instead, securing it between my bra and my skin. He raises an eyebrow and gives me a bemused look.

"Pleasure to see you again, Sasha."

Cocktail hour is over, and guests are filtering into the elevators for the rooftop reception. Gordon heads to the bar for another refill, and I head upstairs to find my table. At 7 p.m., the sky is just beginning to turn a dusty blue. Pink and orange streaks hang across the west side of Manhattan. Golden yellow lights flicker on in buildings below us. I watch Mary-Kate and Toby's first dance as Mr. and Mrs. Warren, then drown myself in a second martini as couples stream onto the dance floor. My phone dies, so I can't even retreat online.

Jonathan maneuvers into the open seat to my right. I fix him with a stone-cold gaze copied directly from his mother.

"Will you dance with me?" he asks.

I give a short, hollow laugh. "You must be kidding me."

"I'm not."

"No."

"Sasha, please." He buries his face in his hands, then smoothes his forehead with tense, flexed fingers. He has that same look of frustrated concentration he gets when he receives a particularly bad work email. "I know I hurt you. Just dance with me and let me talk to you. Let me explain."

He looks so goddamn sharp in his tuxedo, like an old Hollywood actor. I'm reluctant to give him an inch, but I'm curious about what he wants to say. I like that for once, *he's* begging *me*.

"Fine. You have one dance."

"Thank you."

The song is winding down and another one starts up. I rise out of my chair and walk to the dance floor. He holds out his arms stiffly, like he's recalling the correct position from the dance lesson Mary-Kate and Nancy forced him to take last month. I step into his arms, and he relaxes, like this is the most natural thing in the world. The sensation of his grip on my waist and his fingers curling over the top of my shoulder makes my brain vibrate in an uncomfortable way.

"I want to apologize," he says, leading us into a slow, rocking two-step. "I messed up. Big-time. And I know this doesn't make up for what I did, but I promise it won't ever happen again."

"Why did you do it?" I ask after a pause.

He tilts his head back and groans. "I don't know. I wish I never did."

"But you did."

Couples slow-dance all around us.

"I felt powerless, okay?" he spits out bitterly. "My job controls my hours, what I do, when I do it. I don't have any say over my life anymore. You don't know what it's like to feel so powerless."

I would push away from him, but the photographer chooses that exact moment to sidle up to us for a shot. I stay put, fuming, in his arms. It'll be an awful photo.

"*I* don't know what it's like to feel powerless? How about, oh, I don't know, feeling powerless to stop my boyfriend from sleeping around?"

"Sasha, shhh. My family is all here."

"You think I give a shit if they hear?"

Jonathan's grandparents, to our left, look over, alarmed.

"You're right. I'm sorry. I'm so, so sorry."

When I don't respond right away, he looks around the room and sighs loudly.

"Did I tell you that you look beautiful tonight?"

"Yes."

"'Breathtaking' is really the right word."

"Mhm."

"I mean it."

"Mm."

"Sasha, damn it, talk to me. I need you to forgive me."

He continues leading me in slow two-steps around the dance floor. I'm sure my teeth are leaving irreparable imprints on the inside of my lip. If I bite down hard enough, I'll be able to focus on the pain, not the man in front of me, not the wedding, not my life.

"Fine. You want me to talk? I'll talk." I take a deep breath and will myself not to cry. If I cry, he'll see how weak I am, how easily he can bend me back into his arms. "You knew my dad cheated on my mom for years. And she hasn't had an easy life—she taught herself English, worked her way up from a minimum-wage job. But you know what the proudest moment of her life was? Leaving him and starting a new life for herself. That's what she considers her biggest accomplishment."

"I know I messed up!" he explodes. He stops dancing. "But I'm nothing like your dad. This isn't like that. Just please. Forgive me."

Nancy strides over to us, nostrils flaring like all hell, hands on her hips.

"What do you two *think you are doing*," she whispers, razor-sharp, through gritted teeth. "You're causing a scene."

Jonathan opens his mouth, then closes it again. His eyes deaden. If he thought he could win me back this easily, he's just now realizing he can't. I might be the first thing he's ever wanted and not gotten right away.

"I was just leaving," I say, crossing my arms over my chest.

"You can't leave!" Jonathan protests, just as his mother says, "That sounds very wise."

I spin around, hold my head up high, and walk back to my table. I pick up my martini and raise it to my lips; fleeing a wedding is no excuse for not taking full advantage of an open bar. But then I see Jonathan rushing after me, scooting around the two dancing flower girls and an elderly relative trying to catch his attention.

"Sasha, please, just listen to me," he pleads, catching my arm.

I try to pull away, but his fingers tighten around my wrist.

"Let go."

"If you'll just listen, I swear—"

In one lightning moment, I slosh the martini glass toward him. The vodka arcs gracefully through the air before splattering across his blinking, sputtering face. He drops my wrist and yelps, and I dart out of the room.

– *Chapter 15* –

I don't charge my phone until an hour later, after I've trudged twenty blocks home in pumps that rub my feet raw and recounted the wedding in exquisite detail to a near-hysterical Caroline. ("You did *what*?") That's when the missed calls flood in from both Eddie and Diane. Was their date scheduled for tonight? I listen to the first voicemail in horror.

"Sasha? I'm waiting by the park." I can just barely hear Eddie's nasal voice over the clatter of tourists and the chimes of Jane's Carousel at Brooklyn Bridge Park. "You never emailed me with D.'s description. There are so many people here, I don't know how I can find her."

Then there's a nearly identical message from Diane, and a second pair of voicemails a few minutes later.

"Shit, shit, shit," I mutter, panic fluttering in my chest.

"I thought you would tell me how to find him," Diane said, her tone turning accusatory.

Eddie dialed in a minute later. "I don't even have her name or phone number," he complained. "I've paid so much money for Bliss and it's given me nothing."

I open my calendar to see what I had written. Sure enough, their date was scheduled for eight o'clock. It's nearly ten. I can just imagine the two of them circling the same stretch of the bustling park, each too shy to approach strangers. *I* wouldn't have the balls to ask random strangers if they were my blind date, and I'm not a shut-in or a forty-year-old virgin. I had realized their date would fall on the same night as Mary-Kate and Toby's wedding; I hadn't anticipated getting swept up into a scene and forgetting to date-sit.

It's probably not polite to call so late at night, but Eddie hauled ass all the way from the Bronx. The least I can do is apologize. I call, hoping he won't answer. But, of course, he answers on the second ring.

"So, there you are," he snaps, not masking his contempt.

"Eddie, hi! I'm so sorry. I won't lie, I messed up in a big way. I know Diane was really looking forward to meeting you."

I can practically hear him shaking his head. "Well, she won't want to give me a second chance now!"

I bite my lip. I know I shouldn't promise anything. If I give my word that Diane will meet him and that falls through, he'll never trust me or Bliss again. But I need to give him faith that this insane process might actually—against all odds—work out in his favor.

"I wouldn't assume that. She might. And if she doesn't, I'll find you someone else. Someone more understanding, more forgiving. You deserve someone amazing."

Eddie exhales in a wheeze. "You don't have to lie to me, you know."

"It's not a lie!" I protest.

But he's already hung up.

Two days later, my lungs are on fire as I run down First Avenue. I dart around a nanny pushing a double stroller and nearly knock over a bodega's flower stand as I zip around the corner. I'm not built for speed. I skid into the brownstone for the weekly matchmaker meeting five minutes late. I can tell from the way Penelope arches one thick eyebrow that this is not acceptable behavior. Yet again.

"Thank you for joining us, Sasha," she calls from down the table.

Cut me some slack. I'm late because my credit card was declined at Dunkin' Donuts. Because, you know, this company hardly pays me. Setting up dates at $120 a pop sounded like a surefire way to pay my bills, feed myself, and even take a stab at chipping away at my student loans. Instead, I'm surviving on a diet of iced coffee, bagels, pizza, and cheap wine. I never got paid for Eddie and Diane's date because it never actually happened. I could quit Bliss and probably make more money working retail or at a restaurant. But those jobs are surprisingly competitive in New York, and anyway, I'm not ready to give up matchmaking just yet. I want to get it right—if not just for my own ego, then for Mindy's and Eddie's sakes.

I slink into an open seat near the door. One of the matchmakers, Jane, is frantic because her client Naomi has a date in five hours, but her match just canceled.

"I need to find a petite Buddhist lesbian in Brooklyn, mid-fifties. Must love dogs, must be available tonight. Anyone?"

Crickets.

I can't focus. It's been two days since the wedding, six days since my breakup, and I'm a mess. Depending on which minute you catch me, I'm either furious at Jonathan, elated by my independence, devastated by the prospect of ending up alone, or so deep underwater I can't feel anything at all. *The Vampire Diaries*, which Caroline sucked me into despite my initial protests, featured a plot line in which vampires could actually turn off their emotions when life got to be too much. (Or, rather, death got to be too much. You know what I mean.) And so those supernatural beings with superior bone structure got to zap out of their heads and walk around as shells, not feeling a thing. I'm jealous.

The room falls silent. I suddenly realize that everyone is looking at me.

"Sasha? We asked how you're doing," Georgie says gently, like I have cancer or something.

"I'm great, thanks," I say, forcing a sunny smile. "All good here. Everything's just fine."

"Do you want to tell us about your progress?" Penelope asks.

"Well, Eddie had a date this weekend." Wait. Shit. That didn't end up happening. "I mean, he was supposed to. But he, uh, asked to reschedule."

"I didn't see a note of that in the database," Penelope says.

"Yeah, it was a really last-minute thing. That's why."

"You need to put any changes into the system in advance," she reminds me. We covered this during my training. "When is he going out again?"

I drum my fingers on the table and look up to the ceiling, as if I'm trying to remember. "You know, we set a date, but I can't recall specifically what we decided. . . . Eddie's just a busy guy. And Diane hasn't picked up when I've tried to call."

In truth, I haven't spoken to Eddie at all since our phone call on Saturday night. I'm supposed to reach out to each of my clients three times a week to see how they're doing, but that's always felt like far too much contact. Since my personal life imploded, speaking to anyone—especially my clients—has felt impossible.

"All right," Penelope says, the tone of her voice implying this is very clearly *not* all right. "Make sure it gets into the database this time. Any other news?"

"Um, yes. I met a potential match for Mindy at my . . . friend's wedding. He's British."

That earns a smattering of applause and cheers. I explain Gordon's background. Penelope seems pleased, and asks me to set him up with Mindy soon.

"Ugh, can you set me up with him?" Georgie asks. "I love British men. So posh."

"Georgie, you know the rules. No dating clients or recruits," Penelope intones.

It sounds like the thousandth time she's said it. My date with Adam is in five and a half hours. I run a hand through my hair and avoid eye contact with both of them. I know that Adam is technically off-limits, but I don't see the harm. He and Mindy aren't interested in seeing each other again. Adam seems genuinely interested in me. And I desperately need a night out to take my mind off Jonathan. What Bliss doesn't know can't get me in trouble, right?

After the meeting, I linger at the table while I call Eddie and Diane to reschedule their date for tomorrow night; the guilt from lying to Penelope spurs me to just get it over with. Then I schedule Mindy and Gordon's date for the same night. Working isn't exactly the distraction I'd hoped it would be, but I have to keep moving. I slip my laptop into my bag, head out of the brownstone, and wander through the East Village, popping into my favorite independent bookstores. Eventually, I find myself on the edge of Tompkins Square Park. I pick out a bench in a corner of the park shaded by a soaring copper birch tree and sit. I manage to appreciate the park's leafy trees and the guy playing the guitar for about two and a half whole minutes before I check Cassidy's Instagram, which has not been updated since I last checked four hours ago.

I pull my laptop out of my bag and open the Word document I've used as my makeshift diary since college. I haven't written in months. I pour out everything: my new job at Bliss, finding Jonathan on Tinder, breaking up with him, the wedding. The words tumble out, and I feel lighter when I'm done. I've missed writing like this. If I could actually make a living as a writer, I would. I'm mostly done dumping out my heart when my phone lights up with a text from Adam.

"Hey there. Just checking that tonight is still cool?"

I count out exactly sixty seconds before replying so I don't appear too eager.

"Of course."

He shoots back a text right away, and my heart leaps.

"I figured I'd ask you for a bar recommendation, but you must be sick of that from setting up a million other couples."

I count out another sixty seconds.

"Only a little. Do you have a place in mind?"

He texts me the address of a dive bar in the East Village. Not exactly Gramercy Tavern, but it's not like that signified anything great for my love life, anyway.

I'm halfway to the bar when I begin to feel shaky. This is my first date with someone other than Jonathan in more than two years. I catch my reflection in the window of a hookah bar on Avenue A, and for a split second, I don't recognize myself. I haven't worn makeup in a week, since I just wind up crying it off. My loafers are sensible and tasseled, the kind of thing I bought when I thought I was going to work in journalism. Now that I'm off my meal plan, I've been eating less, and it shows in the sharpness around my shoulders. This is what I look like now, I guess.

The sidewalks aren't that crowded, but I'm terrified I'll bump into Jonathan. There are eight million people in this twinkling trash heap called New York City, and I doubt Jonathan's ever been this deep into the East Village. But still—what if?! It's weird that I'm going to meet a guy other than him.

Maybe Adam will pay for my drinks. Maybe, if things go well, he'll kiss me at the end of the night. And maybe, if things go really well, I'll go home with him three dates from now and see his apartment and what he looks like naked. It's freaking me out. Didn't Jonathan feel this ticking, neurotic sense of unease when he met Cassidy? How could he not have? I can hardly think about anything else.

Maybe it isn't fair to Adam that I'm still so upset about Jonathan. Maybe I should've canceled drinks. Shit. I check my phone. It's four minutes till eight. Is that too close to call off the date? The more I think about meeting someone who isn't Jonathan, the more the pressure builds up behind my eyeballs. I want to cry. I might like Adam, but he's not my person, not the way Jonathan is—was. Whatever. And now I have to go pretend to be a normal human being whose insides are not currently going through an FBI-grade paper shredder.

Maybe one day, Adam could be my person. But that's a far-off possibility, and the prospect of waiting all those weeks or months or years till I have a relationship like that again is too painful to think about.

I'm halfway down East Fifth Street when I see a tall, tan figure leaning against a brick wall by the entrance to the bar. It's him.

"Hi," Adam says, leaning down to give me a kiss on the cheek.

My cheeks go warm and the watery pressure behind my eyes starts to fade.

"Hi," I breathe.

Next, I feel his warm hand on the small of my back as he guides me through the open door. The bar is lined with red pleather booths on one side and a weathered wood bar on the other. A song I vaguely recognize from the '90s alt rock radio station is playing. The bartender, a redhead in a Grateful Dead T-shirt and faded jeans, calls out Adam's name, and he waves. We get our drinks—vodka soda for me, a Southern Tier IPA for him—and head to one of the booths. The pleather sticks to the back of my thighs as I try to slide over the seat, and I wish I had worn something longer than cutoffs.

There's so much that I want to say, but probably shouldn't: I'm a newly single train wreck; he dated my client; he's fully off-limits. I cast around for anything to say to break into conversation—unlike my Bliss screenings with men, this interaction isn't scripted for me. I'm grateful that he launches into an easy conversation and takes the pressure off me.

"I used to be part of a bar sports league, so we played here a lot," he says, gesturing to the back of the bar, which is lit up with arcade games, a pool table, and darts. "Every Tuesday night."

"Oh, yeah?"

"My team won second place in the nation for Skee-Ball. We traveled to Tampa for the tournament and everything."

I guess I involuntarily wrinkle my nose, because he asks me what my problem is with Tampa.

"My dad lives there," I say, setting my drink down on the table and fidgeting with the rim of the glass. "With his latest girlfriend. I used to spend every summer down there when I was a kid."

"You didn't grow up there, then?"

"No. I grew up in Jersey. My parents split up years ago."

He seems to sense this isn't my favorite subject and is gracious enough to navigate back to safer waters.

"You know, I've been to Jersey just once since moving up north. For a Skee-Ball tournament, actually. The Mid-Atlantic Conference. A bunch of bar sports losers crowded into an old rec center and threw balls around and drank beer. At the end of the day, we walked away with some highly impressive plastic trophies."

"That's very impressive," I say, going along with the joke. "Why'd you stop playing?"

He shrugs. "I was the oldest one on the team. I figured I'd let the kids in their twenties do their thing."

The kids in their twenties. I take a long sip of my drink to stall. "You know how old I am, don't you?"

He squints, like he's trying to remember. There's a definite crease across his forehead, the kind that guys my age just don't have. "I think your Tinder said twenty-seven?"

"Twenty-two."

I run a hand through my hair and try to shake off the potential awkwardness of the moment. I can't read his expression. Is he amused? Or does he think I'm just a kid?

"That's fine." He shrugs. "I think I like you. I swiped right on *you*, didn't I? Not Mindy."

There's a vulnerable look in his eyes, like he's searching for me to agree with him. Oh, god, those eyes. I swallow a sip of my drink to prevent myself from breaking into a shit-eating grin. I don't know how this can happen. Five minutes ago, I was sweating over the feelings for Jonathan I just can't shake off. I shouldn't have mental space to devote to liking Adam—but I do.

"Well, I like you, too," I hear myself say. I can't quite believe it. The words keep tumbling out. "I've liked you since the minute I first saw you. I might have been jealous that Mindy got to go out with you and I didn't. It's funny how it's all worked out, isn't it?"

That all sounded much more casual in my head. Less so out loud. His eyes are the exact shade of melted chocolate under the glimmering bar lights. Normally, I'd feel naked right about now, spilling my guts to him like that. But after the events of the past week, confessing to maybe, sort of, kind of liking somebody in a secluded bar booth is laughably simple.

"And Mindy told you everything about our date, right? You don't mind?" he asks.

I figure he's talking about their makeout by the cab, or maybe the embarrassing number of drinks they downed. "Of course. I didn't set you up as friends."

Everything seems so smooth now. I pick up my drink and slide out of the booth. "Come on, show me how to play Skee-Ball."

He leads me to the back of the bar. The Skee-Ball machine is in the back left corner, and features a low, sloped plank leading up to a series of concentric wooden circles. Each circle has a hole at the bottom with a number painted next to it: 10, 20, 30, 40, 50. Adam flips open his wallet, pulls out a dollar, then squats down and feeds it into the machine. The waistband of his blue plaid boxers peeks above his jeans. The machine whirs to life and lights up pale green, then a series of palm-sized balls rolls down a tube on the side. He turns back to me to explain the game. I like that I have to crane my neck up to meet his gaze—it's a first.

"So, you roll the ball up the center here and try to get it into the holes. Eight balls, eight tries."

"That doesn't sound so hard."

"Oh, you think so? Wanna play?"

"Sure, but I'm gonna lose to a world champion."

"Just a national champion, actually." He smirks, feeds another dollar into the adjacent machine, and picks up his first ball. "Ready?"

I grab my first ball and center myself in front of the machine. "Ready."

I fling the ball up the center line, but it swerves off course, slides to the bottom of the board, and settles into the 0-point slot. His ball glides in a graceful arc, dropping right into the 50-point slot. I study the flick of his wrist and try again. This time, I get a 40. I punch the air.

"Beginner's luck?" he says, flicking his eyes over to my scoreboard.

I score a 30, then another one. The rest is a mix of 0s and 10s. When we're both finished, my score is less than half of his.

"What do you think?" I ask, picking up my cold highball glass from the floor and dipping the straw coquettishly between my lips.

"Not bad at all."

I drop into a mock curtsy. He reaches out to playfully punch my arm. His skin feels electric against mine.

"I'm going to get change at the bar so we can keep playing. Can I get you another drink?" he asks.

"Oh, sure. Thanks." Mine is almost drained.

He approaches the bar. There's a line now, so it looks like it'll be a minute. I slip my phone out of my purse and instantly wish I hadn't. Penelope has sent me a slew of emails. I scan the subject lines: 8:03 p.m. *New client! Gretchen Phelps*; 8:07 p.m. *New client! Chrissy Kodowski*; 8:15 p.m. *New client! Lily Chang*. I want it to all go away. I don't want to care about Bliss right now.

"Everything okay?" Adam asks, returning with the drinks.

"Oh, yeah. Just work stuff." I slip my phone back into my bag and accept the vodka soda. "Thank you so much."

We play another round, and this time, I just narrowly make half his total score. On the other side of the room, I spot a pair of dartboards.

"Ever played darts?" I ask, jerking my thumb at the boards.

"Not in years. Do you play?"

"My dad has a dartboard in his basement. I spent summers as a kid perfecting my game." Staying downstairs was always preferable to heading upstairs and finding him with that month's girlfriend.

"Then by all means, let's go."

I erase the chalk marks on the scoreboards, pick up the two sets of darts, and hand him one. We fall into an easy rhythm: my turn, his turn, retrieve the darts, chalk up our scores, banter back and forth, and repeat.

I like him, and not just because he's off-limits. He's gentlemanly, alluring, attentive, and a good listener. The conversation is easy—we're not grasping for things to say and only coming up with small talk. The chemistry is palpable, hanging between us as plainly as the Skee-Ball machines and the darts do.

"So, what are you reading these days?" he asks. "I won't be offended if it's not my stuff."

"Remind me again where you write?" This is a total lie. I know—I vetted him for Mindy.

"*Esquire.*"

"Riiight, right, right. You mentioned that. I'll have to check that out."

He screws up his mouth and hurls a dart. It misses the board entirely. Mine lands an inch from the bull's-eye.

"Nah, you don't have to read it. It's mostly political news these days, but I get to do some long-form reporting every once in a while."

"No, I'll read it," I say. It comes across a little too earnest. I retrieve the darts. "Bret Easton Ellis, by the way. I just finished *American Psycho*."

"Oh, that's fantastic. Patrick Bateman is almost as slimy as real-life investment bankers."

I laugh, but it comes out like a cackle.

"Your ex worked in finance, didn't he?" Adam asks, looking over with raised eyebrows.

"Every girl in New York has an ex who worked in finance," I retort.

It's his turn to retrieve the darts. He takes his sweet time pulling the needle out of the cork before he turns back to face me.

"I may have done a little Facebook stalking. It's only fair, since I answered all your questions under this whole 'matchmaking' pretense before you asked me out." He makes smug air quotes around the word "matchmaking."

I know I'm turning pink. I like knowing he stalked me, too. I bite my lip and grin.

"Right. The 'matchmaking' thing was all an elaborate scheme to get you to go out with me." I mimic his air quotes.

"You know, Mindy was cool, but you—Sasha, you're something else. You're stunning."

It's my turn to toss the darts, but Adam is right in front of me. I tilt my head back to look up at him and let my arms go slack against my body. There's a nervous, crackling energy between us. I want him to kiss me so badly. He angles his head toward mine. Up close, I can see just how soft his lips are. And then, there's a loud voice behind us.

"Are you using these dartboards?" asks a stocky guy in a Yan-kees hat.

Adam quickly steps back.

"Oh, go ahead, dude."

"We were . . ."

"Just leaving," Adam finishes. He slings an arm around my shoulders. "This girl is killing me so far. I'll never catch up."

He slips his hand into mine without hesitation, and leads me back to the front of the bar. I slide into the same booth we were sitting in earlier, and he sits down next to me. Our bodies are so close, I can feel the warmth radiating from his skin. I fumble for words.

"Um, right, uh, what were we talking about?"

"Something about how I stalked you. Please, let's move on." He pauses, slowly placing his hand on my knee. He glances at the door, then back at me, rubbing his shoulder. "Do you want to get out of here?"

I blush again and look down at his hand on my bare leg. It's un-believable how I ended up here. A half hour before my date, I was leaning into my bathroom mirror, mopping tear tracks, and repeat-ing "I am fine; everything is fine" until my chest stopped quaking with sobs. I'm a mess. And yet, being around Adam is so simple and *right*. Talking to him lights me up from the inside in a way I haven't felt in so long—not even when I was with Jonathan.

"That would be great," I tell him.

Adam smiles and backs out of the booth. He extends a hand for me to grasp as I exit, which is totally unnecessary and yet exactly the type of gesture that makes me feel like a swooning heroine in an old movie. I rise and follow him out of the bar into the twinkling twilight of the East Village.

He leads me a few feet down the block. I back up to the brick wall and drape my arms over his shoulders. I fit precisely into his arms, like he was made to hold me. He leans down to give me the sweetest kiss, but soon it deepens. I arch into him. It feels so easy to keep kissing him, keep reaching for the curve of his neck and the hard line of his jaw. I don't want him to pull away, but he does eventually.

"I don't mean to sound too forward, but I want to invite you back to my place." He runs his hand appreciatively over the curve from my waist to my hip.

Part of me wants to be coy and say no. Make him work for me, so that when I finally have him, he's truly mine. Good girls don't go home with guys on the first date. But I spent so long follow-ing the rules with Jonathan, trying to be the right kind of girl, and that ended up not being much fun. Spilling secrets, throwing drinks—now *that*'s fun. And I bet going home with Adam will be even better.

"Lead the way."

"Really?"

He seems surprised; I feel like some sort of sultry minx. The sensation is intoxicating. He hails a cab and directs it crosstown to Chelsea. The cab barely has a chance to turn the corner before our fingers are tangled in each other's hair and his lips are hot on my throat. I kiss a trail from his ear to below his collar and he groans. Ten minutes later, we come up for air just long enough for him to pay the driver. I can't believe this is really happening. I lean against his building to wait. He grabs me for another long kiss, then fishes for the key in his pocket and fumbles the door open.

"It's a fourth-floor walkup," he explains. "Sorry."

Adam has trouble keeping his hands off me while we climb. I playfully turn him around and push him up the flight. Inside, his apartment is decorated with an IKEA bookshelf and a ratty couch that looks a lot like mine. A video game controller lies atop a messy stack of *Esquire*s and *New Yorker*s on the antique black leather trunk he uses as a coffee table. The focal point of the living room isn't the television, but rather a console table with an old record player and stacks of vintage records.

"What do you listen to?" he asks.

I freeze up, trying to determine what would impress him. I go with an honest answer instead.

"Mostly pop. Or stuff like Lana Del Rey, Lorde, Adele."

"Let's do Lana," he says. He squats down to the bottom of the stack and pulls out a new record, the kind that's designed to look old. "I love this one."

I watch him cue up the record precisely. He chose my favorite album.

"Not too pretentious?" he asks, wincing.

"No, this is perfect."

Adam moves to the nook with a fridge and two bar stools, the kind of space that counts for a whole kitchen in Manhattan, and grabs two cold craft beers. He snaps off the caps with a bottle opener on his keychain and hands me one. We each take a sip, but I'm far more interested in him than I am in the beer. I think he feels the same way, since he wraps a hand around my waist and pulls me close. His finger grazes the underside of my chin, lifting my face up to his. When he finally kisses me again, it feels like a lightning bolt. We end up in his bed, kissing and peeling off each other's clothing. His skin is golden brown, like a toasted marshmallow, and his arms go on forever, from sinewy shoulder to toned bicep to lanky forearm. His fingers skim the edge of my black lace bikini briefs and linger there. I silently thank whatever higher power compelled me to accidentally wear non-fugly underwear without any weird period stains today.

A nagging feeling tugs at the back of my brain. I want this to last. I want Adam to still like me just as much tomorrow, if not even more, and I want to see him again. This can't be it. I wish there were a way I could tell him that and not sound like a stage-five clinger, but I don't know how to string the words so they sound neat and easy. I just—

"Are you okay?" he asks, pulling back just an inch.

I hadn't realized it, but maybe my lips slowed down or my grasps at his torso became less insistent.

"If you want to slow down, that's cool. We can just talk or hang out or go to sleep," he offers.

"I . . ." My voice catches in my throat. "I just like you, that's all. I hope you know that."

He breaks into an authentic smile. "I like you, too, Sasha."

He strokes my arm, and right there, it clicks into place. He's not going to leave me. He's not going to stop talking to me tomorrow. He's a good guy.

I move his hand back to my hip and let his finger curl around the lace there.

"Go ahead."

- Chapter 16 -

I'm still half asleep when I roll toward a warm, broad chest and rest my thigh across a pair of legs. I'm cozy and comfortable for exactly three whole seconds. Then my eyes fly open. Instead of Jonathan's tawny blond hair, I see a head full of dark curls. Holy shit. I'm in Adam's bedroom, naked, skin pressed to bare skin. I pull my limbs back to my side of the bed and stare wide-eyed up at the ceiling, praying I didn't disturb him. We are not yet intimate enough for the Early Morning Thigh Drape. That comes after . . . what, date five at least? I'm not familiar enough with the rhythms and regulations of new relationships to know, which is cruelly ironic when you consider that I'm paid to advise other people on these exact matters.

I try to fall back asleep so I can wake up later, when Adam does, but my heart is pounding too hard to let that happen. My chest is tight and I have to breathe, but I'm worried that he'll hear every inhale and exhale. I force myself to relax, but it's impossible with Adam just inches away. He feels like a furnace—if furnaces had toned limbs and a smattering of chest hair.

Time to employ strategy number two, which is to slip quietly out of bed. I creep over to the desk by the bedroom door, where I apparently flung my purse last night, and dig my phone out of it.

I skim the emails Penelope sent me last night. I already know that being here with Adam is wrong; the glut of Bliss emails just makes me feel worse.

Adam stirs. "Morning," he says, voice mussed with sleep. "You look amazing."

I'm butt naked. Sunlight streams in from the window above his bed and hits me like a spotlight. I run a self-conscious hand through my hair, and discover it's been transformed into a messy lion's mane of curls. I say good morning and squat down to snatch yesterday's bra and underwear from the floor.

"Oh, don't get dressed right away. Come here."

"I can't, I have a . . . a thing."

"You have to go so soon? I don't have to be at work for another . . ." He checks his phone on the nightstand. "Hour and a half."

I don't have anywhere to be for hours, and god, the gravitational force between me and his bed is intense. I drop my bra and underwear, suck in my stomach, and slink back to bed. He nuzzles a kiss into my neck. I want to conjure up something smart and sassy to say, but all I can think about is that this is the first morning since the breakup that I've woken up and not been shattered by the lack of a good-morning text from Jonathan.

"I had a really nice time last night," I say, daring myself to look him in the eye. "Thank you for inviting me over."

"You don't have to thank me. I'm glad you came."

He pulls me into his arms and asks about my plans for the day. Good taste probably dictates that I avoid telling him that I need to schedule another date for Mindy, but it's like when someone tells you not to think of a pink elephant: it's now the only thing on my mind.

"I'm setting up Mindy with my ex's brother-in-law's friend," I blurt out. "Sorry, that must be weird for you to hear."

He actually laughs. "Really, it's fine. I don't mind. It's funny, actually." He kisses my neck and tells me about the story he's working on at *Esquire*.

If every day could start this way, I would probably drink less. (Smoke less, too.) Conversation falls away when he starts to kiss me. He's tender at first, then his lips move more urgently over mine. Half an hour later, I untangle my limbs from his. I dress facing the wall to hide exactly how moronically wide I'm smiling when he asks if he can see me again soon.

When my phone lights up with a call from Penelope an hour later at my apartment, my stomach drops. For a terrifying second, I'm certain she knows about me and Adam. Matchmakers know everything. The good ones, anyway. But she doesn't bring up his name once. She's calling to give me the scoop on my new client Gretchen, who signed up two days ago and asked to be transferred to a new matchmaker almost immediately because Allison had taken a whole seven hours to respond to her initial email. Never mind that Allison is in D.C. for a former client's wedding. Gretchen only tolerates people who are prompt. And Penelope has reassigned her to me. Oy, Gretchen sends me clipped instructions to meet at a wine bar near her home in Carroll Gardens this afternoon.

I make a point of showing up ten minutes early to ensure she won't hate me. She's there when I walk in, of course, perched primly atop a bar stool near the entrance. She's wearing pristine white pants, an item I haven't owned since high school bullies splattered my only pair with tomato sauce. A ruby solitaire stone set in gold sits heavily on her ring finger, like she's daring you to ask if it's an engagement ring.

"How sweet of you to come out here to my neighborhood!" she says, gripping my hand in a firm shake. Not that I had a choice. She forms each syllable delicately, perfectly, precisely. I get the impression she hasn't mumbled once in her entire life. "You must live in Manhattan, right? Girls always like to go there when they first move to the city."

"Oh, I've actually lived here for four years," I begin to explain. I'd hate for her to think I'm some trust-fund baby brand new to the city who throws back Cosmos at some overpriced bar every Saturday night.

But she's already turned around, not listening, and she's leading me to the back of the bar. She pushes open a creaky screen door onto an open-air patio. We sit at a lacquered wood table underneath a wide umbrella. A waiter in a rumpled white shirt comes by to drop off two wine lists printed in an antique-looking font. None of the wines are old enough to warrant that kind of font, but we're in gentrified Brooklyn, so. Gretchen orders a glass of rosé from the south of France, and I indicate that I'll have the same.

"Now, I'm sure you spend all day long asking other people about their lives. So before we get to me, I want to hear about *you*," she chirps. "You're a matchmaker—that must be fascinating."

I smile wanly. There are so many things I can't tell her: that I've been on the job for just a month; that my only relationship ended in a spectacular blow out in the gourmet nut aisle at Dean & DeLuca after my boyfriend cheated on me with an Instagram celebrity; that I'm only twenty-two and don't have a speck of advice for how a forty-year-old should date; that I've never actually seen a happy, stable, monogamous relationship up close. Where to begin?

"Oh, you know. Well. Dating has always fascinated me, so here I am. It's the greatest job in the world." That line has flown out of my mouth so many times now that it's part of a perfect script. I don't even know if it's true.

She pries a little further. Where am I from? Where did I go to school? Do I have any exciting summer vacation plans? The waiter delivers our rosé and I prolong my time between answers with healthy gulps of wine.

"I'm not that interesting," I say. What I mean is this: none of my answers will impress you. "But let's talk about you!"

Gretchen's eyes sparkle. She pulls a crisp manila folder from her purse, removes the two packets inside, and hands me one.

"I did a little prep work to ensure we wouldn't forget to cover any topic during this discussion," she explains.

Inside is the most fastidiously organized document I've ever seen. *Your Master Guide to Finding Gretchen Phelps's Perfect Match!* spans eight pages. A highlighted section on the first page lists a series of nonnegotiable starting points: men ages 35 to 50 who are in good health, registered as Democrats, and live anywhere along the Amtrak corridor ("Willing to travel!" she chimes in). A series of underlined headings designate separate checklists, each more rigorous than the last: there's one for his physical appearance, including potential celebrity look-alikes; another for his personality traits; a third for his lifestyle preferences; and so on. A footnote at the bottom of page two explains that the points typed in larger fonts are more critical than the points typed in smaller ones.

The document is punctuated with cheery exclamation points. "Avoid anyone currently working through emotional baggage, but my ideal match is someone who has enjoyed the benefits of therapy!" she wrote on page three. "My partner should be highly successful

($250K per year, though more would be fine, of course), but *not* driven by financial goals or industry praise. Rather, he should find motivation from within!" she explained on page four. A subheading on page five introduces "Causes and charities I'd love for him to support!"

She included an addendum ("See Figure A") for a list of thirty-eight potential hobbies they could enjoy together, including gluten-free cooking, meditative yoga retreats, and collecting antique coins. Figure B consists of profiles of her past three ex-boyfriends, complete with headshots and screenshots of their social media profiles. The most recent one, she noted, "is a decorated veteran who has served in three (3) presidential administrations and still has time to hand-carve custom wooden furniture as a creative outlet." The packet culminates in Figure C, a page-long biography of herself written in the third person. By the time I skim the last page, I've remembered to close my mouth, which has fallen open in horror. Gretchen clicks open a pen.

"Do you have something to write with? You might want to take notes as we go through this."

To her credit, Gretchen is incredibly impressive. She sped through Princeton with honors, founded her own marketing firm, and volunteers with homeless New Yorkers. She has a robust group of friends and isn't particularly interested in having children, so she's not clamoring for a boyfriend to father a brood—she wants a *life partner*. It strikes me that Gretchen is the type of woman who would call her divorce a "conscious uncoupling." I scribble notes in the margins of her document as she talks, partly so I won't forget the specifics of her match, but mostly so I can regale Caroline with the complete breadth of Gretchen's insanity later over a bottle of wine. I can't help but feel like the more checklists and addendums and figures she includes, the less of a chance that anyone will meet her standards. Not even her freakishly successful exes did, or else they wouldn't be exes.

But a rigorous checklist doesn't guarantee that you'll be happy. Jonathan is movie-perfect, with his gleaming white teeth and sharp-cornered business cards—and yet he still betrayed me. So, I don't have much faith in Gretchen's checklist. I'll do what I did for Mindy and Eddie—find someone not terribly objectionable, set them up, cross my fingers, and collect my paycheck.

Gretchen is in the middle of telling me how self-aware she is when the waiter comes by to ask if we'd like refills. I hesitate; she declines. She waits for him to leave, then smoothes her hand over the packet and flips it shut.

"I want to explain to you why this list is so important to me." Her tone changes; she's a hair quieter, a little more serious. "When I was just about your age—you're twenty-two, aren't you?"

I nod, carefully watching her expression.

"I know. I looked you up before we met. I'm sure you did the same," she says, winking. "When I was about your age, I was dating my boyfriend from Princeton. He wanted me to follow him to Harvard, where he was going to law school. I thought it was very flattering that he asked me to come with him, and I knew he had a lot of potential. So I said yes, and shortly after, he proposed."

So, apparently Gretchen could be lovable. Good to know.

"This was years before Facebook and Instagram and people posting ring photos the moment they get engaged. People were more private about everything back then. I realized I felt nauseous at the prospect of telling my friends and family that I was going to marry him. He wasn't the right guy."

"What did you do?" I glance down at the ruby solitaire on her ring finger. She follows my gaze and twists it lovingly.

"I told him I'd made a mistake. I couldn't marry him. And he went off to Harvard in the fall, and I went to Honduras to teach English."

"Wow."

She sighs. "That's why this list is so important, Sasha. It can't just be *any* man. It has to be the right man. The most compatible match possible. Otherwise, sharing a life with someone isn't worth it."

I feel bad for judging her list. I don't know what to say.

She sits up straighter, not that I had even thought such a thing possible. "My broken engagement taught me another lesson, too."

"What's that?"

She flexes her left hand over the table and admires her ruby ring. "A woman should never rely on a man for a piece of jewelry. Every woman should treat herself to something beautiful, if she can afford it." She lets that sink in for a moment, then opens the packet again. "Now, I'd really like to address some of the more nuanced points in Figure B . . ."

When we emerge from the bar an hour later, she points me toward the F train off to the right and heads in the opposite direction back to her own apartment. I was nervous about the meeting running over into the time when I should be date-sitting for Eddie and Diane, but I just make it. I slip my phone out of my purse and intend to call Eddie, but Adam's name burns bright on my screen. My cheeks flush instantly. He left a voicemail; I can't recall the last time Jonathan did that. I hit play and his warm voice fills my ear.

"Hey there. I just wanted to thank you so much for last night. Is there any way I can push my luck and see you two nights in a row?"

My first instinct is to gush yes and hop the express train to meet him. Then I check myself. Girls are supposed to play hard to get, or something like that. But that feels like bullshit. I don't want to play by the rules anymore.

"Hey," I type. "I had the best time with you last night. As for tonight . . . it may be your lucky day. I'm coming from Carroll Gardens, but I'll be back in Manhattan in forty-five if that works for you?"

I read it over once, twice, then press send. I feel shaky. Cold. Frantic for his response. I walk quickly down the sidewalk, as if speeding up could somehow cosmically make his response come any faster. Guys never write back right away. But what do you know, a minute later, my phone dings, just like I wanted it to. My heart leaps into my throat. It's Adam.

"Brooklyn? Then meet me outside the Nassau Avenue stop in Greenpoint. There's something I want to show you."

Of course, there's a problem. Date-sitting for Eddie means I can't get on the subway because I might lose cell service and won't be available to take his calls. And walking to Greenpoint will take forever from here. So instead, I hail a cab. I can expense it to Bliss later.

Nestled in the cushy backseat, I dial Eddie and he picks up with a congested, "Hello?" I wish I could pass him a tissue.

"Hi! It's Sasha. I'm just checking in with you about your date with Diane tonight." Cheeriness works its way into my voice naturally; I might actually be getting better at this job.

"Well, I'm all set for the date. I'm just a block away from the bar. It's still on, isn't it?"

"Definitely. She can't wait to meet you."

Eddie makes a noise that sounds like *harumph*. I didn't realize that people actually *harumph*ed in real life.

We chat logistics. I'm sending them to a Mets bar, which I figured would be an ideal place for Eddie to feel comfortable. It's not remotely Bliss-approved—it's not upscale, it's just drinks, and there's no complicated adventure for the clients to enjoy (the purpose of the adventure, I've learned, is to break the ice and give clients something to talk about aside from why they're so desperately single that they've hired Bliss in the first place). But I know they'll love the Mets bar.

I text Diane that Eddie is at the bar, and she writes back a few minutes later that she's almost there. I'm relieved. Later, I repeat the process with Mindy and Gordon.

"Hey there, dollface," Mindy answers when I call. "How's your day?"

I freeze, swallow, and fixate on telling her strictly the parts she can hear. "Oh, you know, the usual. Just met with a new client."

"She's so goddamn lucky to have you."

"Aw, Mindy, stop. Anyway, I'm so excited for you to meet Gordon. . . ."

The rest of the ride to Nassau Avenue is peaceful, and I spend an embarrassingly large portion of it thinking about Adam: exactly how he touched me last night, the sturdiness of his body next to mine as we slept, the proper greeting for when I see him today (a hug? A kiss on the cheek? A kiss on the lips? If only I, an actual matchmaker, knew the rules to dating). I decide on a kiss on the cheek.

When I get out of the taxi, I spot him leaning against the wrought-iron fence around the subway stop. He's dressed in slim jeans and a white T-shirt with a black leather jacket folded over the crook of his elbow. If only he had a cigarette dangling from his lips, I'd mistake him for James Dean.

"I can't believe I get to see you twice in one day," he says, looking me up and down. "I'm a lucky man."

I want to appear cool and calm in front of him so badly, but I can't. I eke out a sheepish, "Same."

His fingers graze my hips and encircle the small of my back, pulling me close for a real kiss. The embrace feels like cozying into an old sweater. Adam smells earthy and spicy and masculine. I could keep kissing him forever, but he pulls away. He grabs my hand and interlaces his fingers through mine. We begin walking.

"So, I wanted to take you to the Brooklyn Night Bazaar," he says. "Have you been?"

"No, what is that?"

"And you call yourself a New Yorker. I guess the southern transplant will have to show you."

We stroll a few blocks down the street, past a baseball field with patchy grass and a two-story bar twinkling with lights that glow pale gold in the dusky purple evening sky. The streets are vaguely familiar. I might have been drunk here during sophomore year, when Caroline and I spent every weekend traveling to a new corner of Brooklyn in search of cool apartment parties hosted by fashion majors and dudes who swore they were on the verge of finally finishing their EDM EPs. But it's early now—that kind of crowd won't start flocking to this neighborhood for another few hours—so we have the streets mostly to ourselves.

We arrive at a brick warehouse that stretches the width of the entire block. The bouncer outside asks for our IDs, peers at mine for an extra half second, then stamps our wrists and waves us forward. I'm used to being carded, but Adam is clearly not. Inside, the warehouse is bustling with hundreds of people. The perimeter is lined with vendors: I spot signs for vintage clothing, handmade jewelry, artisanal popcorn, craft beer, a tattoo artist, Ping-Pong, laser tag, and more. A rockabilly band sets up in the far corner.

"This is awesome," I tell him. I like the way my hand feels in his and don't want to let go.

"I thought you'd like it," he says, a self-satisfied smirk spreading across his face. "I figured you'd seen just about every cool date spot in Manhattan, so I thought this might surprise you."

We weave through the booths, admiring handmade jewelry and sharing a bag of sesame-wasabi popcorn that tingles across my lips. He holds up a garish 1950s bowling shirt to his chest and turns to face me.

"Dashing, right?"

He looks downright ridiculous.

"I mean, if you miss the clothing of your childhood, go ahead and get it." It feels dangerous to poke fun at his age, but I have a hunch the joke will land.

"Oh, ouch! Excuse me, I forgot you were in diapers when Clinton was sworn in."

I stop riffling through the rack of vintage Levi's. "Not quite."

"You were, what . . ." He pauses to do the math.

"Not even conceived yet," I fill in for him.

He places the loudly printed bowling shirt back on the rack. He groans. "Right, right."

I study his face. There's a boyish softness to his eyes, but his forehead is faintly creased and weathered. He looks away, sheepish, and I can't help but imagine that I'm the youngest person he's ever been with. He's certainly the oldest person I've been with.

"Let's play Ping-Pong," I say, leading him to the far corner of the warehouse and away from this treacherous conversation. "I can kick your ass at it."

"Oh, really." It's not a question.

"Want to make it interesting and bet on it?"

"Fine. The winner gets a kiss?"

"I was planning on getting one from you anyway," I flirt back.

He lets out a loud, deep laugh that cuts through the buzz of the crowd. "Cocky, huh?"

The Ping-Pong tables are around the corner in a room splattered floor to ceiling with colorful graffiti. I'm so not cool enough to be here. Adam fishes a five out of his wallet to give to the attendant, and she sets us up with a bucket of Ping-Pong balls and two rubber paddles. I serve the ball across the table with a hearty *thwock*; he lunges sideways to hit it back.

"Looking forward to collecting that kiss," I call across the table.

When I beat him, he leaves his paddle on the table and walks over to my side to embrace me. He tucks a lock of hair behind my ear and strokes my cheek with one finger, tilting my chin up to face him. He's close enough that I can feel the heat radiating off his skin. When he finally leans in for the kiss, I want to melt into his arms. There's a nagging voice in the back of my head that reminds me how wrong this is on so many levels: he's my client's former match; I met him through Bliss; I've been single for exactly one week and three hours; and this is most definitely a rebound. But who said a rebound had to be a meaningless fling?

We've paid for a half hour of Ping-Pong and still have twenty minutes to go, so we bat around the ball for a while. He gets better at returning my serves, but not by much. When I win another round, we turn in our paddles and balls and head back to the main part of the warehouse. I like strolling with him through the crowd. It feels so easy and natural and right to be half of a pair with him.

We move on to the remaining few vendors. He slows by a table of druzy pendants and starts chatting up the artist, a forty-something woman in round tortoiseshell glasses. He asks if she makes the pendants herself, where she learned to make jewelry, if she's sold at the Brooklyn Night Bazaar for long. The whole time, his thumb rubs lazy circles on the inside of my palm. It's comforting.

Eventually, we head for the exit. Outside, the sky has turned midnight blue. We walk through blocks of warehouses and low brick buildings. We end up by the waterfront at the Greenpoint Pier. The entire Manhattan skyline is lit up across the East River. It's a spectacular display, with the lights from the new World Trade Center, Empire State Building, and Chrysler Building reflected a million times over in the rippling water.

"It's gorgeous, isn't it?" he asks, coming up behind me and wrapping his arms around me.

I lean my elbows onto the railing and try to commit this moment to memory.

"Breathtaking."

"Just like you."

When we kiss, he dips me way back, like we're in a goddamn Nicholas Sparks movie. I get a head rush, and it's not just from the dip. It's from the sweet vindication of knowing that I'm capable of being treated right, not just ignored, cast aside, and betrayed. This is the moment when karma comes back in my favor. His hands roam my body and hold me tight.

Scientists should package Adam up and sell him to girls who have recently had their hearts broken. Why the hell would Mindy ever pass him up?

As if on cue, my phone rings in my purse. I bet it's either Eddie or Mindy—either way, I don't want to pick it up.

"Going to get that?" he asks, sliding his fingers out of my hair.

"Mm, no."

I kiss him again, but the ringing continues. It cuts off abruptly as he starts to kiss down my neck. The ringing picks up again.

"It's okay, you can get it," he says, straightening up but keeping one hand tucked into the back pocket of my jeans.

"All right, all right. I'm sure it's work."

Sure enough, it's Mindy. He glimpses the caller ID and chuckles.

"Go ahead, talk to her."

I hesitate. I, of all people, know what it's like to be abandoned for a work phone call. I take a few steps away from him and that glorious waterfront view.

"Hello?"

"Sasha! You. Are. A. Genius."

I heave an enormous sigh of relief. "I am?"

"I had the best time ever with Gordon. He's so cute. So smart. So British! Ugh, that accent, it kills me."

"I know, he's pretty fantastic, right?"

"Has he said anything about me?" She sounds nervous.

"Not yet. I'll get the scoop tomorrow."

"Oh. It's so hard to be patient. I'm not even desperate for him to like me or anything, because I know I'm amazing and I can walk away if he's not interested. But I . . ." She hesitates. "I could maybe see this going somewhere. Maybe."

"That's great, Mindy."

"But don't stop setting me up with other guys. I want to renew my package for next month. Two more dates, all right?"

"Sure, let's keep your options open."

Adam leans back on his elbows against the railing and shakes his head quietly, grinning.

"Amazing. 'Night, doll, talk soon! Ciao."

I test out the word. "Ciao."

I slip my phone into my bag and turn back to Adam, embarrassed without quite being able to put a finger on why.

"How was Mindy's date?"

"She sounded happy on the phone. Sorry, is it weird for you to hear about Mindy?"

"I traded up."

He's perfect.

Back at his apartment, we manage to keep our hands off each other long enough to pop open a bottle of wine and settle onto the couch. The clock under the TV reads nearly midnight. Conversation flows easily in a way it never did with Jonathan. It turns out that casual conversations are much easier when you don't have to memorize a glossary of financial terms first—who knew? He listens to my stories about the ridiculous things I hear guys say on Tinder, my travels across Europe during my semester abroad, my failed tryout for the cheerleading team when I was a freshman in high school. He lights up when I tell him about my background in journalism.

"Did you read the short story in this week's *New Yorker*?"

"Oh, er, no."

"Oh, really?" He looks caught off guard. He leans forward to find the exact page he's talking about in one of the magazines on the coffee table. "Well, anyway, this writer's a really big deal."

I half pretend to skim the story. I feel like I did back in my sophomore year of college, when one of my English TAs was young and cute and I wanted to impress him. Adam's eyes meet mine, and I feel like I have to be honest with him before I get any more invested than I already am. I fidget with the corner of my cuticle so

I don't have to look him in the eye when I explain myself. Sharing the secret means the two of us can share its pressure now.

"You know, I'm not . . . technically . . . allowed to date anyone I meet through matchmaking. Company policy and all. It's kind of bullshit, but I just thought you should know."

"You're a stellar employee," he deadpans. "No, really, I don't want to get you into trouble or anything. But I also . . ." He falters. His next words are slow and measured, like he's nervous and wants to be precise. "I really like you, Sasha. I know it's only been a few days, but you're phenomenal."

I try to keep breathing. It's suddenly very hot in his apartment.

"You're not getting me into any trouble, as long as no one from Bliss finds out."

"Are you sure?"

Goddamn, look at those big brown eyes. Like melted chocolate. The thing is, I don't feel great about breaking the one rule Penelope has explicitly laid down. But with Adam right here in front of me, it's impossible to seriously weigh the risks.

"I'm sure," I hear myself tell him. "I really like you, too."

He sets his wineglass on the table, then takes mine out of my hand and puts it down. He stands up and extends his hand to help me up off the couch, then pulls me into a kiss. He picks me up so I can wrap my legs around him. Normally, I'd feel self-conscious of my weight suspended in his arms like this, but he's like a giant. He can handle me.

"So, you're sure this is completely forbidden?" he asks, his words hot on my ear.

"Absolutely."

He carries me to his bedroom, kicks the door closed behind us, and throws me onto the bed.

— Chapter 17 —

The best part about dating Adam might be the texting. I know that's not what I'm supposed to say—it's supposed to be the sex, right?—but a week after our date in Greenpoint, Caroline has requested a girls' night in and the banter over text all day has just been mouthwatering. Caroline and I sit cross-legged on the couch, passing a package of cold, sliced turkey between us, with white wine in plastic Solo cups on the floor. We've paused an episode of *Broad City* we've both already seen while Caroline catches me up on her date last night.

"It was just weirdly . . . great?" she says. She looks both thrilled and confused. "He asked me questions about myself, paid for our drinks while I was in the bathroom, and texted me this morning to ask when he could see me again."

"That is shockingly normal."

She nods vigorously as she rolls another piece of turkey. "I know, right?"

"Should I bother learning this one's name?"

"You know, you might. Owen."

"Do you think you like him? Or are you just marveling that he did all the things he's supposed to do?"

"I mean, I don't know." She tilts her head. "I haven't really thought about it."

She pulls up Owen's Bumble profile and hands her phone to me, and indeed, he appears shockingly normal. He went to school in Michigan. He works in advertising. His pictures suggest that he owns multiple nice-looking sweaters and has an array of equally normal-seeming friends. When I hand the phone back to her, she beams at the screen for a few seconds. I take that time to steal a glance at my own phone; just as I had hoped, a message from Adam waits for me.

It sounds crazy, doesn't it? Girl likes guy. Girl texts guy. Guy *actually texts back right away.* If Jonathan responded in under five hours, I considered that a success.

"What are you up to later, miss?" Adam had written a minute ago.

I can't help my response: an instant grin, flushed cheeks, a pleasant drop in my stomach. I had forgotten what it was like to have a crush, but it's this tornado of all-consuming physical sensations all the time. I crave his texts. It's been a week since I've seen him last, and I miss being close to him. That's what Caroline has been chasing all these years—the giddy joy of letting yourself fall for a person who actually deserves you.

"That's Adam?" Her tone is slightly sharp.

I press my phone to my chest. "How'd you know?"

She rolls her eyes, then picks up her phone with a breathy sigh, pouts, and bats her eyelashes in a cartoonish impression of me. "Come on, Sasha."

"I just . . . *like* him. I can't help it."

Her face falls just the tiniest bit. "I thought—" She looks away, picks up her cup of wine, and takes a sip. "Never mind. It's stupid."

"What?"

"Never mind."

"No, what?"

Her jaw sets in a hard line. "I just thought we'd finally be single together. You know, have fun with it. Like we used to."

I flash back to a night before I met Jonathan. A Tuesday—dollar-beer night at The 13th Step in the East Village, when hordes of NYU kids and twenty-something transplants who have yet to find better places to drink swarm the bar. It's crowded wall to wall with people who slosh back pints between sticky wooden tables. One night, Caroline and I improvised fake names and stories for each new set of guys who stumbled by to slur pickup lines our way. We were Taylor and Danielle, pole dancers fresh off the plane from Indianapolis; or Ophelia and Constance, socialites slumming it at a dive bar à la *The Simple Life*; or Georgia and Marie, long-lost twin sisters separated at birth and adopted by different families, reuniting for the first time in the big city. We did it to meet men, but whenever I think back to that night, I barely remember the guys at all. I only remember feeling my stomach quake with half-suppressed laughter as I tried to keep it together as she reeled off these preposterous stories.

I shift on the couch to face her straight on. "I'll never stop wanting to be your friend," I tell her. "Ever. Doesn't matter if I'm single."

"I know, I know." Caroline gets up from the couch to put the turkey back in the fridge, possibly to avoid looking at me. When her back is turned, I dash off a text to Adam.

"Tonight's girls' night," I type quickly. "Tomorrow?"

Caroline comes back to the couch, brandishing the wine bottle in one hand and a pint of Ben & Jerry's in the other.

"I've seen Adam, like, three times, Caroline. That doesn't change anything about our friendship."

She shrugs and resumes the episode on the TV.

I stumble across the perfect date by accident the next morning. Gretchen emailed me a list of activities and events occurring around the city during the month of August, organized chronologically and then color-coded by theme (restaurants and bars in blue, outdoor activities in green, live music in red, theater in purple, and so on). "Just wanted to send over some suggestions while you're planning my first date!" she wrote, complete with not one but two smiling emojis.

Under the list for today, August 5: the book launch party for my new client Lily Chang, the writer living in Crown Heights, Brooklyn, who dates both men and women. She has a column about dating, which makes her possibly the one woman in the city whose job freaks out dates more than mine does. When we met for drinks last week, she explained that she didn't really care about the quality or compatibility of her matches that much—she just wanted an entertaining story for her column. The mission was daunting, and so I kept putting it off. A week later, I didn't really have any leads for Lily. But the book party would show my support for my client, and it'd be exactly the kind of date that would impress Adam.

"Lily Chang's book party tonight—you down?" I text him.

"You know her?"

I love that he texts back right away. He makes me feel *wanted*.

"She's a client."

"Whoa. I've heard she's awesome. Let's go."

That's how we wind up in the basement of the ultra-hip bookstore WORD Brooklyn. Adam leads me down the staircase, beelines for the table with wine, and settles into the sea of folding chairs with an ease that makes me think this isn't the first event he's attended here. The crowd is very Brooklyn: the guys wear suede shoes and leather jackets even though it's August, and the girls all have Parisian-looking bangs and carry canvas tote bags with the *New Yorker*'s logo or with a cutesy slogan about veganism (EAT BEANS, NOT BEINGS). I spot Lily at the front of the room, looking unbearably cool in a pair of ripped jeans and an oversized vintage Rolling Stones tee. I want to say hi, but before I can, a thirty-something woman in dark lipstick squeezes into our row and perches on the chair next to Adam.

"I thought that was you!" she exclaims, going in for a hug.

"Hey! How's it going?"

"Ugh, you know. Working on a big piece right now. I didn't know you knew Lily." I can't tell if I'm imagining the intimate, singsongy swing to her voice.

"I don't personally," Adam says. He gestures to me. "Sasha works with her, actually."

The woman acknowledges me for the first time. "Oh, what do you write?"

"I'm not a writer. I mean, I was. But it's not, you know, my job right now."

"*Oh.*"

If she had had the slightest sliver of interest in me before, it was gone now.

"Sorry, I should've introduced you. Sasha, Katie, Katie, Sasha," Adam says. Then as an explanation to me, "Katie freelances for *Esquire*."

"And you two are . . . ?" she presses. "Together?"

"Here on a date." He grabs my hand.

"Oh! I didn't realize. You're so . . ." She takes in my denim shorts and shabby sandals with the straps wearing thin. "Cute. Well, have fun, you two." She slides down the row of seats and excuses herself to the table of wine.

Neither one of us knows what to say.

"That was awkward," I announce.

"I didn't know how to introduce you," he admits. "It's too soon for 'girlfriend.'"

"Definitely too soon for 'girlfriend,'" I agree.

Then again, in my head, I've already started thinking of him as my next boyfriend. My birthday is in November, three months away; I kind of hoped he would be around for it. It's probably unhealthy to jump into a relationship with Adam so quickly. But being around him feels easy and right. I'm happy when I'm with him, and I haven't been happy all that often this summer. I don't want to end up like Mindy and Gretchen, alone at forty with no kids and a five-page checklist.

A bookstore employee taps the microphone at the front of the room. "Hey, guys. Guys? I think we're going to get started."

She introduces Lily with a string of compliments that goes on for approximately a minute and a half, and then asks her to read a chapter of her book out loud. Lily has a mesmerizing speaking voice, steady and confident, even—especially—when delivering the dirty jokes that litter every page. She flips her glossy mane of hair over the top of her head as she reads. I can't tell if I want to be able to write like her, or if I just want to *be* her. Lily closes the book and bows her head as the audience claps.

Lily and the event moderator talk about the book, then open up the conversation for questions from the audience.

"Come introduce me to Lily?" Adam asks when it's over.

She's holding court behind a mountain of books at the front of the room, signing each one with a red Sharpie. I tentatively approach her, and when I'm a few feet away, she spots me through the small crowd of fans. When she finishes scrawling her signature into a copy, she gives me a big wave and gestures for me to come closer.

It strikes me all of a sudden that Lily should be dating someone like Adam. I could see them together so easily—they're more age-appropriate for each other, and in the same industry, and they know all the same people. I feel young and small, ridiculous for thinking this thing with Adam could possibly work. My job is to boil down compatibility from an art into a science; I should know when a couple makes sense. But so far, I haven't pulled that off for any of my clients, and I'm certainly not getting it right for myself.

"Hel-*lo*, Dolly!" She looks Adam up and down. "So this is my betrothed?"

"Ha. I'm still on the hunt," I say.

"I'm just a fan," Adam says, reaching out for a handshake. "Big fan. Adam Rubin. From *Esquire*."

"I loved hearing you read," I say. "I wish I could write like you do."

"Dude, do you write? I didn't know that."

"I mean, I used to."

"You could totally write about matchmaking. People would eat that shit up."

She has a point. I can tell Adam is just dying to talk to her, so I let him steer the conversation toward Lily's book. His thumb rubs the inside of my palm as he talks to her—a gesture she doesn't miss. A line is forming behind us, so he grabs a copy of Lily's book and asks her to sign it for him. She obliges.

When Adam and I are outside the bookstore, he cups my chin and kisses me deeply.

"Thanks for bringing me," he says. "You're the coolest."

It's a bizarre sensation, realizing the way you see yourself isn't the way others do. I'm just a kid faking her way through her first job and scrambling to start paying off her student loans. But to Adam, I'm a girl with a sexy career, connections to one of New York's most notorious writers, and the kind of unhinged confidence that led me to track him down in a bar on a sweaty Monday night.

If he sees me that way, it just might be true.

I can't stop thinking about what Lily said. I should write about matchmaking. I lie awake, my brain buzzing, for an hour after Adam falls asleep. My mind churns over exactly what I could write, where I'd pitch my stories, and how maybe—just maybe—this would get my writing career back on track. I didn't like the way that woman Katie's eyes glazed over when she realized I wasn't paying my bills with my writing.

The next morning, as I watch Adam pull on jeans and muss product through his hair, I pitch him my plan.

"You know that I write, don't you?" I ask, trying to sound casual.

"Mhm." He's focused on the hair product.

"I was thinking maybe I'd like to start my own column," I continue, "give guys dating advice based on what I've learned as a matchmaker."

"Huh!" He turns around, wiping his hands on his jeans. "That could be great."

"Do you think that Esquire.com might be interested in a column like that?"

He looks at me seriously. "You have clips?"

He means writing samples.

"Four years' worth."

"Yeah, I could connect you with my editor."

"You'd do that for me?"

"Of course."

I squeal and throw my arms around his neck in a hug. "Thank you, thank you, thank you."

He gently puts his hands on my waist. "I didn't say I could make it happen. My editor will have to say yes."

"I *know*," I say, rolling my eyes. I sink back onto the bed, feeling triumphant. "He will. I know he will."

"You're cocky," Adam says, lifting one eyebrow.

"Yeah, I am. Half my job is knowing how to make men do whatever I want."

"Oh, come *on*."

"I wanted you to go out with Mindy, so you went out with Mindy. And I wanted you to go out with me, and you did." I cross my arms. "So there."

Adam pauses in the doorway, where he had begun putting on his shoes. Instead, he places both shoes back on the floor and dives onto the bed to kiss me.

"What do you want me to do now?" he growls in my ear.

Later, after I've showered at Adam's place, run home to feed Orlando, and installed myself at a David's Bagels to work for the day, I email Penelope to see if I'm even allowed to write about matchmaking. I explain that I was hoping to pitch a column to Esquire .com—not as a full-time job, but just as a freelance gig on the side.

"Esquire?" she writes back. "*Please*. We need all the press we can get."

So, slurping up iced coffee as I go, I draft a sample column. I want to send Adam's editor, Diego Vidal, a sample of what I can do. The words spill out easily; I write about Mark, the investment banker I had met for coffee at Starbucks who only wanted to date thin, busty blondes, giving him a pseudonym. I start by appealing to the average Esquire.com reader who probably would love to date a whole cheerleading team's worth of thin, busty blondes, but then segue into why Mark's approach to dating isn't doing him any favors. He comes across as desperate and gross. The kind of girls he wants just don't want him. He's probably not even getting laid that much. I wrap up by offering readers three suggestions. First, dating is a full-time job (I explain that it's *literally* my full-time job), and so you'll get the best results if you actively put yourself out there on multiple dating apps and in real life. Second, pursue partners who are equally as attractive and successful as you are. And last but not least, if you're still struggling, hire Bliss.

I make Caroline read it over twice, and she signs off on it after just a few minor edits. I send it to Adam, preparing myself for him to hate it. But miraculously, he doesn't hate it at all.

"Goddamn, you're good," he writes back. "Here's Diego's contact info."

Three email drafts later, I attach my sample column and hit send. I've spent so much time watching the men I date pursue their dream careers. It's time I go after my own.

– *Chapter 18* –

Anyone can date. It's not hard. You go out with someone, you go home with someone, whatever. But turning a series of dates into a real *relationship* requires a series of small victories—meeting each other's friends; taking and posting pictures of each other; agreeing not to see other people. Left to their own devices, guys won't ever initiate any of these steps. Girls have to carefully strategize how to move the fledgling relationship forward without freaking out the guy. So on Saturday afternoon, when Adam texts to ask if I'm free to join him at a concert tonight, I take a calculated risk.

Caroline and I are stretched out on a beach towel in Washington Square Park to sunbathe in bikini tops and cutoffs. She flips through *Cosmo* as I draft a second column for Esquire.com, just in case Diego likes the first.

"Hey," I say, poking her arm with my iced coffee cup. "Are you doing anything tonight?"

She looks up from a story about vibrators. "Maybe Victoria and Graham's housewarming party."

And so the post-NYU migration to Brooklyn begins. Victoria and Graham aren't a couple in the traditional way (he was the president of Delta Lambda Phi, the gay frat), but you never see one without the other.

"What about dinner at Hotel Tortuga first?" I ask.

"You know I wouldn't show up to that party without pregaming."

"I want you to meet Adam. Tonight at Tortuga."

She raises her eyebrows. "Wow. Sure, invite him along."

With Caroline's encouragement, I carefully type out an invitation designed to sound as casual as possible.

"Caroline and I are getting dinner tonight at our fave Mexican place. Join us before the concert?"

Before I can lose my nerve, I hit send. I'm too antsy to return to my writing while I wait for his response. Instead, I wait and watch for the three gray dots to pop up that indicate Adam is texting me back. They disappear and I panic. Is it asking too much to introduce Adam to Caroline? Ten seconds later, the dots reappear, and Adam's text slows my pounding heart.

"Sure thing. Just text me the address."

That's how, seven hours later, Caroline and I wind up in our usual booth in the back of Tortuga. I sit on the far side, my back to the wall, so I can watch the door for Adam's arrival. Caroline sits across from me. Her cheeks are pink from the sun. The ponytailed waiter knows to bring us a pitcher of frozen margaritas before we even ask for one. I focus on ladling the slushy drinks into three yellow plastic cups to distract from my nerves.

"Just relax," Caroline whispers, watching me frantically lift the cups to eye level to check if I poured them evenly. "Your stress is stressing me out."

"Sorry," I say.

I set the drinks on the table and fidget with my half-healed hangnail instead.

"It's just me, some bomb-ass Mexican food, and a hot guy who's already obsessed with you," she reassures me. "Chill."

"I just hope you guys get along—" I begin, but cut myself off abruptly as I see Adam enter the tiny restaurant.

He makes his way to the back, ducks down to give me a chaste peck on the cheek, then straightens up and extends his hand to shake Caroline's.

"I've heard so much about you," he says warmly.

"Yeah, same. I mean, obviously," Caroline replies.

Adam slides into the booth next to me.

"Thanks for coming," I say.

He shrugs. "Of course."

To date a guy who shows up when he says he will—it's refreshing.

He takes in the walls papered with crayon drawings, the orange speckled tables, the yellow hanging lanterns. The tables are close together, packed with people who feel comfortable enough here to slip their shoes off and sit cross-legged and barefoot.

"It's like home," I explain.

There's a short lull in the conversation as Adam glances down at his menu. Caroline and I could recite the whole thing by memory, so we stare at him, then at each other, attempting to figure out what to say. I want this to go well so badly. It feels like so much is at stake.

"You know, Caroline probably deserves a finder's fee or something," I blurt out.

"For what? For me?" Adam looks up, amused.

"She sent you that first message on Tinder," I clarify.

"You're a matchmaker who doesn't even make her own matches?" he asks.

"Oh, come *on*. I make enough. Caroline was just showing me how to use Tinder, and there you were," I explain.

"So I was talking to . . . her?" he puzzles out.

That night feels like it took place years ago. So much has happened.

"Well, then me. And then, actually, my coworker Georgie. But then me, in person."

"After you hunted me down like an animal," he says, grinning.

If only he knew the full extent of my stalking. Caroline and I already looked up his parents' house on Zillow (yellow ranch, three bedrooms, two bathrooms) and found his college ex-girlfriend's Pinterest board themed around decorating her infant son's nursery.

"Don't complain. I got you here, to the best pitcher of margaritas in Manhattan."

"Cheers to that," Adam says, lifting his cup.

We all clink drinks. Later, the waiter comes by to take our order, and Adam asks Caroline about her pilot. He says he tried to write one years ago—I had no idea. Their conversation turns to the screenwriting software Final Draft, writers' groups, querying agents. I sit back to watch them find common ground. I can tell when Caroline is bullshitting a guy; it's imperceptible to whichever dude she's nodding and *mhm*ing along to, but I know her too well to be fooled. She looks sincerely interested in what Adam has to say. Her smiles actually reach her eyes. I get a little high on the vision of my favorite person and this new guy in my life beginning to kinda-sorta-maybe get along.

The waiter drops off our plates, each piled precariously with entrées surrounded by pools of guacamole and sour cream.

When Adam looks down at his plate, the waiter mouths a comment behind his hand: "New guy?"

I blush. I can't respond without drawing Adam's attention.

But the waiter isn't done. "He's cute."

For four years now, Tortuga has been my place with Caroline. It didn't matter if we were living together in the dorms or our apartment. Tortuga has always felt like our home away from home. I don't know what they put in the margaritas, but this place has good vibes only. Jonathan would eat here sometimes with us—and later, Mary-Kate and Toby, too—but there was no question who got custody of this place in the breakup. It's eerie to see Adam eating his beef-topped nachos where Jonathan once ate his carnitas quesadillas.

It could work, though. I can see Adam fitting into my life the way Jonathan once did. He's performing the role of Potential Boyfriend with charm and ease; Caroline's dates—like Wesley, the melted-cheese artist at the rooftop party—typically fall flat, leaving me to wonder what she sees in any of them. They embarrass her. But Adam is carrying the conversation, asking Caroline all the right questions, and behaving like a gentleman. I'm proud to have him here. As he eats and talks next to me, he slings his arm around my shoulders and stretches his legs out under the table, like he's getting comfortable.

After dinner, we linger outside the restaurant. Adam has his arm wrapped around my waist; Caroline's a foot away.

"So, there's this band playing at Rockwood Music Hall tonight," he says. "Think The Strokes, but new. Seriously good guitar. I covered them a while ago and the publicist says I can swing by with a few people."

"Great," I say.

"Caroline, coming? I'm sure I could get a third ticket, no problem."

She hesitates and runs a hand through her hair. "I'm going to head over to Victoria and Graham's housewarming. I'll catch you later?"

"Yeah, I'll see you," I say.

"See you soon," Adam says, breaking away from me to give her a hug.

I hope he means it.

Caroline heads east toward the subway as Adam and I round the corner to walk to the Lower East Side. When I thank him for meeting her, he shrugs.

"Yeah, of course. She's cool. And I know how important she is to you."

"Like a sister."

"I got that."

There's a beat of silence. I'm embarrassed by how happy I am that he accepted my invitation to meet Caroline. I want to read into it and assume he must really like me—but I also don't want to get my hopes up and then be wrong. I can't be crushed by two men in one summer.

The publicist, a woman dressed in black wielding a clipboard, is standing behind the bouncer in the doorway of the venue. She calls Adam's name as he approaches.

"You made it!" she squeals. Then, to the bouncer, she explains, "It's fine, they're with me."

I'm not much of a music junkie, but even I have to admit it doesn't suck to be pulled into a hot concert spot by a hot guy on a hot New York summer night. There's already a crowd at the base of the stage where a four-piece band sets up against a red wall—three guys in Adam's mold of white T-shirt and black leather jacket and a girl in a long gauzy dress, clutching a microphone. I'm tall, but not quite tall enough to enjoy the view from the back of the crowd. I rise up on my toes to get a better view.

"Let's watch from the balcony," Adam says, pointing to a stair-case leading up to a second floor.

I follow him through the crowd, up the stairs, and to a two-top overlooking the stage. It's perfect. A cocktail waitress drops off two beers.

"From Sara," she says.

"The publicist," Adam tells me.

The beer is refreshingly cold—and free.

"You know, I never thought this would be my life," he says, lean-ing in close so I can hear him over the din. "I still feel like a nobody from Atlanta who snuck into this dream life."

"I get it," I say. "Trust me, I get it."

Five years ago, I could barely imagine living in New York. And I certainly couldn't imagine the sweet jolt of tracking down a prom-ising match for a Bliss client, or the comfortable silence that comes on a quiet night in with Caroline, or the satisfaction of leaning my head against Adam's shoulder as the band below crackles to life and begins to play.

- *Chapter 19* -

Three weeks later, my first column publishes on Esquire.com. I didn't think anything could top the thrill of seeing my name stamped across the top of the column—that is, until I saw my name printed across a check. At $200 a pop, the column proved more lucrative than setting up a single date. It felt more rewarding, too. It even garnered enough online traffic that Diego asked for a second one.

For column number two, I gave Eddie and Diane pseudonyms and told their story, which was becoming more adorable by the day. I wouldn't exactly describe their first date as smooth—he choked on his mozzarella stick when she called him "brainy" and had to go stand outside the bar, hacking and wheezing, until he coughed up the fried cheese and regained his composure. But by some miracle, they both wanted to see each other again, traversing borough lines for a dinner on Staten Island. And again, when they took a ferry and a subway and a bus to meet for a Mets game in Queens.

"Unbelievable. She . . . wants *me*?" he asked breathily over the phone one night.

Against all odds, she did.

He sounded like a sixteen-year-old girl gushing about a date. They were a long way off from officially calling themselves boyfriend and girlfriend, he told me, but they liked each other enough to go on multiple dates, which is more than I could say for most of my other matches. I had assumed Eddie would be my toughest client, but he turned out to be the easiest. The happiest. He went into his date with Diane without expectations or a checklist, so he was able to appreciate her for exactly who she was. Maybe that's the key to it all—rolling with what life gives you, rather than seeking something that isn't there.

I'm still figuring out what my third column will be about. There's Mindy, of course, who had seen Gordon for a second and third date, but still wanted to see other men on the side. There's Chrissy, the banker who loudly asked to be set up with men interested in bondage and domination (the cardigan-wearing group of moms planning their private-school kids' charity auction at the next café table turned to gape). There's Brett, the gay political consultant with the used-car-salesman smile and impressive speaking gig at the last DNC, who wants a revolving door of buff guys to help him blow off steam after a long day of campaigning. And then there's Margot, the socialite who only dates musicians, who bragged about her long-ago fling with Kanye West and dropped vague references to her friendship with Beyoncé. I set her up with Anna Wintour's favorite DJ, a hunky former model, but she rejected him when he revealed his favorite book is merely *The Da Vinci Code*. "I date *intellectuals*," she seethed.

And there's Wretched Gretchen, as I think of her these days, who wants an accomplished tennis player who spent significant time traveling abroad and happens to be blessed with Jon Hamm's fine bone structure and a whole pile of money; I gave her a private wealth manager who taught tennis lessons at a Swiss boarding school after college and lived in Buenos Aires for a year. She trilled his faults to me over the phone the morning after her date with a perverse note of pleasure in her voice: yes, he played tennis, but he hadn't played regularly since the '90s; yes, he had lived abroad and spoke three languages, but didn't seem passionate about traveling to *her* favorite countries.

She sent me an updated, annotated version of her checklist explaining how Mr. Hedge Fund failed to meet her specifications. And another annotated version when Date #2 failed (she's appalled by his table manners and posture), and another annotated version when Date #3 failed (she said the dark circles under his eyes were "distracting"), and another annotated version when Date #4 failed (she disliked his "aura of negativity"). Lately, I've been fielding daily phone calls from Wretched Gretchen, in addition to highly detailed emails that require thousand-word responses to adequately answer her list of questions. For fun, Caroline calculated my hourly wage when working with Gretchen, and found that I would have made eight times more money flipping burgers at McDonald's. Delightful.

Not all my clients are so memorable. Most of them are what Adam called "*Sex and the City* women." We all know the type: mid- to late thirties, brilliant, tons of friends, high-powered career, schedule packed with boozy brunches and Hamptons weekends and SoulCycle classes. Almost all are Jewish and had intended to get married and have kids five years ago. I scooped up a few particularly dashing specimens on JDate and rotated them through my *Sex and the City* women until I found a match that worked. I set these women up with Mitchell, the pediatrician who actually volunteered with the homeless on the weekends; Ari, the graphic designer with impeccable bone structure; Noah, the CFO with a disgustingly cute terrier, who'd be married by now if he were just two inches taller.

Adam would have fit the bill, but I didn't send him out with anyone anymore. I added a note to his profile in the Bliss database explaining that he was "seeing someone" and should not be contacted by any of the matchmakers.

So. Adam. Adam, Adam, Adam. Paris may be the city of love, but I swear there's nothing more magical than getting to know someone new under the glittering lights of New York City. The West Village was meant for long, winding walks hand in hand, lingering in front of lingerie stores, kissing along the waterfront. His rooftop in Chelsea was made for savoring wine under the stars. Central Park was crafted for lolling about in bathing suits in the grass on sun-drenched Saturdays, and the whole borough of Manhattan was designed expressly for popping into bagel shops to order everything-and-a-schmear piping hot out of the oven.

We spend a lot of time together blushing, insisting how lucky we are to have found each other. When we went uptown to Serendipity for frozen hot chocolate and had that particular discussion all over again, the girl at the next table actually rolled her eyes and coughed loudly in our direction. We switched to a more mundane conversation topic while playing footsie under the table. Infatuation like this happens once in a lifetime.

Here is how New York tests your love, or at least your lust: if you are willing to brave the smell of hot, rotting garbage wafting through Union Square on a ninety-degree summer day in order to cross town to have sex in a cramped apartment without central air-conditioning, you know it's real. You've made it. Congratulations, you may pass Go, collect $200, and head straight to Kleinfeld's to pick out your big white wedding dress. *Mazel.*

And that's how the rest of my summer goes—a frenzy of match-making by day, a whirlwind romance by night. By September, I no longer sleep in my own bed. Caroline doesn't mind; she's been seeing her Bumble match Owen at nearly the same pace. I stay at Adam's place almost every night. He offers me one of his white button-downs to sleep in, under the condition that I wear it without anything underneath, but I opt to sleep naked instead. Stiff white shirts, just like the Financial District, Midtown skyscrapers, and spreadsheets, still remind me of Jonathan in a painful way.

Jonathan tried to get back in touch with me. In the weeks after the wedding, we were tagged in a dozen photos together on Facebook, which made my stomach turn. Next, he tried calling me. I didn't pick up, so he texted repeatedly asking to get coffee and talk things over. I ignored those, too, and got a rush from how good it felt to blow him off. Was this how he felt every time he stayed late at the office when we had plans?

The more experience I rack up as a matchmaker, the worse I feel about men as a whole. I talk to dozens a week, and so many of them are just plain awful. The finance types refer to dating multiple women at once in terms of "diversifying their portfolios." But across every profession, they're all bad. They shoot off texts riddled with spelling errors, demand to be set up with the hottest physical specimens available no matter what kind of garbage *they* look like, and assume that no matter how often I mention my client, I'm really just out to score ass on Tinder for myself.

By contrast, Adam is a dream. He's easygoing, makes me laugh, and brims with stories of his adventurous twenties. He shows up to hang out with me when he says he will. He pays attention. Even if I have to trudge through the depressing singles scene all day at work, I get to leave it behind when I'm with him.

As my thoughts ping between Adam and Jonathan—as they do daily—Diego emails with news. He has an opening on staff for an entry-level writer to cover dating and relationships. Do I want to apply? I send him my résumé immediately. I'm shocked when he replies a few hours later and asks me to do an edit test—industry-speak for a packet of ideas and writing samples.

I slave over the edit test for four days, barely emerging to flick through Tinder during meals, and send it off to Diego before I can second-guess myself out of applying for the job.

– Chapter 20 –

The summer has been hectic, and I miss seeing Caroline as often as I'd expect to see a conjoined twin, the way we hung out in college. My occasional hours in the apartment rarely overlap with hers anymore, so today, the Sunday after Labor Day, she texted me to hang out with her during a shift at Flower Power. I'd been in a few times before, and it's always dead quiet, save for the occasional willowy woman toting a yoga mat and a bottle of kombucha who pokes her head in but doesn't buy a thing. Sure enough, the shop is empty when I arrive. Flower Power lies a few steps down from the quiet, tree-lined stretch of East Ninth Street. It's dimly lit inside, with wooden floors that creak and walls lined with jars of shredded this and flakes of that and powdered whatever to cure your aches and pains and appease the gods. It smells like the inside of Shailene Woodley's dreams.

Caroline is perched on a bar stool behind the counter, watching someone's Snap Story on her phone.

"Hi," she says, without looking up from the screen. "One second . . . ugh. Have you been following Kylie Jenner's Snapchat today?"

"No. Should I?"

"No, you wouldn't actually care. Take a seat, I want to hear about your week. It's been, like, a week, right? Crazy. I never see you anymore."

I slip behind the counter and take the bar stool next to hers. She fills me in on the latest. Apparently, a mildly successful television writer followed her on Twitter, which her mother believes is a sure sign that a network is about to pick up her pilot (um, sure). She likes Owen, but he hasn't offered to be exclusive yet, so she responded to all "wanna have sex?" messages from Tinder fuckboys with "No, I'm looking for a serious relationship." Two of them wrote back variations of "Oh, cool, good luck with that." Two didn't respond, another three pressed for sex, and one asked for nudes. But at least she was entertained. Also, depressed. The highlight of her week was when the Duane Reade checkout guy forgot to charge her for a pint of Ben & Jerry's on Tuesday.

"So, anyway. That's that. What have you been up to?"

"I met some of Adam's friends last night. One of them, Ryan, invited us over for dinner."

"Like, at his apartment?"

"Yeah, for a dinner party."

"Like, he had a dining room table?"

"Yeah. And matching chairs."

Caroline bites off the corner of her nail and thinks this over. We get by with a portable card table and two folding chairs.

"Wow." She sounds bored.

I know she's tired of talking about Adam, but I need to gush about him to someone—it's not like I can gush to the matchmakers or any of my sad, single clients.

"So, anyway, Ryan works in consulting and has a really nice one-bedroom in the East Village with his girlfriend. They invited over a few couples, and—"

Caroline sputters to keep from choking on the herbal tea she's drinking.

"Couples? You're a couple now?"

"Well, I mean, not technically. But I feel like we will be soon."

She doesn't smile. "Sasha, it's been, like, what, three weeks since you broke up with Jonathan?"

I cross my arms defensively over my chest. "Almost six."

I've actually counted.

She looks like she's about to fire back, but a customer wearing faded overalls pushes the door open. Caroline gives me a withering look, then turns to greet her customer in a sugary-sweet voice.

"Hi, welcome to Flower Power. Are you looking for anything in particular today?"

The customer shakes her head and wanders over to examine a wall of glass canisters holding dozens of varieties of herbs: agrimony, alfalfa, ashwagandha root—and that's just half of the *A*s.

"All right. Let me know if you need anything."

Caroline swivels back to face me. "Girl, I'm just worried about you," she whispers. "You've hardly had time to get over Jonathan."

"I'm fine," I whisper back.

"You're not. You must be miserable."

"Caroline, I said I'm fine. I'm really happy with Adam." I bite down hard on the inside of my lip to keep from snapping at her.

"You're not. Relationships take time to get over."

"Oh, right, I forgot. You've had so many long, fulfilling relationships, you would know, wouldn't you?"

She recoils. It feels like I've slapped her, and I want to apologize, but she also just *doesn't get it.* The most significant relationship she's ever had was with a guitarist in an NYU band during sophomore year who never wrote any songs about her and ghosted after six months of sleeping together. She still talks about him sometimes—wistfully, even—but claims to now think his music is "kinda overrated."

"Look, Caroline, I'm sorry. I shouldn't have said that."

"No, you shouldn't have," she snaps. "But you did."

The customer approaches the counter with a small dark vial with a sticker that reads JOY IN A BOTTLE!

"I was just curious if you could tell me how this works. The ingredients are just water and alcohol."

Caroline takes the bottle from her and examines the fine print on the back.

"Well, yes. But it looks like there's also trace amounts of St. John's Wort and lemon balm, which are both mood lifters."

The customer looks skeptical.

"It's very soothing," Caroline adds, handing the bottle back to her, barely concealing the annoyance in her voice.

"Hmm." The woman runs a finger over the price sticker: $17.95. "Thank you," she says, turning on one Birkenstock and heading out the door.

There's an awkward silence in the shop.

"I never tell you what to do with your relationships," I say quietly, staring straight ahead so I don't have to look her in the eye. "So don't assume that you know what's best for mine."

She gapes.

"Are you kidding me? You're a *matchmaker.* You make a living telling other people what to do with their relationships, which is hilarious, because yours are a mess."

I roll my eyes. The thing is, she's right.

"I know, I know. But my relationship with Adam isn't a mess."

"You dumped Jonathan and rebounded with an off-limits guy

who's eleven years older than you are that very same day. Come on, that doesn't sound great."

Again, true. I know that I've only been with Adam for a few weeks, but it feels like so much longer than that—so much more important than that.

"But I really like him."

"I'm sure you do." She sighs. "And I liked meeting him, too. But it just doesn't seem healthy to jump into a new relationship right away, especially when things ended so disastrously with Jonathan. You were a wreck."

Now would not be the right time to tell Caroline that I still Insta-stalk Cassidy Greer. There's definitely a male hand lingering in the corner of the photo she posted last Thursday—it's holding a fucking homemade organic biscotti—which sent her followers into a frenzy of rumors. Is she dating someone? Who is it? Or is that maybe just her brother? Does she even have a brother? No, she's definitely seeing someone. Ugh. I can't tell if it's Jonathan's hand. I think it is. I bet it is. I hate her.

"Look, I'm not trying to pick a fight," she continues. "I'm just concerned about you. I think you're clinging to Adam to avoid being single."

"Mm. Thanks." I pause. "I have to go. Mindy asked me to go shopping with her on her lunch break. She has another date coming up this weekend and needs something to wear. Hope the rest of your shift is okay." I gather my purse and my phone and get up to leave.

"Love you!" Caroline calls as the door swings shut behind me.

I hate fighting with Caroline. I care about her more than anyone, and I know she feels the same way about me. But all those years of living together and sharing everything means we know exactly how to hurt each other. Friendship doesn't cover what we have—we're more like sisters, or at least I think this is what it must feel like to have a sister. I can see whatever we have stretching out forever. And that stability, that security, makes it easier to toss cruel comments back and forth. Forgiveness is a given.

I wind through the bar- and boutique-lined streets of the East Village to Union Square to catch the uptown 4 train to Blooming-dale's, where I'm planning on meeting Mindy at 1 p.m. The subway pulls into the station just as I reach the platform. I hop on and squeeze into a seat next to two people wearing bright sneakers and backpacks examining a subway map. Tourists.

Inside Bloomingdale's, I see I have texts waiting for me. The first is from Mindy.

"Running two mins late!!" she writes. "So sorry, see you soon."

The next is from Mary-Kate. I've barely heard from her since the wedding—partly because she and Toby spent two weeks in Tulum on their honeymoon, and partly because I don't know where our friendship stands now that Jonathan and I are no longer together.

"Babes—I need help narrowing down jewelry choices for an accessories story we're doing in the magazine. I love them all and can't pick just one haha. Pick your favorite . . . thx!"

She sent the text and an accompanying photo to her group thread of bridesmaids. I guess this means our friendship can still stand, if I'd like it to.

The other bridesmaids have all chimed in already. I tap open the photo. Six rings rest on a plush black background—a round diamond set in rose gold, an oblong sapphire set in platinum, a pear-shaped diamond with a glitzy halo. Most of them are too ornate for my tastes, but the simplest piece catches my eye. It's an emerald-cut stone set in yellow gold.

"The yellow gold one's gorgeous," I write back.

"Classic. Chic. Tiffany's. Great choice," Mary-Kate shoots back, adding a fanfare of diamond emojis.

It's a weird note for Mary-Kate to resume our friendship on, but that's how Mary-Kate operates. She doesn't like to dig into uncomfortable emotions. The more she can avoid experiencing actual feelings, the better; she and Jonathan have that in common.

"Hi, dollface!"

Mindy's voice rings out across the store. She hurries toward me, clad in a flamingo pink dress and metallic silver pumps.

"Again, so sorry to keep you waiting." She kisses me once on each cheek. "Work is insane right now. And I can feel myself getting sick, too, which absolutely cannot happen. I refuse to be sick right now. So, let's shop! I want to wear a new dress for my date, and I only have an hour before my next meeting."

I follow her as she flies expertly through the women's floor, picking up a purple dress with a full skirt, a little blue off-the-shoulder number, and a heap of black dresses. She never pauses to look at the price tags. She foists the dresses on a twenty-something saleswoman, who hauls them to a fitting room. I linger behind Mindy, feeling the soft cashmeres and slick leathers, trying to keep up the conversation like I'm a girlfriend and not hired help. But the conversation is one-sided—she gabs fluidly about Rosh Hashanah services, her friend who is inexplicably moving out of a rent-controlled Upper East Side apartment, the açai juice cleanse she wants to try, and so on. We dissect her previous dates with Gordon, wringing as much meaning as we can out of the kind way he treated their waiter and the length of his good night kiss outside her apartment.

Our conversation never veers toward my own life. She knows the basics, like where I'm from and where I went to college, but I don't offer anything more. It's cleaner this way. I lean against the door opposite her fitting room and watch as she twirls out in each dress.

"I'm obsessed with this one," she announces, trotting out the third black dress. It has a slit that reveals enough leg to make me worry about a wardrobe malfunction. "But I wonder if it might be too much."

"A little much, yeah," I concede. "It's just dinner."

"Well, why not make an entrance?"

She walks to the three-way mirror at the end of the row of fitting rooms and steps up onto the pedestal, twisting to see the back of the dress. Then, she gives me a panicked look and rubs a hand over her stomach.

"Oh, god. I really don't feel well. I need to—"

She covers her mouth and sprints down the hall to a small black trash can. She picks it up, tosses off the lid, and vomits inside. The fitting-room attendant leaps back. I feel like I'm obligated to help, but the prospect of running toward a bucket of vomit is just . . . ew.

"I'm so sorry," Mindy says to the attendant, panicked, picking up the lid of the trash can and setting it back down on the carpet, covered. She wipes her mouth with the back of her hand. "I think I'm coming down with something."

I approach her timidly and rub her back in small circles. Her face is drained of color.

"I'm so embarrassed," she says quietly. "Let's go."

She scurries back to get changed. The fitting-room attendant gives us the fakest smile I've ever seen and a faux-cheery "Hope you feel better!" on our way out.

"I'm so sorry," she says as we exit onto Fifty-Ninth Street. She disappears around the corner, and I take the subway downtown to my place for an afternoon of phone calls and Tindering.

I'm so lost in my own world—headphones in, music on full blast, sunglasses on—that the figure in a sharp-shouldered navy blue suit leaning against my front door hardly registers. I'm about to breeze past him when he snaps into action, shoving his BlackBerry back into his pocket and taking two quick steps toward me.

"Hi," Jonathan says, a look of bemused confidence spreading across his face.

I hate the effect he still has on me. My stomach drops, the exposed skin on my shoulders tingles. This is a primal response, fight or flight, and I'm supposed to be running away. But my feet feel glued to the sidewalk. If I ignore him and head inside now, I'll never find out what he wants—and I can't help but be curious. I take a step backward, crossing my arms tightly over my chest.

"Hi," I respond.

"I know you're probably wondering what I'm doing here." He's eerily calm.

"Considering you normally don't leave Goldman Sachs's bat cave during daylight hours? Yes."

He takes a deep breath, and there's something about the measured quality of his voice that makes me think he's practiced exactly what he's going to say.

"I haven't been able to stop thinking about how we left things between us, and I want to tell you again how sorry I am. I really ruined everything. I ended it with Cassidy and I deleted my Tinder. I'm not going to mess around anymore, I promise. That was the worst mistake of my life."

I squeak out something like "Oh."

He takes this as an encouraging sign. His eyes blaze blue.

"I shouldn't have ever taken you for granted. I know that there's no excuse for what I did, but I want to make it up to you, if you'll let me. I want to spend the rest of my life making it up to you, because you're worth it. I don't know a single other person like you, Sasha. You make me see the world differently, and you laugh at my nerdy jokes, and you support me, no matter what."

I start to understand what's about to happen, but I don't know how to process it. This is the grand romantic gesture I'm supposed to want, but I'm not sure I want it anymore. Behind Jonathan, a shirtless homeless man with a full beard pushes a grocery cart full of trash. I should be paying attention to the sincerity in Jonathan's eyes and the vulnerable tinge to his voice, but I can't. I feel paralyzed. It's like my entire future—and Jonathan's future, and maybe even Adam's future—is wrapped up in what's about to happen, and I don't feel confident enough to give Jonathan an answer right now. I don't know what I want; I only know that I'll have to decide fast.

"I know this is crazy, but I couldn't let another day go by without doing this. I have to put this out there, even if you hate me, even if you say no."

He drops to one knee and pulls a small black velvet box out of his pocket. I'm both flooded with panic and entirely numb; I can see my hands trembling, but I can't feel my fingers. He flicks it open to reveal a ring that glints brightly in the sun—the diamond I had selected from Mary-Kate's text today rests two feet in front of me, nestled in velvet, clasped in Jonathan's hands.

"Sasha Goldberg, will you marry me?"

— Chapter 21 —

I crash through the front door of my apartment. My knees shake. Orlando, alarmed by the noise, leaps up from his reclining position on the couch and scurries away. I can hear the rush of the shower at the end of the hall.

"Caroline? Caroline?" I drop my purse on the floor and fly toward the bathroom. I pound on the door with the side of my fist. "Caroline? I really need to talk to you."

Damn it, she doesn't care if I see her naked. I wrench open the door. She yelps.

"Oh my god, Sasha, is that you?" She whips her head around the shower curtain. Thick trails of eyeliner and mascara have pooled in smudgy streaks below her eyes, and she has shampoo suds in her hair.

I don't mean to break down, but I do. I try to steady my trembling hands long enough to open the black velvet ring box. She gasps. I'm heaving to catch my breath.

"Jonathan. Two minutes ago. He proposed." My voice is getting higher and more hysterical by the second.

"Oh my god, Sasha. What did you say?"

"I didn't know what to say! I couldn't say yes, but I didn't want to say no, either."

I snap the box shut. I don't even want to look at it.

"You—what?!"

"I don't know, okay?" The acoustics of the bathroom's cramped tiled walls make my wail sound so mournful, or maybe I really am that sad. "I didn't know what to tell him."

She tips her head back into the stream of water to wash the shampoo out of her hair.

"Give me two secs. I'll be right out, I promise."

I'm only slightly indignant that she doesn't hop out of the shower immediately. I try to sit on the couch in the living room, but sitting requires more stillness than I'm capable of at the moment. Orlando saunters in to sniff at my feet. When I scoop him up, he sits in my arms for a minute, but then spots a fly on the wall and wriggles away to chase it. It's stupid to feel rejected by a cat. I pace around the living room and think this through, trying to make sense of this ugly mess.

Jonathan's proposal is crazy. We're not together. I don't want to be the kind of girl who tolerates cheating, and taking him back sends the message that I can be walked all over. What would happen if I said yes? Would I come home one day ten years from now to find Jonathan in bed with another girl? Only then, it could be worse. We'd be living together. Married. With kids. I couldn't be like Mrs. Colton. And besides, I'm with Adam now. It's only been a few weeks, but it feels different—in a good way. Jonathan made me feel like a nuisance, like I had to beg for scraps of his time and attention, but Adam makes me feel special, desired, important—a treat to be savored. I don't have to mask who I am, messy and modest beginnings and all. That matters. I can see this relationship with Adam—and it definitely will be an official relationship soon, won't it?—going somewhere.

But it would be wrong to cast aside more than two years of history with Jonathan because of a few weeks of fun with Adam. Falling in love with Jonathan was the most satisfying experience of my life. He messed up, but he's trying to make things right. And even while I'm falling for Adam, I miss the familiarity I had with Jonathan: the way I knew which colleague emailed him based on the volume of his groan; the way I could predict when he'd fall asleep watching a movie; the way I could determine what he'd order on the menu at any given restaurant with perfect accuracy. I suppose I could have that with Adam one day. But it wouldn't be the same. He wouldn't be Jonathan.

When I call my mom, I feel like a little kid reaching for her security blanket. She's not a fan of Jonathan and she's always advocated for me to enjoy being young and single, so I don't expect her to have a real discussion of the pros and cons with me. I only want her to tell me it'll all work out in the end, no matter what I choose. I want her to lie to me. The phone rings and rings, but ultimately sends me to voicemail. The message tone dings and I panic.

"Mom, Jonathan proposed, call me back," I blurt out. Then I hang up.

I hear the shower turn off, and a minute later, the click of the bathroom door. Caroline's damp feet slap against the wooden floor as she scrambles down the hall. She's wrapped in a purple towel and hasn't yet bothered to scrub the rivers of eyeliner off her cheeks.

"So, I've been thinking, and I realized you can't tell me this story without a drink," she announces, reaching on tiptoe for the bottle of vodka on the highest shelf of our liquor cabinet. She hands it to me without a glass or chaser.

We sit on the couch and I twist open the bottle, taking one quick gulp before explaining what happened.

"He was waiting for me outside our building and apologized for making me feel neglected, for cheating. Then he got down on one knee and pulled out the ring and asked me to marry him."

"Holy shit." Caroline grabs the bottle from my hand and takes a swig.

"I was so stunned, I didn't know what to say. He couldn't have been down there for more than, I don't know, ten seconds? It felt like forever. I told him to get up."

"So you said no?"

I take another gulp and shake my head. "No. I told him I needed time to think over what he said."

"But you kept the ring." Caroline reaches over to grab the box and flips the top open. "*Fuck*, this is gorgeous."

I can't deny that. Engagements are starting to pop up on my newsfeed (already, holy shit). I don't really know how much engagement rings typically cost, but something this special must not have been cheap.

"I didn't want to keep it. I tried to give it back to him, but he literally refused to take it. He shoved his hands in his pockets."

"Whoa."

"My hands were shaking so hard that I almost dropped it."

"Put it on, let me see," she says, handing the box back to me.

"Oh, no. I can't. I didn't say yes."

"So?"

"Wearing the ring would make it feel too real."

"Come on. You're not even curious what it looks like on?"

She snatches the box back and pinches the ring out of its velvet case. When she jams it onto my limp finger, a chill rushes down my spine.

Last year, I found Jonathan's class ring on the bookshelf in his bedroom. It was a dark, burnished gold covered in black inscriptions. I slipped it onto my thumb, the only finger big enough to keep it from sliding off. He never expressly gave me permission to take it, but I loved wearing it; I relished how heavy it felt on my hand. I liked catching glimpses of it bobbing up and down over my keyboard when I typed notes in class. I felt smug when girls did double takes and asked about it.

"Oh, it's just my boyfriend's class ring," I'd say, trying to sound a lot more casual about it than I felt.

Wearing his ring made me feel so fabulously committed and *adult*. Three weeks after I took it, I blacked out at a party, lost it, and thought it was gone forever. He was probably furious, though he didn't say so. It turned up under my bed two days later, and I gave it back immediately. Neither of us ever brought it up again. Wearing his jewelry symbolized too much.

But now, I have this diamond. The ring is a hair too small, requiring an extra twist and tug to remove it. I tuck it in the box.

"What are you going to do?" Caroline asks.

I let it all tumble out: how I can't let myself go back to Jonathan, even though I miss what we had together, and how much I like Adam. It's hard to process everything. I'd been swimming along, not knowing when I woke up this morning what today would bring.

Caroline's lips are pressed together in a thin line.

"Do you love Jonathan?"

It's the same question Mrs. Colton asked me at the wedding. Time hasn't made it any easier to answer.

"I did. I really did. Maybe I do. I don't know, I . . ."

Judgment creeps into Caroline's face. When Jonathan neglected me, she always told me I deserved better. The worst of it came last year when Jonathan and I went through a rough patch. He had blown me off yet again, and Caroline called him a "seventy-percent-off boyfriend." Like I scooped him up from the dregs of the sale rack because no one else wanted him at full price. I've never been able to forget that.

I struggle to explain it to her.

"I love him in the way you're always going to care about the first person you fall for."

She considers this. "But you don't love him now, do you?"

"I'm . . ." Ugh. Why is this so hard? "I'm angry at him."

"As you should be."

"Oh, trust me, I know he's a dick. He messed up. But so what? He's human. He wouldn't propose if he didn't want to spend the rest of his life with me."

Caroline stares. "Are you apologizing for him?"

I take another swig from the bottle instead of answering. It's easier.

"Sasha, he went behind your back and fucked another girl. When you invited him to your parents' place for the weekend, he lied, avoided it, and fucked her again. How could you even consider marrying a guy like that? You did the right thing by dumping him. I was so proud of you."

Oh, god. That day was so brutal. Sometimes, when I'm trying to fall asleep, I see the precise number of degrees his face fell when he realized I was leaving him. The way the fire dwindled out of his eyes. The heavy set of his jaw. The gourmet nuts scattering everywhere. Even today, downstairs, when I didn't immediately accept his proposal, his face fell like that. Caroline is still ranting about every minor injustice he's ever committed, ticking them off on her bitten-down fingernails as she goes.

"Remember that time he swore he'd help you move, but then backed out at the last minute to work? It was a Sunday! Remember that time he fell asleep and forgot to come to our housewarming party? Remember that time he begged you to go all the way downtown to his apartment in the middle of the night because he was horny, even though you had an eight a.m. final the next day?"

"Caroline! Enough."

I can tell she has another dozen infractions at the ready, but she stops, and settles back onto the couch, arms crossed.

"He's not perfect, okay? I get it. I'm just saying . . . I can't make a decision here without factoring in all those years that he was really, really great to me."

"Two. You spent two years with him. That doesn't mean you owe him the rest of your life."

I hastily wipe away a plump tear before it rolls down my cheek.

"You're my best friend, and what I need from you right now is support. Not judgment. I know you have your issues with Jonathan, and that's fine, but that's not what I need to hear today. I need someone who's on my side."

She folds me into a long, tight hug.

"I'm always on your side," she murmurs.

My phone screen lights up with a text from Mary-Kate.

"Soooo . . . sis?!?! WE'RE GONNA BE SISTERS!!!!"

I read it aloud. Caroline groans.

"Forget about her. Responding will just stress you out."

There's another notification for a text I missed an hour ago from Adam.

"Hey! Are we still on for tonight?"

We had made tentative plans to get dinner, but the prospect of sitting across the table from him tonight makes me sweat.

"Could I actually take a rain check? Don't hate me, I'm just not feeling well and should probably stay in tonight."

The three gray chat bubbles pop up right away.

"Do you want me to come over? I could bring you chicken soup if you're sick."

"Thanks, but Caroline's taking good care of me. Have a good night!"

"You sure?" he replies.

"I'm good, but thank you so much for offering." I don't have the mental energy to deal with him right now. One man at a time.

"We could play doctor. ;)"

"Ha. But I'm actually sick. Another time."

It comes down to this: I loved Jonathan. And I might love Adam one day. Right now, I feel lost. But now is when I need to make the biggest decision of my life.

"I just need time to think," I tell Caroline. "I hate men. Can we just forget about this for now and drink a lot and snuggle with Orlando and pretend my life isn't a soap opera?"

"Of course."

While researching date spots recently, I stumbled across Professor Thom's, a Boston-themed sports bar on Second Avenue that gives any couple on a Tinder date two-for-one drinks. Caroline and I both set our Tinders to match exclusively with girls in a one-mile radius. We play glam-sad Lana Del Rey music videos too loudly and drink vodka tonics out of coffee mugs as we swipe until we find each other. It takes nearly an hour, but it works. I squeal when I find Caroline and swipe right triumphantly. She swipes back and starts up a fake conversation, scripting it so we can make the bartender believe we are perfect strangers. ("Hey, I'm Caroline. How's it going?") Five minutes later, we're out the door. Whatever we were fighting about this morning at Flower Power seems an eternity away.

This is the difference between a best friend and a boyfriend: a boyfriend isn't legally family until he puts a ring on it; a best friend won't ever be legally attached, but she's been family since day one.

When Caroline and I float into the bar, it's not even six. The pub is empty, save for two gray-haired guys in the back. Televisions tuned to the Yankees–Red Sox game line one wall, and the other is decorated with sports jerseys. We take clumsy seats at the bar.

"We're on a Tinder date," I announce unsteadily to the bartender, a slim, bearded guy in a Red Sox shirt. I shove my phone screen toward him so he can read the Tinder conversation. "See? Can we get free drinks?"

"We just met," Caroline says, dramatically draping her hand over mine on top of the bar.

He laughs. "Sure, whatever you want."

We probably didn't need to go to all the trouble of matching.

Caroline and I settle in and gossip about a couple we know that's moving to a studio in Bushwick together after just three months of dating. It sounds disastrous. I give it three more months before she's posting sad quotes on Instagram and he's writing Facebook statuses asking if anyone needs a roommate. The bartender comes by when our drinks are nearly empty to offer another round.

"The next one's on me," he says, "even though you're clearly not on a Tinder date."

"Excuse me, this is a very romantic first date and we are having a wonderful time," Caroline insists, grabbing my hand for emphasis.

"You two have straight girl written all over you. And you know each other too well for this to be a first date." He squirts tonic water into two glasses.

"Well, this might not be our *very* first date," Caroline concedes.

I lean forward onto the bar. "Fine. You're right. We're straight. That doesn't disqualify us from another round, does it?" I ask. "We really need it tonight."

"Oh, yeah?" He sets the glasses down in front of us and grins. "What's the occasion?"

Caroline and I exchange glances.

"My ex-boyfriend proposed to me today."

"She didn't say yes," Caroline adds quickly.

"But I didn't say no, either."

The bartender raises his eyebrows and whistles. Bartenders, I imagine, must hear a lot of shit at work. Just like matchmakers do.

"That calls for some shots. Hold on, I have just the thing for you."

The rest of the night goes by in a giddy blur. Later, I will vaguely remember stumbling out of the bar, needing to pee so badly, and trying to hit up the legendary French fry joint Pommes Frites for drunchies before remembering it burned down in a gas explosion when we were in college. I think we Ubered the nine blocks home, but I can't really be sure.

Here's what I am sure of. When I wake up the next day at noon, I sit up in bed and feel like someone kicked me in the head. I scroll through eight frantic texts and two voicemails from Mom, all variations on "What??? Call me immediately!!!" I'm too worn out to respond with anything other than a short text: "Don't worry, I didn't say yes yet. I'll call you soon."

In the shower, when I should be scrubbing the smell of vodka off my skin, I spend fifteen minutes under the stream of hot water replaying Jonathan getting down on one knee. I don't feel any closer to an answer than I did yesterday; my mind is even more muddled than before. I get dressed and push the ring onto my finger just to see how it feels. My fingers are swollen from the hot shower, and the gold band scrapes painfully past my knuckle on the way down.

– Chapter 22 –

As I scarf down my usual order at David's Bagels, my hangover notches down from an eight to a six. I walk to Bliss for the weekly check-in. I'm finally catching up to the other matchmakers in competence. At last week's meeting, I reeled off potential matches' names and recalled which downtown hotel bars took reservations in advance and which were walk-ins only without thinking. Georgie expressed an interest in setting up her client with a guy I screened from JDate last month, and I could recite his list of deal-breakers with perfect clarity: no workaholics, no one who wants children within the next five years, and no one who has a problem with polyamory (good luck, Georgie).

I enter the brownstone's dining room and take a seat at the middle of the table. The grandeur of Bliss's headquarters hasn't quite worn off on me yet; I try not to gawk too much at the intricate crown moldings and the tall glass vase with white orchids in the middle of the table. We go around the room, updating one another on our progress for the week. When it's my turn, I mention Mindy's upcoming date and quote aloud from Wretched Gretchen's latest email. This week, she sent me a note titled "Helpful suggestions!" with a list of fourteen questions I should be asking men to ascertain the degree to which they are emotionally over their exes.

Penelope rolls her eyes.

Allison shakes her head. "I can't," she says. "I literally can't with her."

I bury my face in my hands, groan, and start explaining where I'm at finding Wretched Gretchen's ultimate dreamboat, but Georgie flags me down.

"Oh my god. Sasha. Stop."

"What?"

Oh, no. I drop my hands into my lap.

"Do you have news for us?"

Fuuuuck. I had forgotten to take the ring off before leaving the apartment. I decide to play dumb.

"Yeah, Wretched Gretchen has gone completely insane."

"No, come on, you know what I mean." Her voice is soupy, gossipy, the sonic embodiment of the flirty banter she uses to lure potential matches on Tinder. "What are you wearing on your *finger*?"

I don't want to spill more of my personal life than I already have to my coworkers, but I also can't think of a convincing way to explain why I'm wearing the bling.

"Um, it's a family heirloom? It was my grandma's?"

Georgie, who had been slouched down in a chair next to Penelope, springs up from her chair and races over to me. For someone so tiny, she moves frighteningly fast. She grabs my hand out of my lap and examines the ring.

"*Girl.* That's some grandma. Didn't you break up with your boyfriend a couple of weeks ago?"

The room goes quiet. No one's texting or typing anymore—all eyes are, horrifyingly enough, on me.

"Well . . ."

She doesn't give me time to answer. "Is this from him?"

"Um."

Allison squeals first. "Oh my god. It totally is!"

Georgie looks at me incredulously. "Is it?"

Even Penelope drops her usual businesslike façade and leans forward on her elbows, eyes glowing. "Is it?"

I feel like I'm facing a firing squad. Lying seems too complicated, so I pinch my eyes shut and go with the truth.

"I broke up with my boyfriend last month after Georgie found him on Tinder, but he apologized and wants to get back together. For good."

A silence falls over the room for a moment, then it explodes into a cacophony of cheers and whoops. A few of the girls scramble over to my seat to see the ring up close. It's exciting, but terrifying. With every "Oh my god" and "Congrats!" this whole mess feels more real. The girls ask if we've set a wedding date and accuse me of hiding my engagement on Instagram, and I feel sick. The flurry of attention should be exhilarating, but it feels all wrong.

"I didn't say yes," I admit, swallowing. "Things are complicated between us right now."

The noise dies down. Georgie gives me a knowing nod.

"Say yes for the rock alone," Zoe encourages.

"Seriously," another matchmaker chimes in.

"I think it's super romantic," Allison says. "I wish my ex would come back like that."

Penelope looks amused. "Ladies, let's get back to work. We have so much to get through today."

I zone out for the rest of the meeting. If I really were engaged, that would happen over and over again, on Facebook and with my high school friends and at family reunions. I'd be treated like the girl who has it all: the hot, successful fiancé, the sparkling ring, the fabulous job, the perfect life—when that's only what it would look like on the surface. The fear that Jonathan and I might not last would lurk underneath. I understand now how Gretchen must have felt when she got engaged—and I *never* expected to find any common ground with her.

When the meeting wraps, I try to hustle out the door, but Georgie catches up with me on the stoop.

"Hey, wait!" she calls.

I spin around.

Her usual obnoxious confidence is gone, and I notice for the first time how childlike her petite frame really is. She looks embarrassed to have chased me out here.

"I just . . . You're not really engaged to him, are you?"

"Not really. Maybe? I'm still figuring it out." I know I sound stupid, but what else can I say?

A group of other matchmakers stream out the door past us, straining to hear our conversation. Georgie, god bless her, waits till they're out of earshot before speaking.

"I know it's not my place, but you can't marry him, Sasha."

"You're right, it's not your place at all," I retort, crossing my arms over my chest.

It's one thing for Caroline to weigh in on my potential engagement, but Georgie—the only girl on the planet besides Chrissy Teigen who can actually pull off sex hair—doesn't know the first thing about my life.

She backs away, palms up. "Look, I'm sure I don't know the full story. But I remember when we found him on Tinder. We're matchmakers, Sasha. We know how to read men's intentions."

I snort. "Yeah, right."

"Tinder is full of guys like Jonathan. They're all slimeballs. I've been in your shoes, remember? I know what it's like to think you can't do any better than the guy right in front of you, even if he sucks."

She gives me a sad smile. I lean back against the wrought-iron railing of the stoop.

"He doesn't *suck*. He just made a mistake."

"Look, I've never met the guy, but it sounds like he sucks. If you set, say, Mindy up with a guy, they hit it off, started dating, and then a couple of weeks later you found him on Tinder, wouldn't you warn her?"

"It's not the same." Georgie is pissing me off.

"Why not?"

"Because I love him, all right?"

The words burst out and hang there. It's the first time I've let myself acknowledge that I love him since we broke up. I hide my hands in my pockets.

"Just because you love him doesn't mean you shouldn't leave him."

She says this like her twenty-six to my twenty-two makes her some fountain of wisdom. Across the street, a twenty-something guy in a dark suit hustles down the stairs of a brownstone and into a waiting Uber. He checks his phone as he ducks into the car. Another Jonathan. The city is full of them.

"I have to go," I say, stepping around her tiny frame. "I have work to do."

"I know you're going to make the right decision!" she calls.

Yeah, yeah. Like that's so easy.

To get my mind off my train wreck of a life, I head to The Bean, a coffee shop up the street, to churn out matches. At The Bean, the baristas all have bad chest tattoos, the customers own tiny adorable dogs they tie to their tables, and the cold brew is double the price it should be. I order a coffee and sit down with my laptop to tackle my inboxes.

I message back some dudes on Tinder, Bumble, and FetLife.com for Chrissy, the BDSM-loving banker. Her first two dates were less than ideal: she thought one guy was too short and slight for her plus-sized frame, and the next was a guy she called "the most arrogant idiot she's ever had the misfortune of meeting." Her third match needs to be totally baller.

"It sounds like you've been to some incredible places," I type back to the advertising guy who bragged about his vacations to Thailand, Iceland, and Morocco in his profile. I've been chasing him for three days now, but I'm not totally sure why. It's not like there's anything particularly special about him, other than the fact that he's single and is responding to my messages at a timely clip. Every online dater on the fucking planet claims they *love to travel*.

"Where do you want to go next?" I ask him.

"Age is just a number. I don't think you're too old for me at all," I lie to the forty-seven-year-old I'm wooing. I haven't told him I'm chatting him up on Chrissy's behalf yet, since I get the vibe he might not be into a plus-sized girl. (He keeps stressing he likes "fit" girls, as if there is no way any girl above a size twelve has ever entered a gym.) I note that he has a baseball cap jammed firmly on his head in every photo. "Bald?" I jot into my spreadsheet where I track potential matches.

I coax a Bumble guy into agreeing to a phone call so I can learn more about him. His name is Vince, he's a forty-two-year-old chemist, and he's not scared off by the concept of a blind date. I need to suss out if he's potentially interested in tying up Chrissy or throwing her around. There are zero non-awkward ways to do this, so I futz around with softball questions about what kind of personalities he's attracted to and what he does on the weekends before asking about his preferences in the bedroom in a straight monotone. He fumbles.

"Excuse me?"

"Like, are you into rough sex, or are you more gentle, or do you have any particular fetishes?"

I flush pink, but pretend this is a very normal question to ask a stranger just ten minutes after first speaking on the phone. If I act casual, so will he. The guy at the table next to me stops typing on his laptop and cocks his head an extra five degrees toward me to listen. Bro, chill.

"Oh, uh, just, um, normal stuff, I guess," Vince says.

"Normal stuff. I see." I don't bother hiding the disappointment in my voice. I stop typing notes on my laptop.

"I mean, most of the time," he confesses, his voice dropping low. "Give me one moment. Let me close the door to my office."

I get an earful of his interest in role-playing, taking "classy, intimate black-and-white portraits," and, yes, dominating women. I feel a lot like I imagine an OB-GYN might—I know way too much about the sex lives of people I'm not having sex with. In addition to passing Chrissy's requirements in the bedroom, he also seems tall and broad enough to make her feel dainty, and he appears to have hobbies other than bragging about his international vacations to single girls online. Phenomenal. When I've heard enough to check off my boxes, I tell him I'll be in touch soon.

Next, I dive into my email, fending off Wretched Gretchen with another thousand-word email, reassuring her that no, I'm definitely not using any online dating sites or apps to locate men for her (I definitely am), and yes, I've reviewed the most recent version of her checklist (I skimmed it; I want to kill her), and yes, I'm quite confident that the next match will be better (ugh), and that yes, I understand that if I can't deliver a fantastic match next time, she'll have to be transferred to a new matchmaker (please!). I should spend a good chunk of time tracking down a new guy for her this afternoon, but I've hit a wall. Sometimes, matchmakers need to help their clients figure out what they want. But that's clearly not the case here. I know what Wretched Gretchen wants—I just have no clue where to find a 5'10" half marathoner with zero baggage from past relationships and a passion for parasailing, or whatever she thinks she needs. I need to talk to Penelope about developing a new strategy for working with her, since clearly, what I'm doing isn't working.

Dwelling on Wretched Gretchen stresses me out, but the perfect antidote waits in my text messages. Eddie sends me a selfie of him and Diane. Their heads press together into the frame and they wear matching toothy grins. "We're calling each other boyfriend and girlfriend now. Thank you so much. Can you please cancel my Bliss membership?"

I'm still beaming from Eddie's good news—fine, and also mourning the lack of income—when I get an email from Diego, the *Esquire* editor. For a short message, it packs a dizzying punch.

"Sasha, I liked your edit test. When can you come in for an interview?"

I jam my clenched fist over my mouth to stifle a shriek.

"Did you do this?" I text Adam frantically, adding a screenshot of the email.

"Nope. That's all you," he writes back.

I've never been to Adam's office, but I wonder how close he and Diego sit. Close enough that they're laughing over my texts together?

"Seriously," I text.

"I'm serious," he responds.

If Adam didn't ask Diego to offer me an interview, that means I earned it on my own. I had pitched stories culled entirely from my real life, about online dating and cheating and age gaps in relationships. Miraculously, Diego had liked them. A chill runs down my spine. I write him back a ridiculously earnest and polite email, expressing gratitude that he had even considered my edit test and letting him know that my matchmaking schedule is flexible. I could be in his office at any time.

I'm not even sure that I want to leave Bliss. I haven't even been matchmaking for two full months; the high of holding people's love lives in my own two hands hasn't worn off yet. But the daily rigor of the job is sinking in. My thumbs ache from swiping; my feet are blistered from running between neighborhoods; there's a crick in my neck from spending so much time on the phone. I'm beginning to feel like a robot who sees people as strings of database numbers; I'm too emotionally exhausted from dealing with clients to give my fullest attention to Caroline; and I can feel myself hating men—truly despising them—with a vitriol I've never felt before. Given all that, I'm still barely making enough money to get by. It's not that I want to leave matchmaking, but I can't stay at Bliss forever and retain a grip on who I am.

Diego confirms an interview slot for tomorrow afternoon. I enter it in my calendar and try to relax, but I can't. The stupid diamond ring is staring me in the face, like it's taunting me to make a decision. I take the subway downtown to Tiffany on Wall

Street. Tiffany is a soaring granite building with a majestic, robin's-egg blue flag out front and a lanky doorman in a black suit with a matching blue satin tie. I look disgusting (unwashed hair, grubby jeans, flip-flops) but the doorman gives a gallant smile. I suppose he's seen tourists look worse. I have a hunch that this is where Jonathan bought the ring. Just being here makes my stomach churn.

I approach a salesman and ask whom I could speak to about diamonds. He directs me to the diamond department on the second floor. I wind through a group of preteens fawning over the Elsa Peretti Bat Mitzvah jewelry and take the elevator up one level. Upstairs, it's serene, empty save for one couple poring over a case of rings and two saleswomen. One, a fifty-something blond woman with a Farrah Fawcett cut and a name tag that reads DEB, greets me with a cheery hello.

"Is there anything I can help you with today?" she chirps.

"Actually, yes. I . . ."

Jesus, how do I even begin to explain this?

"I . . . was recently given a ring that I believe may have been purchased at your store."

I awkwardly splay out my fingers like engaged girls do to show off their rings, and Deb takes my hand. She peers at the ring and coos.

"Ooh, yes, beautiful. I believe I sold that to a gentleman just yesterday. You're a lucky girl!"

I emit a sound that could possibly be considered a laugh. A display case of diamond rings rests between me and Deb; a dozen rings for a dozen happily-in-love couples who will probably get married with no drama, and maybe ten or fifteen years down the road, they'll fall out of love, have a nasty divorce, and take off the rings for good.

Deb has kind, dark eyes rimmed by fine lines. She wears a thick strand of pearls around her neck and looks like the mom who always had homemade sugar cookies lying around her kitchen. Meanwhile, my hair has frizzed in the humidity and I've been hovering on the edge of a panic attack for the past twenty-four hours.

"I don't know exactly why I'm here." I don't even feel like I'm inside my own body.

"Do you want to exchange your engagement ring? You know, some girls do that after the proposal. They go for a bigger diamond." She actually winks.

"You know, I'm not even really sure if I'm engaged," I mumble. "I didn't say yes. My ex-boyfriend proposed to me yesterday."

Deb's eyes go wide.

"We were together for more than two years, but when I found out he cheated, I dumped him," I explain. "And I've been seeing this new guy, who I'm really falling for, and I can't help but wonder if I'm missing the opportunity of a lifetime if I say no to my ex. He really could be the one, although I'm not even sure I believe in 'the one' as a concept at all, you know? Well, maybe you don't. You work here. I guess I'd hoped that you could give me some advice. Ha. I'm sure this all seems ridiculous to you."

I take a deep breath and slide my hand off the glass counter. I sound unhinged.

"Oh my goodness." Deb covers her mouth and shakes her head. "I don't know what to tell you, hon."

"So you were here when he bought this?" I ask, probing for any useful scrap of information that might help me make a decision.

"I was. Young guy, dark blond hair, in a suit—that's him?" Deb confirms.

"Yeah. Did he say anything about me?"

She tilts her head, like she's trying to recall. "I don't know if he said anything that stood out specifically. He seemed excited. Maybe a little nervous. I assumed it was typical pre-proposal jitters."

My hangover is returning with a vengeance. The couple at the other end of the counter is now trying on rings: he has a dark crew cut and glasses; she looks like an Anthropologie catalog model, with a wispy bob and floral A-line dress. I stare up at the ceiling and try to breathe, willing my heart rate to return to normal. Deb looks concerned.

"Do you ever get guys in here who need to return rings? I mean, if the girl says no."

"I suppose it could happen."

"But it doesn't. Not really, does it?"

"No," she concedes. "It doesn't."

I slump my elbows onto the counter and bury my face in my hands. If I give Jonathan the ring back, I make him the most pathetic man in the world. I don't want to do that to him. I try to explain this all to Deb, and she gives me a sad smile.

"You know, it's very kind of you to consider his feelings," she tells me. "Some girls might be tempted to exchange the ring for store credit and go on a wild shopping spree."

"I couldn't do that."

She raises an eyebrow. "He splurged. You could exchange this for several pretty pieces."

I examine the ring again. "How much is this?"

She pulls up the electronic receipt on the computer behind her and writes out the number on a small slip of paper. She slides it across the counter.

Instantly, I'm nauseous. A cold sweat breaks out along my spine. The ring costs what I spend on rent in a year—and I live in *Man-*

hattan. Everything spills out: I tell Deb about our perfect start in Paris; my job as a matchmaker; the horror of finding him on Tinder; that Instagram bitch Cassidy; my infatuation with Adam; how confident Jonathan looked outside my building yesterday. By the time I've finished, Deb is glassy-eyed, carefully dabbing at the corner of her eye with the back of one finger.

Nothing screams *train wreck* quite like making the Tiffany saleswoman cry.

I pinch the ring between my middle finger and thumb and slide it off my finger. It leaves two millimeter-wide indents on my skin.

"Do you have a box for this? I don't want to wear it home."

"You're giving it back to him?" she says, a note of alarm in her voice.

I sigh.

"I don't know. Maybe. Wearing it just makes me feel uncomfortable, so I'd rather put it away till I make a decision."

"I have a feeling that your story isn't over," Deb says, reaching across the counter to squeeze my hand. "You're both just so lovely."

I give her the ring. She nestles it inside a new black velvet box and drops it into that little blue bag that every girl in the world is supposed to want. I don't know at what point my life derailed into a rom-com (rom-com gone wrong?), but none of this feels right anymore. Three months ago, my life was simple. I wasn't a matchmaker. I wasn't having a covert affair. I wasn't wandering around Manhattan with ten thousand dollars' worth of bling from a guy who fucks other women. I miss goofing off late at night in pajamas with Caroline over cheap wine. Married women don't do that, do they?

Before I leave, Deb steps out from behind the display case to give me a hug.

"I know you're going to make the right decision," she says softly. "I just don't know what that is. Only you do."

If only I knew.

I take the elevator down to the first floor and slip out past the doorman, past the group of tourists in matching T-shirts holding selfie sticks. I dart between them to cross the street. For a moment, I'm tempted to drop by Jonathan's apartment, just to see if he's there. But I'm not ready to face him yet.

I call my mom, and this time she picks up.

"Mom? I need to come home."

Chapter 23

Even though it's rush hour and the train is crammed with commuters sweating through their dress shirts, I find the ride to New Jersey soothing. It's important to get out of Manhattan every once in a while to clear your head and remember that some exotic locales featuring strange concepts such as backyards exist. New Jersey also puts the entire width of the dirty Hudson River between me and Jonathan. The sight of Mom's silver Kia in the train station parking lot is almost enough to make me tear up. Sometimes, a girl just needs her mom.

When I climb into the car, Janet Jackson is warbling on the car radio. Coffee cups are stuffed into every cup holder. Mom leans across the middle console to hug me tight. I inhale her vanilla perfume. She smells like home.

"Explain," she orders, when she lets go of me. "Tell me everything."

"For starters, I'm not really engaged. I mean, he asked. But I haven't said yes yet."

Mom reverses out of the parking space, then turns carefully and shifts forward to drive. I tell her about my off-limits fling with Adam, about Jonathan's proposal—how I'm now dodging both of them. She interrupts with questions and gasps and clucking *tsk tsks*. I had told her that Jonathan cheated when it happened, but when I bring it up again, she wipes away a tear. She's stopped at a red light when I pull the blue Tiffany bag out of my purse and show her the ring. She looks at it with apathy. It dwarfs the diamond chip she wears on her hand.

"So, he's rich," she says, shrugging and handing it back to me. "Nothing we didn't already know."

Even though she's never been Jonathan's biggest fan, she listens carefully when I explain why I might say yes. I'm grateful that she's at least letting me talk about Jonathan like he's a real option. The decision might be clear-cut for her, but she lets me work through my own thoughts out loud.

We pull into the driveway. The headlights illuminate the little white house. I climb out of the car and start toward the four steps up to the front door, but Mom intercepts me with a hug. I've been bigger than she is for years now, but in her arms, I want to melt down to little-girl size again. She holds me close for a long time, stroking my hair. We walk into the kitchen together and she flicks on the lights. I peer cautiously into the living room, but it doesn't look like anyone is home.

"Steve's at poker night. It's just us," she says, as if sensing my discomfort. She points to the kitchen table. "Sit."

It's not that I don't want Steve to know. I just can't deal with explaining everything all over again. Mom takes a tub of caramel swirl ice cream out of the freezer, then grabs two bowls and spoons and comes to sit with me. She scoops out ice cream for both of us, giving me all the best caramel bits. I dig in immediately, savoring the cold, creamy texture and the luxury of food that I don't have to pay for.

"I'm just too young for all of this, Mom. I can't get married."

"I was married a year already at your age."

I hate when she pulls that card on me. I make a face. "Hardly by choice."

"It was a choice to find a better life for myself. For me, that was necessary. For you, it doesn't have to be."

"I know that."

She takes a long look at me, hand hovering halfway between her bowl and her mouth. "Do you?"

"What do you mean?"

She licks the ice cream off the spoon slowly, as if she's trying to work out the best possible way to phrase whatever's running through her head.

"You have the freedom to be with anyone you want, princess. Why be with someone who doesn't give you the attention you deserve? Who doesn't accept you for who you are?"

"I know that Jonathan loves me. He just made a mistake. And anyway, if I say no to Jonathan, there's no guarantee that anything will work out with Adam. What if he's no better in the long run?"

"You shouldn't worry about that. Have fun. Think of all the things you could do if you were single! All the things I wish I'd done . . ."

This is what it means to be a mail-order bride's daughter: all of Mom's dreams for herself rest heavily on my shoulders. She wants me to focus on a lucrative career so I can buy a comfortable home and travel the world. Marriage doesn't need to be a priority. When she read me fairy tales as a little girl, she always improvised the endings. Cinderella never ended up with the prince; Snow White awoke with a hug from a friend.

I agree with her in theory—I don't need a man. But I can't help if I *want* one. Or two.

"You should be single for a while. Have your fun."

"Mom, no one thinks being single is *fun*. That's the whole reason I have a job."

She shakes her head. "You don't know what you could be missing."

"Do you know how many of my clients would skin me alive in order to be engaged right now? They're so lonely, they'd do anything."

"Weren't you lonely when you were with Jonathan?"

She has a point. I push my ice cream away, slump my forehead down on the table, and close my eyes. Whenever I think about a future with Jonathan, I can't see him actually in it. All I see is me, alone in his apartment. Me, ordering takeout for one again. Me, alone holding a screaming kid with his bright blue eyes. It didn't used to be like that—not when we were first in love, spending that unusually icy spring bundled up in our school-issued apartments in Paris. But the loneliness is all I've been able to feel for a long time now.

"Marriage doesn't always last forever," Mom says. "But you shouldn't enter a marriage if you can already see its expiration date."

I look up and there are tears in her eyes. I always thought I understood what Mom went through when she met and married Dad. She took a gamble that she'd grow to love Dad so that she could escape a life of poverty in Russia. She left behind her family, her friends, her hometown . . . everything she knew. She learned English and moved halfway around the world for a better life. She wasn't like the women who hire Bliss matchmakers. For her, marriage had nothing to do with love and everything to do with opportunity.

I spent all these years trying to be nothing like Mom, but now I feel like I've backed myself into the same corner: pinning my hopes on a rich guy I can't reasonably rely on to make me happy.

I sleep in my childhood bedroom, dressed in pajamas from high school and slutty red underwear, which I had put on this morning in a misguided attempt to make myself feel better. I pass most of the night watching the glow-in-the-dark alarm clock on the nightstand flash times that get later and later. It's almost sunrise when I reach a decision. The finality of it prickles in my chest.

- *Chapter 24* -

If your boyfriend consistently neglects you for the sake of sucking his boss's cock or whatever investment bankers actually do all day, a good way to manipulate him into responding to your texts immediately is to leave him hanging for thirty-six hours after he proposes. So, when I text Jonathan that I'm ready to talk, my phone lights up with his reply within seconds.

"Fantastic. Tonight? I should be able to finish up here early," he writes.

I'm stretched out on my couch, scratching Orlando behind the ears. I wait a good three minutes before texting him back, savoring every second that Jonathan must be panicking. It feels nice to have the upper hand. No wonder the patriarchy is so reluctant to give it up.

"I'll meet you at your apartment at 7," I text.

I know that's too early for him. I don't care.

"Can it be 8?"

Then a second text pops up.

"No, you know what? This is important, I'll make it work. See you at 7. Love you."

I don't respond. He who texts last cares the most, and everyone knows that caring is the quickest way to lose power in a relationship.

Anyway, I'm busy. At 3 p.m., a security guard waves me through a turnstile in the cavernous lobby of *Esquire*'s building and directs me up an escalator to a set of elevators. Diego is waiting for me upstairs in the elevator bank, leaning against a gray wall and sternly typing on his phone. He straightens up when he sees me.

"You must be Sasha," he says, offering a firm handshake. "Diego. So great to finally put the face to the name."

"Thanks so much for having me."

He swipes a card to open the door and leads me past a set of desks into a glassed-in conference room with a jaw-dropping view of Central Park. He unbuttons his gray tweed sports coat as he sits at the head of the table and gestures for me to take the chair to his right. From my seat, I can see past Diego's shoulder into the office; Adam is craning his neck. He gives me a big, cheesy double thumbs-up, and I feel like my heart could explode. I pull a folder with three crisp copies of my résumé from my purse and slide one to Diego.

I prepped for the interview by reading everything Esquire.com has published on the subject of dating for the past year, drilling answers to potential interview questions, and grilling Adam over text about what I needed to know. (His tip: Avoid calling men "terrible." Noted.)

I can't help but size up Diego the way I do whenever I meet anyone new now. Clear skin, thick head of hair (though graying at the sides), and most important, no wedding band. He's friendly, but keeps a professional distance. He probably doesn't make enough money for Gretchen, and he's too short for Chrissy. Would Lily be into him? I can't tell if he's too corporate for her.

"You know, I'll be frank with you," he says. "I don't typically consider candidates unless they've built up a serious portfolio of work—not even for entry-level positions. We can afford to be competitive here. But your columns are doing amazing things for our traffic. If you can keep us spiking like that, that's worth more than experience."

"Oh, thank you. But actually, I do have a portfolio from college." I gesture to my résumé. "I interned for People.com in college, and I wrote for my school's blog."

He looks almost apologetic. "Right. But college and internships are a different game. Anyway, the *good news* is that I like your work. And obviously our readers do, too. The bad news is that if you want to work here, you'll need to do more than write from your match-making experience. Can you do that?"

I know how to hold my own with men who think they're hot shit. Matchmaking taught me that. I smile and plunge ahead with an answer.

"Absolutely. Writing for a big site like this is a lot like matchmaking, isn't it? It comes down to understanding what people want—what your readers want, what my clients want. Based on traffic, we already know that they're interested in dating advice from a woman's point of view. So it's just a matter of applying that same perspective to the rest of your dating content: viral stories, sex tips, funny listicles, and more."

Diego nods and scribbles something down on his copy of my résumé.

"I'm not a one-trick pony, if that's what you're afraid of," I add.

I'm not nervous, exactly. In the worst-case scenario, I don't get the job, but I keep working at Bliss. But the dream of working full-time as a writer has been reignited; it'd be tough to come so close and not make it happen. The rest of the interview isn't hard. He seems impressed when I can recite past Esquire.com headlines from memory, and I think I nail the question about how the site could improve. He tells me he's still considering another candidate, but will be in touch soon with his decision.

He walks me back toward the elevator and pauses by the door.

"By the way, how do you know Adam?" he asks.

Maybe I'm reading too much into it, but Diego sounds like he's pretending to seem casual.

"Oh, he didn't say?" I wish I could turn around and look at Adam for reassurance.

"No."

My mind races for the appropriate answer. I can't tell him the full truth.

"I set him up on a date with my client. It didn't work out between them."

"Ha. That's too bad. He's a good guy."

"Yeah, I think so, too."

At 7:10 p.m., I rap twice on Jonathan's door and pull myself up to my fullest height. The doorman had recognized me and waved me through the lobby without buzzing Jonathan first.

"One minute!" Jonathan calls.

I'm ten minutes late as a power move. I stare purposefully at the charcoal gray carpet flecked with red and blue, and focus on not passing out from nerves. The door clicks open and I snap my head up to face him.

"Hi," he breathes. "Come on in."

He holds the door open and stretches an arm to give me a hug.

I step into his embrace and he bends his head into the curve of my neck. I bet he can feel how hard my heart is pounding, even through my top and his undershirt, button-down, and blazer. His apartment is a mess, with a stack of suits still in dry-cleaning bags thrown over one arm of the cream couch, and an uncapped, half-full bottle of Scotch on the coffee table. A pile of unopened mail sits next to a bag of Chinese takeout splotched with grease stains.

"Sorry," he says, grabbing the bag and scuttling to the kitchen to toss it. "I've been meaning to get someone in here to clean. I just haven't . . . I, uh, it's been kind of rough around here lately."

He's flustered, scratching the back of one leg with the toe of his shoe and mussing a hand in the back of his hair. My purse is slung in the crook of my elbow, held as a protective barrier between us. The words I'd prepared all day are stuck in my throat; I don't know how to begin.

"I meant to straighten up," he says, "but I literally just walked in—you know that deal I was working on, the one with the oil company? Huge crisis with them at the last minute. The office has been slammed for days working on deadline, and . . ."

He trails off when he sees me lose interest, then tries a different tactic.

"You have no idea how glad I am you're here. I wasn't sure you'd really show up."

"Well, I'm here."

"And you're good? How is everything?"

"Fine. Great. I am totally fine and great."

He nods and rocks up onto the balls of his feet. He shoves his hands into his pockets, then rocks back down to his heels. There's an extra foot of polite space between us.

"So, I know I probably kind of caught you off guard the other day."

I actually laugh for the first time in two days. "Um, yeah, you could say that."

"I meant what I said, you know. I love you, and I want to spend the rest of my life with you. We'd build the best future together. I hate myself for hurting you, but I want to fix what I've ruined."

He closes the gap between us and tucks a piece of hair behind my ear, running a tender finger down my cheek. I'm too on edge to exhale. He leans forward gingerly, then kisses me, pulling me tight against him, hands firm on my hips. It would be so easy to melt into him here, let my guard down, and tell him I love him.

But I can't do that.

Instead, I remove his left hand from my hip and take a shaky step back.

"Jonathan, stop. I can't marry you."

His face falls and his eyes turn stormy. If he thought I'd say yes, he doesn't know me well enough at all. Two months ago, I'd have been scared that no one would ever love me the way Jonathan does. And after spending my summer fixing up single New Yorkers, I should be afraid to turn down his proposal. But I'm not. I'm not that girl anymore. I know myself well enough now to realize that even with a proposal and a ring and a promise to change, Jonathan and I aren't compatible.

I pull the glossy blue Tiffany bag out of my purse, but he doesn't take it from me.

"Keep it," he says quietly.

"I can't. It's over, Jonathan."

"Sasha, no, come on. You don't mean that. I want to be with you."

Every ounce of anger I've felt toward him over the past two years hits me all at once: the nights he canceled plans to put in face time at the office, the countless dinners I spent sitting across the table in silence while he emailed his bosses, his nauseating betrayal. I don't know how I didn't see it before: he's not the one.

"I don't really mean that?" I echo. "Are you kidding me? I'm capable of having my own opinions, you know."

"No, that's not— Just, ugh, just please, stay."

"I have to go." My voice might sound hollow, but at least I'm not groveling like he is.

"Just stay the night," he asks softly. "For one last time. For me."

I hesitate. It would feel so good to curl up in bed with him. He'd be the big spoon, and his arm would drape across the groove of my waist. I could listen to the steady *tick tock* of his heart as we drift into sleep, just like we've done a thousand times before. I'm tempted, but I can't. I place the Tiffany bag on the coffee table. After all this time together, this is it.

"Goodbye."

I turn and walk away. I open the door, force myself to not look back, and let it swing shut behind me with a heavy thud. I speed-walk to the elevator and jam my finger into the button until it dings and the door slides open. It's empty, mercifully. When I reach the lobby, the doorman waves goodbye to me. He doesn't know it will be for the final time.

Only once I'm safely outside do I let myself slump against a brick building and relax. I'm prepared to heave with sobs. But the tears don't come. I'm not sad—just overwhelmed. And I'm proud of what I've done. If the thought of marrying someone makes you want to vomit, he's not the right person for you.

And then I get a text from the right person.

"Hey, sugar. I just started cooking. Want to join me for dinner?"

Chapter 25

Adam is leaning against the doorframe of his apartment, one brown leather loafer crossed over the other, waiting for me. A song by LCD Soundsystem wafts into the hallway.

"Hey there, beautiful," he says, kissing me.

I try to forget that Jonathan had kissed me just an hour ago. It doesn't matter anymore; he doesn't matter anymore. There are more important matters at hand, like the scent of garlic sizzling on the stove and Adam's finger curled around my belt loop.

I lean down to nudge off my shoes so I don't have to look him in the eye. It's too soon for me to tell him about Jonathan. I don't want to scare him off. I line up my shoes in their usual spot against the exposed brick wall of his living room (porn for New Yorkers like me) and straighten up.

"So, the interview—talk to me."

I can't help but beam. "It went well! I think. I mean, did Diego say anything?"

"He thought you were smart and eager. I told him I wouldn't send him any dummies."

"If I got the job, would that mean we'd work together?"

He hesitates. "I mean, it's a pretty independent job. I'd work on my pieces, you'd work on yours."

"But we'd work for the same company, in the same office."

He wrinkles his nose. "Is that weird? That's weird, isn't it?"

"I didn't say it was weird."

I sling my arms over his shoulders and tilt my head up for a kiss to shut down the conversation. I'm not completely insane—I *know* it's risky to work with someone you date. (Or to date someone you meet through work, for that matter. Obviously.) And maybe this is my naïveté talking, but it feels like the rules don't apply to me and Adam. I hear all my clients talk about how difficult and awful dating is, but when I'm with him, everything just feels easy. I can't explain it to someone like Caroline because she's never felt this way before; you either get it or you don't.

"Now, can I put you to work in the kitchen?" he asks.

"I can microwave a mean frozen pizza, if you happen to have one of those lying around."

"Come on, that's not real food. You can chop vegetables, can't you?"

"Vegetables . . . those things that grow out of the ground? Yes, I believe I can do that."

He rolls his eyes. "I'll give you the cheese instead. More your speed."

"Thank you."

He hands me a hunk of mozzarella, a wood slab cutting board, and a knife. "Bite-sized pieces, please."

"Coming right up, chef."

He turns back to the stove to stir the garlic with a wooden spoon and drizzle in more olive oil. I like watching him work in the kitchen, especially on nights like tonight, when he's rolled up his sleeves to show his muscled forearms and sexy, capable hands. I admire him for a second, then get to the cheese.

"You're not one of those crazy New Yorkers who uses their oven for storage, are you?" he asks.

"Adam, I would never. That's ridiculous." I make a mental note to transfer my old textbooks from the oven to my closet before I see him next. They would make such a mess if they caught fire.

I finish slicing the mozzarella, and he approves my work. I graduate to cutting morsels of sweet Italian sausage. And when I'm finished, Adam requests that I perform the one kitchen task I can pull off with ease—uncorking the wine. I pour us each a glass of cabernet sauvignon, hoist myself up onto the counter, and continue to admire his confidence in the kitchen.

He finishes preparing the meal, two cavernous bowls of pasta tossed with sausage, mushrooms, onions, and gooey cheese. We eat on a pair of bar stools facing the kitchen island, and he recaps the day's biggest news stories for me—one of the many perks of dating a writer. When he tells stories, he lights up, waving his fork around as he gestures. It's entertaining to watch someone who actually *cares* about what they do, rather than keeping track of business deals and the financial markets just to . . . what, make more money? I push away thoughts of Jonathan and tell Adam about my phone call with Vince yesterday, when I tried to suss out what he likes in bed. He bursts out laughing and shakes his head.

"I can't believe you actually get paid to do that," he muses. "Your job is unbelievable. And none of your clients care how old you are?"

"I mean, it's not like they know."

He pauses, fork midway to his mouth, and makes a face. "Come on. They have to know."

I straighten up in my seat. "I could pass for older. You thought I was, what, twenty-seven when we first met?"

"You didn't even know what JNCOs were until I told you . . . you learned about the O. J. Simpson trial in history class . . . your mom still pays your phone bill. Sorry, Sasha, but you're not fooling anybody." He laughs at all of this, making me feel even worse.

I hate when he brings up my age. It knocks my confidence. "Okay, fine. But look at the perks of my age: I could stalk you on Instagram right away, I'm cute enough that creepy old dudes swipe right on me all the time, I have the energy to work around the clock. That counts for something, doesn't it?"

"Whatever you say, kiddo."

After dinner, we fall into one of those new-couple dazes on the couch, where he kicks his feet up onto the table and I curl sideways with my head on his chest. He strokes my hair with his left hand and pretends to find something to watch on Netflix with his right, but neither of us really cares what's on the screen as long as we can stay like this. Eventually, he puts on an indie drama that neither of us feels invested in so we can drift in and out of kissing without missing any of the plot. We've spent a dozen nights just like this, cooking and watching movies, and it's starting to feel like a routine. I love how comfortable this is.

I check my phone when the movie is over, and there are two texts from Mindy. I'm praying she isn't going to cancel tomorrow's date, because that would require rescheduling it.

"Are you free to meet for coffee tomorrow?" she wrote an hour ago, followed by "???" a half hour later.

"Sure. What time?" I write back.

She texts instantly to schedule an 11 a.m. meeting at the Starbucks near her office, dashing off a frenetic "Thank you!!!!"

"Work?" Adam asks.

"Yeah. It's Mindy."

"Tell her I say hi."

I roll my eyes and wriggle around in his arms to face him. "I'd rather not get fired."

"Riiiight, right, right. So, let's concoct a story. Say we met by chance."

"That's intriguing, but no."

"Why not?"

"We live on opposite sides of the city, we don't go to any of the same bars, we have zero mutual friends, we don't work in the same industry . . ." I tick off each reason on my finger.

"We actually did meet on Tinder, you know."

"You know, typically when people lie about how they met, it's so they *don't* have to say they met on Tinder."

He shrugs. "Whatever works for us."

Us. The word sends a shiver down my spine. I like it.

Adam has a hungry look in his eyes that I know means just one thing. The conversation about how we fake-met falls by the wayside as he kisses a hot trail down my neck and unbuttons his shirt. I tug off my sweater.

"Jesus, look at you," he says, marveling, running his hands down my chest and wrapping them around my waist. "You're the most gorgeous girl in the world."

I make sure there's enough time between leaving Adam's place and meeting Mindy for coffee to shower. It seems tacky not to rinse off the mingled scent of sex, sweat, and Adam's cologne before seeing her. Mindy is early, wiping crumbs off the Starbucks table with a brown paper napkin when I walk in. She vaults out of her seat to hug me.

"Hi!" She swoops in to perform a double-cheek air kiss, stopping short to avoid smudging her scarlet lipstick across my face.

"Love the lipstick," I say, half because I do, but half because I know the compliment will make her beam. I'm right.

"Do you want something to drink?" she asks. She looks better than she did the last time I saw her, but only because she's sitting upright instead of curled around a Bloomingdale's trash can. The line stretches nearly to the door right now. Even though I could probably get away with expensing my drink to Bliss, I decide to skip it. There's something about the way Mindy is digging her nails into the sides of her cup that makes her look anxious; I don't want to make her wait any longer for this conversation than she already has.

"Nah, I'm fine. I don't want to wait in line," I say, pulling out a chair. "How are you feeling? Better?"

"I'm fine." She nods, slipping the cardboard sleeve off her cup and twisting it around her fingers. "I asked you to meet me because we need to have a serious conversation."

"Sure," I say cautiously. I have a bad feeling she's about to request switching to another matchmaker.

"You know, it's funny, I came to Bliss because I want to get married and have a family. I mean, I'm not getting any younger here. I've had my fun, I've built up my career, and I'm just so beyond ready to meet someone great and settle down. That's the only thing I want, Sasha. That's it."

Shit. I know where this is going. She's upset because I haven't found her future husband yet.

"I was so obsessed with chasing this vision of a boyfriend and a big Manhattan wedding and taking my husband with me to Lamaze classes. So cute, right? He'd coach me through labor and we'd have all these cute little Jewish babies. I thought that's how my life was supposed to go. But it's not going to work out quite like that, and weirdly enough, it's all thanks to you."

Her usual breakneck pace of speech comes hurtling to a stop, and suddenly, she's not fidgeting anymore. She's sitting very still, beaming. I think I'm being praised, but I'm not sure why. There's something I'm missing.

"What do you mean, thanks to me?"

"Well, I wasn't fully honest with you earlier. I guess I was embarrassed. I mean, I'd just met you, and I didn't want you to think I would jump into bed with a guy the first chance I got, you know? I didn't want that to color your perception of me if you're working for me. I hardly ever do this."

"Do what?"

"Sasha," she says, leaning across the table and clutching my arm like we're best friends sharing a juicy secret. "Remember that first guy you set me up with? Adam? We slept together. I just found out I'm pregnant."

"Oh my god." I can't hide the horror in my voice.

"Don't worry! This is all good news. I'm ecstatic," she reassures me.

"You slept with Adam?"

"I know. It's crazy, huh? It happened just once, after our date."

"This is unbelievable," I croak.

"Look, honey, no need to freak out," she says with a laugh. "I know you're young. When your friends get pregnant, you probably send them a sympathy card and ask them when the abortion is. But this is different. I'm thrilled."

"No, it's not that. I'm so happy you're happy." I force a smile. "It's just . . ."

I squeeze my eyes shut and try to think back to my first date with Adam, a week after his date with Mindy. What exactly had he said? *Mindy told you everything, right?* I hadn't even thought to ask what "everything" meant. I didn't know I needed to.

"What?" Her expression sours. "You don't think I'd be a good mom?"

"No! Honestly, I'm jealous of your kid. You're going to be an amazing mom." I mean that. "It's just . . . does Adam know?"

"Not yet," she admits. "I don't even have his number. That's why I asked to see you. You can give me his number, right?"

"Yeah, of course."

I pull up his number on my phone and slide it across the table so she can copy it. Starbucks is playing a cloying Ed Sheeran song that's all wrong for this occasion. It's been, what, almost two months since their date? They must have gone back to his place, not hers, since she made such a big deal of pointing out that she didn't like his couch. Which means she's been in his apartment. Which means I've been having sex in the same bed where Mindy and Adam conceived their *child*. This is all so revolting.

"I don't need anything from him emotionally or even financially," she says, tucking her phone back into her purse. "I mean, he's what, a writer? Right."

"He's technically an editor." I don't mean to say it. It just slips out.

"What?"

"At *Esquire*. That's his job title. Editor."

"Oh, right, whatever. An editor. Anyway, I don't need anything from him—I just want to tell him for his sake, in case he wants any sort of relationship with the baby."

"Right. Mindy, there's something you need to know," I say in a strained voice.

"Yeah?"

I hate that I have to tell her, but it's the right thing to do. If she doesn't hear it from me, she'll hear it from him. At least this way, the conversation is on my terms. I take a deep breath. This is it.

"One of the reasons I love working with you so much is because we have such similar taste in men. It makes my job very easy. I liked Adam from the moment I met him, so I figured you would, too." I swallow and look down. "After you told me you weren't interested in seeing him again, I called him for feedback on the date—it's standard matchmaking procedure to hear from both people. He said he'd be up for a second date if you were, but he never said anything about you two hooking up. I didn't know how, um, involved you two were. I didn't think you'd ever cross paths with him again, so later, after my boyfriend and I broke up, I asked him out."

"On a date?" she asks sharply.

"You could call it that."

"For yourself?"

"Yes."

She narrows her eyes. "Did you sleep with him?"

"You've got to believe I had no idea that you hooked up with him."

"Sasha, did you sleep with him?"

To my horror, I start to feel tears welling up. "Yes."

"More than once?"

I consider my answer for a brief moment, but it wouldn't be right to go with anything other than the truth. "Yes. We've been dating," I admit.

"I can't believe this," she says, shaking her head slowly.

"I know. The odds of the whole situation . . ."

"I'm not talking about the odds," she snarls, eyes blazing. "I can't believe you would throw yourself at your client's sloppy seconds."

Mindy's anger scares me. I know I'm in the wrong; I know I deserve every reprimand and nasty comment she wants to hurl my way. I never wanted to hurt her.

"I would never have done anything had I known that you guys had a fling. How was I supposed to know?"

"It doesn't matter how much you knew! Do you know how unprofessional that is?"

I start to retort, but I have no defense. I look down at the table. "I know. I'm so sorry."

"I just don't understand how you could think it would be appropriate to set me up with someone because you have a little crush, then snatch him out from under me the second I say I'm done," she says, pressing her fingers to her forehead and screwing up her face like she actually cannot comprehend such a thing. She doesn't call me a slut out loud, but the word is just begging to escape her lips.

"Mindy, I'm so sorry. I'm so, so sorry."

She crosses her arms over her chest, purses her lips, and stares at me. "End it," she orders.

"Excuse me?"

"If you're sorry, you'll end things with Adam."

I feel like I've been pummeled repeatedly for months on end, and I'm one heartbreak away from disintegrating into dust. The prospect of losing Adam, who's brought so much joy into my life when I really needed it, is too painful to consider.

"I can't do that."

Two nights ago in New Jersey, I had wondered if I really needed Adam—now that I'm on the verge of losing him, I know I do.

Mindy exhales heavily. "I'm not dealing with this right now. Cancel my membership."

"Of course. I'm so sorry, I just—"

Mindy pushes her chair back. It scrapes loudly against the floor. People stare as she rises from the table, snatches her purse from the back of the seat, and storms toward the door. She throws me one last nasty look over her shoulder.

"Oh, and Sasha? I'm calling your boss."

– Chapter 26 –

Mindy's threat wasn't empty. I sulk the forty blocks home from Starbucks in hopes of clearing my head, but the walk fills me with even more self-pity and rage. By the time I jiggle open my front door, there's already an email from Penelope waiting in my inbox. I groan, then trudge to my bedroom and collapse flat on my back on my bed. I hold my phone above my face and tap open the email. Penelope's tone is even more curt and clipped than usual.

From: penelope@bliss.com
Subject: We need to talk.
Meet me at the brownstone tomorrow. 2 p.m. sharp.

Shit.

"Caroline, you home?" I call.

No answer. Orlando leaps up on the bed with a *mrow* and sniffs at my face. I scratch the mink-soft spots behind his ears and he purrs loudly. At least I can do right by him, if no one else. I consider explaining to Penelope what really happened over email, but that requires more chutzpah than I can muster right now. I'm worn out.

From: sasha@bliss.com
Subject: Re: We need to talk.
Of course. See you tomorrow.

I know I have every right to be furious at Adam for not telling me about sleeping with Mindy, but I can't make myself really feel it. I don't want to be mad at him. I don't have the energy to be angry at yet another man for sleeping with another woman. If I call him out for what he did, that means pushing him away. I'm already about to lose my job. I can't lose him, too.

I don't understand why Adam didn't tell me what happened. And I don't know if it's possible to salvage my job. I'm on the verge of tears, but I'm too worn out to cry. Instead, I zone out in front of Netflix until I have to press the "Are you still watching?" button twice. Adam calls in the middle of an old *Law & Order: SVU* episode, just as Olivia Benson is interrogating the bad guy. He never returned the text I sent on my way over to coffee with Mindy—something mindless about which Thai place we should order takeout from tonight. The phone rings four times, basically for an eternity, before I muster the guts to pick it up.

"Hi," I say.

He hesitates on the other end of the line. "We need to talk tonight."

"You talked to Mindy." It's not a question.

"Yeah, she called me. It's . . . wow."

I exhale and focus on picking at a piece of cat hair on my bedspread.

"I'll be there tonight," I say. "I'll get pad Thai from Ngam. And wine. Do you want red or white?"

"Don't worry about it."

"No, really, I don't mind picking something up on my way over."

"Seriously, don't worry about it," he says quietly. I can't quite read the tone of his voice. "I'll see you at seven."

Something about the click of the phone when he hangs up makes my eyes water.

Two hours later, I show up at his apartment with two steaming tubs of pad Thai and a nine-dollar bottle of red—I splurged. I rise up on my toes to give him a kiss when I walk in, but he doesn't kiss back the way he usually does.

I try to go through the pleasantries of polite conversation: how are you, how was your day, how was work? He responds with monosyllables. I don't know what to say. I spoon the noodles onto two plates and uncork the wine in silence.

"Sasha, we need to talk about Mindy," he announces.

I give him a plate and a glass and sit on the bar stool next to him. I slosh my wine around.

"Why didn't you tell me you slept with her?" I ask quietly.

"I thought you knew."

"She never told me. All these times we've talked about her—you never brought it up."

He stares, opens his mouth to say something, and closes it.

"I'm sorry. I didn't know you hadn't heard. It never came up. It didn't mean anything to me. It was just sex."

I've heard that before. It still hurts the second time around.

He shakes his head, twisting a fork into the noodles and shoveling a bite into his mouth. I tell him what happened in Starbucks this morning. I don't want to throw Mindy under the bus with the story, but I have to tell him how terribly she reacted.

"Adam, I could lose my job. Mindy is furious at us."

Bizarrely, he doesn't seem fazed. He swallows his wine and shakes his head. "No, she's not. She's fine. Excited, even."

"She hates *me*. She already tattled on us to Bliss, and now Penelope wants to see me tomorrow."

"When she came by my office today to tell me about the baby, she was in a really good mood," he offers.

He grins. Wait, he's *happy*?

"You know, it's weird," he says. "I was freaking out. I mean, Mindy meant nothing to me. Nice girl, but, you know, no real chemistry there. And it's not like this is ideal timing, or the ideal person. But, well, everyone I know is settling down and doing this whole kid thing. I wanted that someday. It's just working out differently than I thought it would."

"I can't exactly imagine you with a baby in this apartment."

"Why not?" He shrugs.

I glance around at the sparse furnishings, the minuscule kitchen, the two empty six-packs by the door waiting to be recycled.

"You live in a fourth-floor walk-up? And it'd be a pain to drag a stroller up here?"

"I could move," he says simply.

I stare across at the exposed brick wall, wishing it contained some sort of answer written there that would help me make sense of all of this. Adam's from the South. People have babies young all the time there. And it's not even like thirty-three is too young to have a kid. It's just . . . he's Adam. He's mine. And a baby doesn't fit into that.

"This is insane," I tell him, reaching for my wine. It's too dry and woody to swallow in gulps, the way I want to. I don't even know how to pick out wine. Another thing that Adam learned in his twenties that I haven't yet.

"That's why I wanted to talk to you tonight. About where this is all going."

"It's going straight to a sitcom," I joke. "Like one of those shows you see advertised on billboards that get canceled after one season. Like, the zany chronicles of a matchmaker watching her boyfriend struggle to raise a baby with her favorite client."

He's silent. He doesn't return my playful look.

"I meant where we're going. We need to talk about us."

"Oh." I put my fork down.

He angles toward me on his bar stool, resting his hand on my knee. He clears his throat.

"Sasha, you're a great girl," he begins.

I feel woozy. I know where this is going, because I've delivered this exact same speech to dozens of people on the phone after my clients lost interest in them. Adam reels off a string of my good qualities: I'm "so hot," allegedly, and also driven and charismatic. I know the next word in the sentence is going to be "but," followed by a carefully crafted excuse designed to soften the blow to my ego while simultaneously shifting the blame away from him.

"But I just need to focus on what's going on with Mindy and the baby right now," he explains, stroking my knee. "I'm not in a position to be a good boyfriend to you."

I feel like an idiot. I had assumed that nothing would have to change between us—Mindy would raise the baby herself. Hadn't she told me this morning that she didn't want anything from Adam? I bite my lip and look away. The tears I've been holding in all day trickle out from the corner of my left eye, and I brush them off my cheek.

"That's not true," I protest. "You're fantastic."

He spins the bar stool away from the counter and leads me to the couch, where I snuggle up with my back against his chest like we do when we watch movies. He strokes my hair and kisses the top of my head, like I'm some pet.

"I'm sorry," he whispers in my ear. "But I have to give Mindy a chance. I'll regret it for the rest of my life if I don't."

I squeeze my eyes shut, thankful that he can't see the tears brimming up from his perspective. I don't quite know how I got here—dumping a potential fiancé one day, getting dumped the next. I still feel shaken from what happened with Jonathan; it's too much to process Adam leaving me, too. I feel like the *Titanic*, Mount Everest, and the Empire State Building dropped their combined weight on my chest. I shift on the couch to face Adam.

"I'm not asking you to give up your baby for me," I say, speaking slowly so my voice doesn't shake. "But that doesn't mean you have to give up on us. You never wanted to be involved with Mindy. You said it yourself after your date."

He considers this, staring down at the stupid, ratty college couch Mindy hated. He bites his lip, his dark brows knitted together. "I don't know what to tell you, Sasha. Don't get me wrong, you and I have had fun."

"Nothing has to change," I plead. "We can still be together."

I know our time together was short, but it mattered to me. I felt like I could be exactly myself in front of Adam in a way I've never felt in front of any other guy—not Jonathan, not any of the boys I knew in college, not any of the hundreds of men I've faked my way through conversations with as a matchmaker. This is real to me.

There was a morning not too long ago, a Sunday, when the sun creeping in through his bedroom window woke me up before he stirred. We had nothing to do all day but stay tangled up in the white bedsheets, his hand on my ass while he told stories and made me laugh. I knew it was going to be a blissful day, but for now, I could just watch him sleep. His lips were parted slightly and he made the softest of baby snores. His body was so warm next to mine, and there was a natural space between his bicep and his chest for me to snuggle into, so I did. I laid my head on his chest and listened to the easy rhythm of his heartbeat. There was a moment, a minute before he woke, where I just knew I could do this forever. I tunneled into the future, and it wasn't terrifying, the way it was with Jonathan. It was calm. Comfortable. Happy. I know it's too early to love him, but I think I do anyway.

I reach a hopeful hand toward his thigh.

"This doesn't have to be the end," I beg softly.

He looks at me so tenderly, I could shatter. "You knew it had to be like this. Didn't you?"

I can't form words, just a mortifying sniffle.

"You're so young, Sasha. You don't know what you really want yet. I'm not it, trust me."

"That's not fair. You can't tell me what I do and don't want."

He's treating me like a child. I get that a relationship with him would have its challenges—of course it would. I knew from the beginning that pursuing Adam would be complicated. But that doesn't mean I don't want to give it a try. He was worth chasing and he's worth hanging on to.

"Maybe one day, things will be different," I suggest, wiping at my nose. "We can pick up where we left off."

Adam closes the space between us on the couch, gazes into my eyes, then tucks the pad of his index finger under my chin. He kisses me softly.

"I'm sorry," he says again. "I'm so sorry."

When he kisses me more deeply this time, a searing pain erupts in my chest. I weave my fingers through his hair tightly. I don't care if I pull too hard. He caresses my cheek with one hand and pulls me closer with the other, grasping insistently for me. Adam's mouth on mine is hot and passionate. He kisses a trail down my neck, and I gasp at how good it feels. I slide my hands over his shoulders, then his back, feeling for the tense muscles there. I can't believe this is the last time.

I feel the sturdy warmth of his palm on my chest. His fingers skim the edge of my bra through the thin cotton of my shape-less black dress, then slip under the material to graze my skin. He breaks away just long enough to push the dress up over my hips and tug the garment over my head. I let him, then rush forward to undo the buttons of his shirt. I want to be with him forever, but if I can't have that, I want to be with him right now. It's not enough, but it'll have to do. And maybe, just maybe, this will remind him that we're right for each other.

Afterward, he holds me. His feet hang off the arm of the couch.

"I think I love you," I mumble into his shoulder.

"I know." He sighs into my hair.

It doesn't change anything. When I've gathered up all the com-fort I can from his warm, bare skin, I get up, find my dress, and start putting myself back together. He slips into pajama pants and ties them low on his hips. I leave my dinner on the counter. He picks up my purse from the floor and hands it to me. In the doorway, he starts to kiss me again, but I pull back first. If I don't tear myself away now, I never will.

"Goodbye," I say.

He echoes my words, then closes the door and lets me disappear down the hall. I push open the creaky door to the staircase and take the three flights down quickly.

I still feel shaky when I exit onto Twenty-Sixth Street. I walk east across Manhattan, pausing at every pizza place I pass. I've barely eaten anything all day, and hunger gnaws at the pit of my stomach. When I'm close to home, I buy not just a slice, but a whole box.

Back at my apartment, I call out for Caroline, but there's no answer. She's not in the living room or kitchen. The bathroom down the hall is empty. There's no light streaming out from under her bedroom door. Not even Orlando comes to greet me, and he always pokes his head into the living room when he hears me come in. Always. My phone, which constantly buzzes with Bliss emails and dating app notifications, is suspiciously quiet.

I am alone.

I rest the pizza box on the ottoman in front of the couch and eat a slice oozing with cheese and grease. It's so oily that by the time I finish one slice, my fingers are slick and my skin feels slimy, but I keep going. By slice two, Orlando emerges to sniff at the box. I click my tongue and tap the empty space next to me on the couch hopefully, but he gives me a look of quiet disdain and stalks past me.

By slice three, I start to see the problem with matchmaking: nobody really knows what they want. Adam said he wanted to have a little fun before settling down. He said he wasn't interested in dating a JAP. And here he is, two months later, dumping me to have a baby with the queen of JAPs, Mindy Kaplan, who once admitted to me that she still wears her Camp Ramah sweatshirt from 1997 to bed sometimes. Mindy told me she wanted a suited-up finance guy. Adam couldn't be further from that. I could interview people all day about what they're looking for in a match, but humans are just so damn unreliable.

Wretched Gretchen's downfall, in the end, is that she's trying to engineer herself a husband through sheer force of will. She thinks if she can quantify and calculate her ideal match, he'll wander into her life. In reality, her lengthy checklist covered it all, really, except for the messy, magical bits—the things that make you fall in love. People are more than the sum of their parts.

Then there's Caroline, who's sure she knows what she wants: a boyfriend, *duh*—that's how she would say it, rolling her eyes. She desperately wants someone to give her love to, but it hasn't occurred to her yet that not everyone she meets is worthy of it. She's learning, I guess. We all are.

I used to think I wanted Jonathan: normal, successful, all-American Jonathan. It turned out that I just liked the idea of him—the package he came in, but not the actual brain and heart and soul that made him a real person. And that's the problem. Jonathan was the dream guy who failed me. He didn't know he wanted me till it was too late. Adam was never supposed to be mine, but I wound up wanting him the most. And maybe, even though I'd never admit this out loud to him, I just liked the idea of Adam, too.

Bliss taught me to believe that finding your dream partner is the hard part—hard enough that it's worth forking over $700 a month to a crew of so-called experts. But the hard part, I'm learning, is reconciling your dream guy with the stark reality in front of you. They don't always match. Maybe they never do.

The next afternoon, I'm trudging down First Avenue past the sketchy massage parlor, the Chinese takeout joint, and the falafel place on my way to the Bliss brownstone when my phone rings. Caller ID shows an unfamiliar number with a New York area code, but I pick up anyway.

"Sasha? It's Diego. How are you?"

I mean, awful. But he doesn't need to know that. I step over a pile of dog shit (at least, I hope it's dog shit) on the sidewalk and try to sound chipper. "Great, how are you?"

"Fine, thanks. I'm calling because I'd like to offer you the position at Esquire.com. I can give you thirty-five thousand a year, plus benefits."

He's kidding. He must be kidding. He's not kidding? I got the job?! The salary is nothing to be thrilled about, but it's the most anyone has ever offered me for anything. I doubt I'd make quite that much in a year at Bliss. It feels like winning the lottery.

"Thank you! Wow. This is amazing."

"I'm sure you'll need some time to think it over," Diego begins.

"No, not at all. I want to work for you. When can I start?"

The certainty of my own voice scares me. I feel phenomenally lucky—minutes away from probably being fired from Bliss, and suddenly offered the dream job that I never fully believed to be within my reach. I'm afraid I'm going to wake up any second now, drenched in a cold sweat in bed, to find that Diego never really called.

"Oh!" He sounds startled, but *real*, at least. Solid. I'm not hallucinating his offer. "Awesome. I'm glad to hear you'll be joining us. Can you start in the next week or two?"

"Sure."

Exactly *how* I'll wrap up my current position is another story. But I'll figure that out soon enough.

"Of course, of course. We'll be in touch regarding the start date."

It's only after the call ends and I'm drifting downtown in a sun-drenched, giddy haze that the reality hits me: I'll be working with Adam. Who will be raising a baby with Mindy. Who thinks I'm a sloppy harlot. It's not ideal. But this summer toughened me up. I can deal with it.

I had been dreading my meeting with Penelope, but not anymore. Now, regardless of what she says, I'll be fine; I'll leave bliss for *Esquire*. I practically skip up the five steps of the brownstone and knock a jaunty rhythm on the front door. She doesn't smile when she opens it.

"Sasha." She grimaces. "Come on in."

Penelope doesn't waste any time. She's too busy; even during the brief ten-minute meeting, her phone sits between us on the velvet couch in the brownstone's study and flashes twice a minute with new messages. She doesn't offer me anything from the glass dish of chocolate truffles on the coffee table. It's a good thing she makes me too nervous to think about what just happened on the phone with Diego; otherwise, I'd be smiling all over the place.

"I have to let you go," she says, her eyes boring into mine as if she's daring me not to squirm. "You made quite a mess with Mindy Kaplan."

Then, silence. It stretches for longer than is comfortable. I'm ashamed to tell her; if I explain it out loud, whatever happened between me and Adam might lose its magic.

"I know I made a mistake," I admit. "But Adam and I aren't seeing each other anymore. I know that what I did was terribly unprofessional, and it reflects poorly on the company. It was never my intention to hurt Bliss or upset Mindy. I'm so sorry, Penelope."

"You knew about our policy—no dating clients or recruits."

"I did."

She shakes her head. "It's a shame, really. You had such a unique story. And you really did show such promise. You're not a bad matchmaker, you know."

"Really?"

"Really. Until now. Your database access will be turned off today and your clients will be transferred to other matchmakers."

Penelope rises from the couch and smoothes the front of her purple pencil skirt. Apparently this meeting is now over. She grabs her phone and coffee in one hand and extends the other one toward me. I get up and shake her hand.

"Thank you so much for taking a chance on me," I say.

I follow her out of the wood-paneled study and past the dining room with the glittering chandelier into the foyer. My interview here feels so long ago.

Penelope opens the door to the brownstone. Outside, I can't help but laugh. In the past three days, I've turned down an engagement, gotten dumped, lost my job, and found another. Nothing feels certain anymore.

I take the steps down to the sidewalk slowly for the last time, running my hand along the beautiful wrought-iron banister. There's nowhere in particular I need to be, no clients to manage, no boyfriends to call on. For a moment, I don't know where to go or what to do with myself. But then the solution clicks. My feet carry me to Flower Power, where Caroline is working a shift. As I walk, I flick through the dating apps on my phone and delete them one by one. I don't need them anymore.

– Acknowledgments –

I'm so thankful for my brilliant editor, Kaitlin Olson, whose vision and attention to detail shaped *Playing with Matches* into what it is today. I love that she immediately understood and embraced what I wanted this novel to be. Every writer dreams of working with an editor like Kaitlin. Many thanks to everyone at Touchstone Books, including Susan Moldow and Tara Parsons.

Thanks to my fabulous agent, Allison Hunter, whose passion, creativity, and energy know no bounds. I'm so lucky to have had her as my advocate, fairy godmother, and de facto therapist through this exhilarating and occasionally stressful process. Thanks to everyone at Janklow & Nesbit Associates, including Clare Mao for her assistance, and Brenna English-Loeb for changing my life overnight by fishing my manuscript out of the slush pile.

I wrote, sold, and edited this book while at Seventeen.com. Special thanks to all my colleagues, especially Troy Young, Kate Lewis, Kristin Koch, Elisa Benson, and Betsy Fast, for encouraging my foray into fiction and pushing me to grow into a stronger, savvier writer. And thank you to my colleagues at Elite Daily and Bustle Digital Group, including Theresa Massony, Kylie McConville,

Kate Ward, and Bryan Goldberg, for celebrating this milestone with me.

Thanks to my mentors: Ann Shoket, who's always inspired me to dream bigger and work harder, and Kaitlin Menza, whose savvy guidance has shaped my career.

Thanks to my professors at NYU, including Jessica Seigel, whose tenacity and warmth I'll never forget, and Marie-Helene Bertino, who told me to "keep going" when I turned in a fourteen-page short story about a young matchmaker struggling to make it in Manhattan.

This novel would not exist without E. Jean Carroll, Julia Armet, and the rest of the team at Tawkify. They taught me the magic behind matchmaking; I'm wiser and bolder because of it. I'm also grateful to Melissa Schorr for her column "Dinner with Cupid" in the *Boston Globe Magazine*, which sparked my interest in matchmaking a decade ago.

Thanks to my friends: Roshan Berentes, Morgan Boyer, Annie Kehoe, Kelsey Mulvey, Elyssa Goodman, Emily Raleigh, Dana Schwartz, Devin Alessio, and Emma and Devon Albert-Stone. They each cheered on my early drafts, gave no-bullshit pep talks on days I was ready to give up, and popped champagne to celebrate when I found success. The heart of this story is about friendship, and I couldn't have written it without them by my side.

The Orenstein, Hart, and Sykes families are far more functional and wonderful than the families portrayed in this book. Their love and support keep me going. I wish that my grandmother Rose Orenstein, who passed down to me her passions for literature and New York, were here to read this.

My sister, Julia Orenstein, was my first and most trustworthy reader. When I began my first draft, I wasn't confident in my ability to write a novel, but she always was. Julia's unwavering enthusiasm for the stories told in this book is one of the most meaningful gifts I have ever received.

One million thanks to my parents, Audrey and Jack Orenstein, who instilled an appreciation for reading and writing in me from a young age, modeled the importance of pursuing what you love, and showed me what drive and determination look like. From suggesting the perfectly cheeky title to editing every draft, their influence is woven into every page of this book.

Hannah Orenstein is a dating editor at *Elite Daily*. Previously, she was an editor at Seventeen.com. At twenty-one, she became the youngest matchmaker at a top dating service. She was born and raised in Boston, studied journalism and history at NYU, and lives in Manhattan with her fat cat, Eloise.

Playing with Matches

Hannah Orenstein

– For Discussion –

1. Sasha's secret about how her parents met is revealed in the first chapter, but it comes up again and again throughout the book. How does that origin story influence her views and decisions when it comes to relationships, if at all?

2. How do you think the technological developments in dating (apps, websites, etc.) have changed the process—for better or worse?

3. From the get-go, Sasha knows that she and Jonathan come from different worlds, but says she "feel[s] a thrill" when she thinks about his success and "normalcy," especially when other people realize they're together. How much do you think other people's perceptions of our relationships dictate them?

4. When Sasha first meets Adam, she is setting him up with Mindy, but when it doesn't work out, she goes out on a date with him instead. Do you think that crosses a line? What would you do in that situation?

5. How do you think men and women approach dating similarly and differently?

6. One of Sasha's clients, Gretchen, is very specific about what she's looking for in a partner. What would you expect or hope for when starting a new relationship? What would you be flexible about? Do you think that criteria or chemistry is more important?

7. *Playing with Matches* is primarily about Sasha's romantic entanglements with Jonathan and Adam, but are there other kinds of love she experiences? How do those relationships influence her?

8. Sasha has a few key clients—Mindy, Eddie, and Gretchen—for whom she struggles to find matches. Who would you rather have the challenge of setting up?

9. Have you ever set up a friend? Have you ever been set up? Discuss the risks and the rewards.

10. Adam and Sasha have to keep their relationship a secret, as it violates Bliss's rules on dating clients. Would you be able to conceal your relationship like Adam and Sasha? What are the pros and cons of hiding something like this?

11. Compare and contrast Caroline's and Sasha's approaches to dating and relationships. Do you think that one is better than the other?

12. When Sasha considers getting back together with Jonathan, Caroline voices her disapproval by listing the times he has let her down as a boyfriend. Do you think this is appropriate? Is her honesty necessary?

13. At the end of the book, Mindy surprises Sasha with news that she's pregnant. Sasha's response changes everything. How would you handle that situation? Do you think Sasha does the right thing?

14. The title *Playing with Matches* is multilayered, a twist on the expression "playing with fire" and the idea of "matching" with someone on a dating app. Having finished the book, what other subtle meanings or messages do you think emerge?

You're a dating editor at *Elite Daily*, and were once a young professional matchmaker yourself. What elements of those experiences helped you to write *Playing with Matches*?
I knew that I wanted to write a novel of some kind, but I wasn't sure what it would be about. The minute I got hired as a matchmaker, I knew I had stumbled onto something really special. My job was a lot like Sasha's: I spent my days scrolling through a massive database of New York's singles, swiping through dating apps, and setting up dates.

If you're a person who can afford to hire a matchmaker, you're likely in your thirties or older. I was just twenty-one at the time, and so I was never interested in any of my clients or matches. But people kept asking me what would happen if I wanted to date one of them. That question became one of the central conflicts of *Playing with Matches*.

In my own experience, even if I had met someone like Adam, it wouldn't have been an issue. I recall my boss saying, "If a hot, successful man lands on your desk and you *don't* take him for yourself, there must be something wrong with him!"

Sasha expects that when she starts working at Bliss, she'll be attending exclusive events and pounding the pavement to find potential clients and matches. Instead, she learns that a lot of the job is being on apps and recruiting people that way. How did you think to put that twist on the process?
I think most people would be surprised to learn two things about matchmakers: first, that there are so many of them; second, that a lot of them use dating apps! Every matchmaker works differently, and not all of them are on Tinder, but I certainly was. (And on Bumble, Hinge, Coffee Meets Bagel, JSwipe, etc.) I spent hours a day swiping, conversing with matches, and meeting men for coffee

to screen them for my clients. Most guys assumed I was either a bot, trying to sell them a membership, or using matchmaker as a "cover" and really just on Tinder to score dates for myself.

There's a long tradition of young female coming-of-age stories set in New York City, on-screen and in books. Were there any influences you drew on during your writing? How much did you want to draw on them, if at all?

Oh, absolutely! *The Devil Wears Prada* by Lauren Weisberger was certainly an influence. Her protagonist Andy Sachs inspired so many people to aspire to the magazine industry. It would be incredible if Sasha Goldberg could do the same thing for matchmaking. There were other books that I devoured and admired the same year I wrote *Playing with Matches* that probably had some influence—all either female coming-of-age stories, stories set in New York, or both: *The Royal We* by Heather Cocks and Jessica Morgan, *Luckiest Girl Alive* by Jessica Knoll, *Normal Girl* by Molly Jong-Fast. And on-screen, I loved how unapologetically millennial *Girls*, *Broad City*, and *Trainwreck* were. That was something I consciously wanted to incorporate into my own work.

There's a tendency in pop culture to portray young women like they "have it all." Sasha seems to on the surface, but is really just trying to figure it all out. What did you like about writing a female protagonist at this age and stage of her life? What was most challenging?

I wrote the first draft when I was twenty-two, and a lot of mundane details about Sasha's life were pulled directly from my own: like her, I made friends with the owner of the wine store to get sale-rack bottles for even less money, I was really impressed by people who could afford (and have room for) dining tables, and I used a "No Scrubs" lyric in my Tinder bio.

And like Sasha, I ate pork nachos at Hotel Tortuga, ate breakfast at David's Bagels, played Skee-Ball at East Village dive bars on dates, hung out at Think Coffee and the Strand, and shared an apartment on First Avenue and Eighteenth Street with my best friend from college. I wanted this book to feel like a love letter to all my favorite places in New York.

The challenging piece of that was to accurately portray someone struggling to pull her life together as a twenty-two-year-old recent college grad in New York . . . while I was trying to pull my life together as a twenty-two-year-old recent college grad in New York. During my first conversation with my agent, she was like, "Adam is so obnoxious because he's this older guy stringing along this younger girl." And I was thinking, "Oh, *that's* obnoxious? I didn't realize that!"

Now that you've written your first book, do you have any ideas or plans for others? What subjects, situations, or characters would you like to tackle next?
Yes! I'm always interested in women's careers, relationships, and friendships, and how they all intertwine.

— Enhance Your Book Club —

1. *Playing with Matches* joins the ranks of great romantic coming-of-age stories like *Something Borrowed*, *Good in Bed*, and *Eligible*. Choose one of these books to read in your book club, and compare and contrast their depictions of dating, love, and growing up.
2. Create a menu for your book club meeting inspired by Sasha and Caroline's favorite girls' night foods from the novel. Or, if you're in New York City, visit Hotel Tortuga, David's Bagels, or Brooklyn Bazaar.
3. *Playing with Matches* has all the elements of a classic romantic comedy. Poll your book club and see which rom-com is the group's favorite. Then, as you watch it together, mark down the similarities and differences between it and *Playing with Matches*.